Big Lake Blizzard

By Nick Russell

Nick Russell
1400 Colorado Street C-16
Boulder City, NV 89005
E-mail Editor@gypsyjournal.net

Also By Nick Russell

Fiction
Big Lake
Big Lake Lynching
Crazy Days In Big Lake
Big Lake Blizzard

Nonfiction
Highway History and Back Road Mystery
Highway History and Back Road Mystery II
Meandering Down The Highway;
A Year On The Road With Fulltime RVers
The Frugal RVer
Work Your Way Across The USA;
You Can Travel And Earn A Living Too!
The Gun Shop Manual
Overlooked Florida
Overlooked Arizona

Keep up with Nick Russell's latest books at www.
NickRussellBooks.com

Author's Note

While there is a body of water named Big Lake in the White Mountains of Arizona, the community of Big Lake and all persons in this book live only in the author's imagination. Any resemblance in this story to actual persons, living or dead, is purely coincidental.

*To my friend Chris Yust,
because everybody needs
a Hillbilly in their life.*

Chapter 1

"He's beautiful!"

"Easy. Just relax, he's not going anywhere."

"Now don't you blow this, Brad! We've come a long way and I've spent a lot of money. If you miss, I'll kick your ass."

"He's gonna do just fine, don't you worry 'bout that, Lenny. This kid is good."

"Shit, you don't know him like I do! He couldn't pour piss outta a boot if the instructions were written on the heel!"

"Shsss! You'll spook him before he gets out in the open!"

Eye still glued to the spotting scope, the guide put his hand on the young man's shoulder, feeling him tremble even through the heavy jacket. Snow had started to fall thirty minutes earlier and already the jacket was covered with large flakes.

"Easy, kid. Give him just another minute and he'll come out into the open. Just center the crosshairs behind the shoulder like I told you, and when I tell you, squeeze the trigger. Got it?"

"Yes, sir."

"You better have it, you little piss ant. Like the man said, squeeze the trigger, don't jerk it. If you blow this shot I'll…"

"Shsss! You're gonna blow it if you keep talking, Lenny!"

Ninety yards downhill and across the small meadow the big buck stepped out of the shadows of the forest, sniffing the air carefully for any sign of danger. Satisfied, he dropped his head and began to graze.

Behind the rock outcropping where the three men huddled, Brad's stomach lurched and he tasted bile in the back of his throat as he tried to hold the bolt-action rifle still. He didn't want to kill the magnificent animal, Lord how he didn't! But he knew he had to or else suffer the wrath of Lenny Dewitt. And given the two options, he was more afraid of his father-in-law than he was of pulling the trigger.

"Okay kid, he's ready. Take a breath, let it half out, and just squeeze the trigger. He's good as dead and hanging on your wall already."

Brad didn't want the animal hanging on his wall, reminding him forever of what he did to it. But he knew that if he missed the shot, it might as well be him hanging on Lenny's wall. Proof once again that he didn't measure up. He could already hear the ridicule in Lenny's voice as he told Chuck and Richey about how Brad had pussied out. Again. And he could hear his brothers-in-law's guffaws as they sneered at him for being less than a man. Again.

He took a breath, let it out, and managed to keep the scope's crosshairs steady as he started to take the slack out of the trigger.

BANG! BANG! BANG!

Three shots rang out in rapid succession, splitting the stillness of the late afternoon.

"Get out of here. Run!"

The words were not needed. Before the second shot had been fired, the buck had sprung back into the shadows of the forest and was already out of sight. The buck stood over three feet tall at the shoulder and weighed close to 300 pounds. With its massive rack stretching out above him, the animal still moved with surprising speed as it nimbly made its way through the Ponderosa pines that covered the mountainside, putting as much distance as it could between itself and the hunters behind him.

"Son of a bitch!" Lenny screamed. "What the hell are you doing?"

"God damn it," said the guide in frustration, standing up and looking down into the meadow. "What the hell is wrong with you, you crazy bastard?"

"You're not killing anything out here today! Get out of here!"

Below them, the figure who had suddenly burst out of cover halfway down the hill stood defiantly, hand still gripping the revolver.

"Emma? Is that you?"

"I told you, Jake, you might as well give those men their money back, because I'll be out here every day until the season's over."

"Who is that bitch?" Lenny demanded to know.

"Emma Moyer. She's the one who jumped all over us at the gun shop the other day when you bought your ammo. Another one of those damn tree huggers trying to save the world and everything in it."

"You just cost us a trophy buck," Lenny shouted at the woman, his face red with rage.

"Go home. Go back wherever you came from," the woman in the clearing yelled. "Take your bloodlust and get out of here!"

"Give me that damn rifle," Lenny said, jerking the Remington from

Brad's hands. "I'll show that crazy bitch who she's screwing with!"

Jake grabbed his arm and said, "Calm down, I'll talk to the sheriff and the game warden. Interfering with a licensed hunt is illegal."

"Calm down, my ass! That bitch just cost me ten grand!"

He yanked his arm free and quickly raised the rifle to his shoulder, firing off a shot that plowed up a furrow of dirt and snow two feet to the woman's left. She yelped in surprise and threw herself sideways behind the cover of a thick pine.

"Are you nuts?" Jake shouted, trying to wrestle the gun from Lenny's hands. The two men struggled while Brad stared at them open mouthed. Jake managed to get the rifle away, but Lenny charged him with murder in his eyes. The hunting guide slammed the butt of the Remington into the larger man's stomach in the old vertical butt stroke every Army recruit learns in basic training. Lenny sank to his knees clutching his stomach as a big woof of breath left him, then toppled to his side.

Jake reversed the rifle and pointed it at his client. "Back off, Lenny! I won't have any of that kind of bullshit out here on my hunt! You can have your damned money back and get the hell out of my sight."

Downhill, the woman carefully peeked her head out from around the tree's thick trunk. "You tried to kill me! I'm going to the sheriff, Jake Gibbons! You've gone way too far this time!"

"I didn't fire that shot, Emma. My crazy client here did. Or I should say former client! But what the hell are you doing running around out here shooting a gun at us in the first place?"

"I didn't shoot at you, I shot up in the air! Besides, my gun's loaded with blanks. I told you I was going to stop the hunt!"

"Well you stopped it alright," Jake shouted back. "You're crazy, Emma! It's a wonder somebody didn't shoot you, running around acting like that!"

"We'll see what the sheriff has to say about this," the woman shouted.

"Yeah, well we'll both be talking to him," Jake told her, as she turned and stalked away.

By then Lenny had caught his breath and struggled back to his feet, though he was still bent over in pain.

"I'll sue your ass for everything you've got," he warned the guide. "Nobody treats Lenny Dewitt like that!"

Meanwhile the snow had continued to fall and the sky was growing darker by the minute.

"No problem, you can have your money back. I'm done with you. But first we need to get off this damn mountain," Jake said. "I'll take you two back to your motel."

"I'm not going anywhere with you, you prick," Lenny said.

"What are you going to do, walk back to town?"

"Better than spending another minute with you!"

"Grow up," Jake said, as he started to collect their equipment. "It's over a mile back to the trailhead and then six miles to town. I'll have you there in an hour or two."

"I don't need you for a damn thing," the big man said. He picked up the rifle from where Jake had set it down, as the guide shot him a warning look. But he hung it from his shoulder with the wide leather sling and turned to his son-in-law. "What? You just going to lay there like a damn bump on a log? Get your ass in gear!"

Brad realized that he had not moved from the time the first shots rang out and Lenny had snatched the rifle way from him. He scrambled to his feet and brushed the snow off of his clothing.

"Kid, try to talk some sense into this idiot," Jake said.

"Come on, Lenny," Brad said. "Let's just get our stuff and we'll have Mr. Gibbons drop us off at the motel, okay?"

"Shut up, you little turd!" Lenny shouted at him. "Why Sherry ever got messed up with you in the first place I'll never know. Damn little faggot!"

"Enough!" Jake shouted. "Now, I'm responsible for you until we get off this damn mountain, so you can either shut up and come with us or I'll truss you up and carry you out like a quartered elk. And don't think I can't do it!"

Lenny started to reply, then saw the look in the guide's eyes and clamped his mouth shut in a thin, hard line.

They silently trudged down off the far side of the hill and came to the trail where they had left the horses tied. Not a word was said as they climbed into the saddle, even when Brad couldn't make it the first time and tumbled out of the stirrup, landing on his rear end as he tried to swing up onto the big sorrel mare. He would have preferred the ribbing he would have normally received for his blunder over the tense silence of the trio.

When they made their way back to the trailhead, Brad helped Jake load the horses into the trailer, though how much help his clumsy efforts were was subject to debate. Still, the young man made the effort and Jake figured he had enough to deal with in the rest of his life to need any more criticism. Jake closed the trailer door, then climbed into the cab of his crew cab pickup and started the diesel engine.

"Now where the hell did he go?"

Brad looked around the small parking area but there was no sign of his father-in-law.

"Maybe he needed to take a leak," Jake said and honked the truck's horn.

"Lenny. We need to get a move on. Let's go!"

No sound came from the shadows in the trees around them.

Jake held the horn down again for a long time then looked at Brad in frustration.

"Any idea where he wandered off to?"

"I don't know," Brad said. "He was here when we started loading the horses."

"Come on, Lenny," Jake shouted, "it's snowing harder and looks like we've got a bad storm coming in. This ain't no time to play games!"

They waited and shouted several more times, then Jake walked around the small parking area looking for footprints, but if there were any to be seen they had been covered by the rapidly falling snow.

"Do you suppose the stubborn SOB actually started walking back to town?"

"I don't know," Brad replied. "You saw how he is, he's not used to anybody treating him like you did. Most people just back down when he gets that way."

"Damn it!" Jake said as he climbed back into the truck. "Let's see if we can find him on the road before he freezes his stubborn ass off."

He pushed in the clutch, put the truck in gear, and pulled out onto the Forest Service road, headed toward town. Driving slowly, they watched for Lenny. It only took a few minutes for the snow to cover the truck and trailer's tracks.

***

Twenty minutes later at another parking area half a mile further up the mountainside, Emma Moyer coughed and panted as she waded through the snow and broke out from the tree line into the parking area. *Damn thin air!*

Then she cursed under her breath as she stood looking at her car, her hands on her hips. All four tires were completely flat.

Wonderful! Just what I needed. Those bastards!

Emma was not having a good day. First that maniac hunting with Jake Gibbons had fired a shot at her, then she had banged up her knee when she threw herself under cover, making her hike back to the trailhead long and painful. She ached all over, and it seemed like every inch of her body was punishing her. And now this!

Richard had told her not to drive the Prius so far off the main road. The hybrid was a great car in town, and good for the environment, but it was totally unsuited for the rough roads that crawled through the forest. The little car had bottomed out more than once on the drive up the Forest Service road, and Emma had had to fight it to maintain any kind of momentum.

Not that the biggest gas guzzling four wheel drive machomobile would have done her any better with four flat tires. She unlocked the driver's door and pushed the button to pop open the hatchback lid and walked to the back of the car, grumbling to herself about bloodthirsty hunters and stupid cars. Shoving aside a stack of newspapers she had forgotten to drop off at the recycling bin next to the fire station, Emma pulled up the rear cargo mat and a plastic tray to be greeted by an empty space where the car's tiny temporary spare tire should have been.

Damn it, Richard! You promised me you'd pick up a new spare when the other one went flat two weeks ago. Thanks a lot! Typical Richard, walking around with his head in the clouds.

She had no idea how it could have helped the situation even if the lone spare tire had been there, but it only added to her frustration and anger. Sometimes she just wanted to scream.

For a moment she wished she had a cell phone, then felt like a hypocrite since she had led the losing battle to keep the two new cell towers from being erected in Big Lake. But she probably couldn't have found a signal this far from town anyway. Now what? Take her chances and try walking back to town, or wait for help to find her? Richard was down in Tucson visiting his daughter, and nobody else knew she was out here. Well, except for Jake Gibbons and his hunters, and they would just love to see her now, wouldn't they? That would sure give them a laugh!

I'd rather try to walk out or sit up here and freeze to death than give the bloodthirsty bastards the satisfaction of asking them for help!

It had been a long day and Emma was weary and couldn't think straight. Was it better to stay with the little shelter the car offered or try to make it back to town? She was still debating her situation when she heard a noise behind her and turned to see the figure staring at her, a high powered rifle cradled in the crook of one arm.

"You scared the hell out of me!" Emma said. "Did you do this?"

"You just love to go around making trouble for people, don't you?"

Anger replaced exhaustion and Emma shot back, "And your kind just doesn't care about anything but what you want, don't you?"

"You've been warned, but you just won't listen, will you?"

Emma wanted to scream out all of her rage and frustration, but the snow was coming down harder and she realized there was no time to argue. "Listen, this isn't the time to talk about what you believe and what I believe. This storm is a bad one and we need to get back to town while we still can."

"You're right, no time to waste talking." Suddenly the rifle was pointed at her.

"Now wait a minute! This is crazy! Don't…"

"Let's see if you can run as fast as those deer you love so much."

The sound of the rifle's safety clicking off seemed incredibly loud in the silent parking area. Emma felt her bowels turn to water as the rifle was brought up to shoulder level. She screamed, then turned and ran for the forest, hoping to get some cover between herself and the gaping maw of the rifle's barrel. But she only made it a few steps when the rifle roared and a long flame shot from its muzzle. She felt a massive blow to her back, the last thing she would ever feel. Emma pitched facedown, unaware that the rough bark of the tree scraped her cheek as she fell. Blood pooled out below her, steaming in the cold mountain air before the snow covered her body.

Chapter 2

"I don't care what you say, it's a bad idea and I won't have it!"

"Chet, it's not a bad idea, it's a good thing! We've needed this for a long time. And besides, there's nothing you or this Council can do about it anyway," said Bob Bennett, Big Lake's Town Attorney.

"What's good about it? Sending a message that women in Big Lake routinely get abused? How is that going to help our image? What message does that give to the rest of the world?"

"Women do get abused," Christine Ridgeway said. "They get abused in high-rise condominiums in New York City and they get abused in fancy summer cabins and run-down house trailers in Big Lake. All we are doing is providing a safe refuge for them when they need it."

"This is not New York City!" declared Councilwoman Gretchen Smith-Abbot.

"No ma'am, it isn't, but abuse still happens here. You and Mayor Wingate can hide your heads in the sand and believe we all live in LaLa Land, but that isn't the case."

"*Go git'em, Hillbilly,*" Sheriff Jim Weber said under his breath, thankful that somebody else was the target at this week's Town Council meeting. God knows he had spent more than his fair share of time in the hot seat. Not that he wasn't there to support Christine in her efforts to convince the Council and the community that SafeHaven was needed and served a good purpose. But sometimes it was nice to sit back and let someone else take the heat.

"Well, all I see this place doing is promoting the Devil's feminist lesbianism master plan," said Hazel Fuller, a little bird of a woman who was a staple at every Town Council meeting.

"Feminism and lesbianism are not synonymous. Nor are they part of the Devil's master plan," Christine replied, "I'm not sure what his master plan is, or even if he has one, but I do know that domestic abuse is evil and that these women and their children need a place where they can be safe."

"The Bible says that a woman must submit to her husband!" Hazel said stubbornly, her arms folded tightly across her chest. "This place of yours encourages them to do just the opposite. It's sinful!"

"We're not getting into a discussion about religion here," Kirby Templeton, the senior Councilman warned Hazel, "And I have not opened the floor to audience participation yet." Hazel glared at him as he turned to Christine, "Miss Ridgeway, I think most of us here on the Council, and in the audience tonight, agree that SafeHaven will be an asset to our community. We're looking forward to working with you in any way we can."

"Now you just hold on there a minute," Chet interrupted, "I'm the Mayor of this town, and you don't speak for the entire Council. I want a vote on this!"

"Darn it, Chet," Kirby said, unable to keep the frustration out of his voice. "You just don't get it. We can't vote on this, because there is nothing to vote on! It's a done deal."

"I want a vote," the mayor insisted, unwilling to budge on the issue.

"Bob, will you try to explain it to him one more time?" Templeton was having a hard time keeping the irritation out of his voice.

"As I have explained over and over again, Lucy Washburn's will was very specific." Bennett said. "She wanted her house and her three rental cabins to be used as a shelter for battered women and their children. She ordered the sale of the remainder of her rather substantial holdings, with the proceeds be put into secure investments to support a nonprofit organization that she had already established to provide for the long-term operation of the shelter. The monies are also to be used to help the shelter's clients establish themselves in an independent life, pay for continuing education programs for them, and to help fund scholarships for their children. The land is zoned for it and there is nothing that this body can do about it, even if we wanted to."

"Lucy Washburn was always a kook," the mayor interrupted.

"Be that as it may, aside from yourself and Councilwoman Smith-Abbot, I'm not sure anyone else on the Council has a problem with SafeHaven," Bennett replied. "Miss Ridgeway's sole purpose in being here today is to answer any questions we may have about the shelter."

"Well, I have a problem with it," Hazel Fuller said from the audience, which consisted of herself and three or four citizens with nothing better to do with their time on a Tuesday evening. "I just know that this place will become a hotbed of prostitution and drug activity! The Good Book says…"

"Enough!" Templeton said with a raised voice that he seldom used as he rapped his gavel. "It's snowing hard outside and we all have better things to do with our time. If nobody else has anything to ask Miss Ridgeway, I move that we adjourn this meeting."

"Seconded," said Frank Gauger, a retired postal worker and longtime councilman.

Before the mayor could object, Templeton called for a vote and the motion to adjourn was approved over the votes against it of the mayor and his faithful ally, Councilwoman Smith-Abbot.

Christine Ridgeway accepted the handshakes of several councilmembers, then turned to the sheriff and said, "Wow! Now I know what you've had to deal with all this time. Those two are a piece of work!"

"Welcome to my world," Weber told her. "I guess the good thing is that even the members of the Council who usually back the mayor were not with him on this one."

"Only because they like me more than they hate you," Christine said. "That's because I'm so much prettier!"

"I won't argue with you on that one," Weber told her, as he held open the door and they stepped out onto the sidewalk.

"Brrrr! It's getting nasty out here," Christine said, pulling her gloves on. "Tell me again, why did I let you talk me into leaving sunny and warm San Diego to come back to this one-horse-town where it is now snowing all over my petite little frame?"

"Because we both know you were going bat shit crazy over there in the land of quakes and flakes. And because we need you here. Now get your petite little frame into your car and get home before this gets any worse."

Christine, who hadn't actually been petite since about the age of maybe eighteen months, got into her Isuzu Trooper and started the engine, then turned on the windshield wipers to clear away the two inches of snow that had covered the vehicle during the Town Council meeting.

Turning back to Weber, she said, "Seriously Jimmy, I do need this. For the last ten years I've just been spinning my wheels caught up in all of that bureaucracy and feeling like I was never accomplishing anything. And after Barry died, I just didn't care any more. I need to care! I need to make a difference in somebody's life!"

She blinked away tears, lost for a moment in time, and then her characteristic good humor resurfaced and she pulled Weber into her ample arms and hugged him. "I love you, you little twerp!"

"Love you, too," Weber told her, then stood up and closed the Trooper's door. "You going to be okay driving home?"

"I've got four wheel drive and all this weight to hold me down, I'll be just fine. I may have spent the last decade tanning on the beach in my bikini, but I'm still a country gal deep down inside. I grew up driving these roads in all kinds of weather. Now stop worrying about me and get yourself inside out of this cold."

"Just thinking about you in that bikini makes me feel warm all over," Weber told her, and Christine laughed.

"Lord, ain't that an ugly picture, Jimmy? See you tomorrow." She blew him a kiss and drove away.

Weber watched as his friend's taillights were swallowed by the falling snow, then walked across the parking lot to the Sheriff's Office. Deputies Buz Carelton and Dolan Reed were standing just inside the door with cups of coffee in their hands, watching the snow build up through the office window. Buz handed Weber a second cup as he stepped inside and brushed snow off his coat.

"You boys don't have anything better to do than that?" Weber asked. "Why aren't you out there fighting crime and keeping the world safe for democracy?"

"Because we're old and it's cold out there," Dolan told him. "Besides, every time you go to a Town Council meeting we have to hang around to see if you're still our boss by the time it's over. We never know when Chet's going to finally get his way and demote you to dogcatcher and give Archer your job."

Weber didn't know which was worse, his ongoing feud with the mayor, or the idea of his bumbling deputy, who happened to be Mayor Wingate's son, having a position with any responsibility more than directing traffic at the crosswalk in front of the primary school or brewing the office coffee. Though he had to admit, as he sipped from his cup, for all of his faults, Archer did make a good pot of coffee.

If he took any offense to Dolan's remark, Archer didn't show it. Then again, Archer seldom showed any emotion or interest in anything except what he was having for breakfast, lunch, and dinner, and any donuts or sweet somebody brought in to share with the rest of the staff.

"So did the mayor whine and snivel about the shelter?"

"Did you ever know Chet Wingate not to piss and moan about something?" asked Mary Caitlin, Weber's administrative assistant, who had been at the Sheriff's Office since her husband Pete had held Weber's job. "That man would be miserable if he didn't have something to be unhappy about."

"Oh yeah," Weber assured her. "He knows that a women's shelter is going to make Big Lake look bad to the tourists, and we can't have that. And then we had Hazel Fuller going on about it turning the local women into lesbians and prostitutes, and about how women should submit to their husbands because the Bible says so."

"That old biddy is obsessed with hookers," Dolan said. "Wasn't it just last summer she was going on about hookers working at the boat launch?"

"And out of the library bookmobile," Weber added.

"Well, you know and I know that this community needs a safe place for women when they've got trouble," Mary said. "I can't tell you how many battered women and their kids we've taken in over the years."

Weber couldn't guess at the number either, but he knew that his former boss and his wife had opened the doors of their home to many people over the years, not only abused women and children, but troubled teenagers as well. When Weber's own parents had been killed in an accident, he took a hardship discharge from the Army only six months into his second enlistment as a military policeman, and came home to take care of his teenaged sister. Pete and Mary Caitlin had become surrogate parents to both of them.

"Isn't it about time you got home, Mary? Old Pete's got to be getting hungry by now."

"Oh, that man's always hungry. I swear, he could eat an entire cow and then ask me what's for dessert. I don't know how he stays so darned skinny!"

"It must be all that good lovin' you're giving him," Weber said, and Mary scowled at him and as she pulled her coat off a hook on the wall.

"Is that all you ever think about?"

"It's all any of us think about," Weber told her, and Dolan nodded.

"We're guys, Mary, it's our job," the deputy said.

"Well, get your mind out of the gutter and back into your vehicle," she told him. "The way this storm is shaping up, we're bound to have a bunch of fender benders with all of the skiers in town. Damn flatlanders don't know how to drive in the snow."

"But they all drive those fancy SUVs with four wheel drive," Buz said. "Don't that mean they can go sixty miles an hour in the middle of a whiteout?"

"No, they can't," Dolan said. "But that don't mean they won't. They never seem to understand that four wheel drive will get you going, but it don't do a durned thing to help you stop."

The deputies laughed, and Weber was glad to see that the tension between the two longtime friends had eased up since the announcement that Dolan's teenaged daughter Gina was carrying Billy Carelton's baby. The two fathers had come to blows over the situation in the middle of the breakfast rush at the ButterCup Café, an incident that had set tongues to wagging in the small town. It gave Mayor Chet Wingate even more ammunition to use against the sheriff in their next confrontation before the Town Council.

"Well, I'm out of here," Mary said as she reached for the door, only to step back as it was opened and Jake Gibbons came in, stomping snow off his boots.

"How's it going, Jake? What brings you out in this mess?"

"Not good, Sheriff. We've got trouble. Big trouble. I've lost a hunter."

Mary sighed and took her coat back off. "Looks like Pete's going to have to get by with leftovers tonight. Looks like it's going to be a long one."

Chapter 3

"Start at the beginning and tell me what happened," Weber said, after pouring Jake a cup of coffee and getting him settled in a chair.

It was hard for the guide to relax long enough to talk and he fidgeted as he related the story of the day's hunt, the confrontation with Emma Moyer, and then the incident with Lenny Dewitt and his subsequent disappearance.

"It's bad enough with Emma running around like a crazy woman shooting that damn gun of hers off to scare away the deer," Jake said with obvious agitation. "But that damn client of mine is a total nutcase. I was afraid he'd kill her, and I think he would have if I hadn't gotten that rifle away from him!"

"Emma's doing what she thinks is right," Weber told him. "You know her, she's always got some cause. But you're right, she could get herself shot pulling a stunt like that."

"Hell, if it was me and somebody popped up out of nowhere blasting away with a gun like that, I might shoot back just in reaction," Buz said.

"Well, I'll deal with Emma," Weber assured the guide. "And I'm sure Mark Santos over at the Game and Fish Office in Pinetop will want to hear about that. But what about this client of yours? Are you sure he didn't get back to town under his own power?"

"He wasn't at his motel when I dropped his son-in-law and my horse trailer off, and my brother Sam had his two sons out. They got back before we did and they hadn't seen him."

"And you're sure you didn't miss him coming back into town?"

"Miss him? Do ya think I'm an idiot, Sheriff? That I'd drive right past him and not even notice? Me and Sam are professionals! We've never had a client get hurt before, let alone lost."

Weber raised his hand to calm the man down. Jake Gibbons was several years older than him and they had a nodding acquaintance at best. But both Jake and his twin brother Sam had reputations as good men, hardworking and honest. It was obvious that the situation had unnerved him.

"I didn't mean that, Jake. But you said he's a stubborn blowhard. Could he have heard you coming and got off the road before you spotted him?"

"Man, I looked and looked. I drove up and down that road half a dozen times and didn't see any sign of him. Sam's out there now, still looking. I guess he's contrary enough to have hid on me, but in a storm like this, a man could get lost and get himself in bad trouble in no time at all."

Weber knew the man was right. A lifetime in Arizona's mountains had taught him that when the big winter storms rolled in over the Mogollon Rim, dropping as much as three feet of snow, things could become very dangerous. More than one hiker, hunter, or unwary motorist taking a shortcut down an untraveled back country road had never made it out alive. And the storm that was closing in on Big Lake looked to be a bad one. He pushed the intercom button on his desk and told Mary to round up the troops and have every deputy report in to begin the search for the missing man.

* * *

While the rest of the deputies assembled at the Sheriff's Office, Buz and Dolan followed Jake up the mountain road toward the trailhead where Lenny Dewitt was last seen. Weber sent Deputy Tommy Frost to the Mountain Mist Motel, where Lenny Dewitt, his sons, and son-in-law were staying, to see if they had any idea of where the man might be found. "After you're done there, canvass the bars and restaurants in case he's in one of them," Weber told the young deputy, though he knew that Tommy had the initiative to have taken that next step on his own.

Chad Summers and Deputy Robyn Fuchette were the first to arrive after Mary's summons, and Weber apologized for calling them in on their day off. Close on their heels were Weber's two newest deputies, Dan Wright and Ted Cooper. Both recently commissioned deputies, both came with experience and so far Weber had been pleased with their job performance.

Ted Cooper, whom everybody simply called Coop, retired after 20 years as an Army MP and was a good, solid lawman who brought a lifetime of experience and investigatory skills to the Sheriff's Office. At 40 years old, Coop was in excellent physical shape and still wore his hair short, in the military fashion. Having served as an Army MP himself, Weber felt an affinity to the man.

Dan Wright had been a star on his small college's football team, but not good enough to get offered a scholarship to a major university or a pro contract. He worked his way through school, graduated with a degree in criminal justice, and was immediately hired by the police department in his small Colorado hometown. Three years later he left after a short, failed marriage to the chief's daughter, when it became apparent that the strained personal relationship with his boss was too uncomfortable for everyone involved. To his credit, the chief had called around to other departments in the region to help him find a new position and had given Wright an excellent reference. "He's a fine young man and an excellent officer," the chief had told Weber, "and if it weren't for the whole damn family thing, I'd keep him on forever. But you know how it is in a small town."

Indeed Weber did know all about small town politics, and he was happy to have the new deputy to finally bring his office to full staff. For the first time in over two years his deputies were working regular schedules and getting their much deserved and needed time off. Old timers like Buz, Chad, and Dolan had told him that it was a treat to have two days in a row off to spend with their families. But they all knew that when an emergency arose, it was all hands on deck. And somebody lost and on foot in a winter storm in the mountains definitely qualified as an emergency.

After a quick briefing on the situation, Weber called Dolan on the radio and asked if they had found any sign of the missing hunter.

"We're at the parking area now where he was last seen," Dolan replied. "No trace of him but we've got a good four or five inches of snow on the ground and it's coming down hard. Any tracks he may have left are long gone. Jake is freaking out. His brother just pulled in, he's been up and down the road three times and even back to the motel and there was no sign of the man. Do you want us to drive further up the mountain?"

Weber wasn't familiar with the Forest Service road they were on but Chad Summers was an experienced hunter who had spent a lot of time in the mountains in pursuit of deer and elk.

"What's the road like past the trailhead there?" Weber asked him, and Chad studied the map.

"It gets worse the further up you go, and within a mile or so it just peters out. And it's steep enough that anybody on foot with any sense at all should realize they are headed away from town. Of course, we don't know if this guy has any sense. Sounds like he's a hothead who doesn't put a lot of thought into anything he does."

Weber was just keying the radio's microphone to tell Dolan to check uphill as far as they could safely travel when Mary Caitlin turned to him from the telephone console and said "Hold on, he just turned up at the motel. I've got him on the phone."

Weber took the phone and introduced himself, and then told him that they were in the process of launching a full scale search and rescue operation for the man.

"Jeez, what's the big deal? I got a ride from a couple of guys in a pickup. We stopped at a bar and I bought them a couple of drinks to thank them."

Weber wanted to tell him that it was a big deal, that he had called in his deputies on their time off to launch a search party, but he had dealt with enough people like Lenny Dewitt in his time to know that the message wouldn't get through anyway. Instead, he said, "We need to have a talk about you shooting at Emma Moyer."

"Who? You mean that crazy bitch up on the mountain? She shot at us first! And I want that goddamn Jake Gibbons arrested! He assaulted me!"

The man's voice had raised while he was talking and Weber decided that he really did not like Lenny and was looking forward to having a word with him, face-to-face. But that was going to have to wait because Mary interrupted him to tell them they just gotten a report of a rollover accident with injuries on the highway just outside of town.

"Mr. DeWitt, don't leave town anytime soon."

"And where the hell am I supposed to go?" asked Lenny. "It's snowing like a son-of-a-bitch out there. And we've still got deer tags to fill out, with or without that crazy assed guide. And I'm not done with him yet either, he owes me!"

Lenny was still yelling into the phone when Weber hung up on him and headed for the door.

Chapter 4

The Mitsubishi Outlander, or what was left of it, was laying on its roof in the ditch alongside the highway amid a litter of broken glass, spewed suitcases, skis, and poles. Tommy Frost had been the first deputy on scene and had put flares out in both directions to warn oncoming drivers of the accident scene. When Weber pulled up, he pointed his spotlight toward the wreck, where two young men were crouching over a young woman who lay in the snow.

As Weber got out of his Ford Explorer another young woman rushed up to him and cried, "You have to help my friend! She's bleeding really bad!"

"Ambulance is on its way," Weber assured her. "Are you injured?"

Even in the near dark, Weber could see the dark blood spattered over the woman's down jacket and hands, but the sheriff saw no obvious injuries.

She shook her head and said, "No, this is Jill's blood. You have to help her!"

Weber quickly made his way down the ditch to the injured woman as Dan Wright and Ted Cooper pulled up in their marked units. Dan began directing traffic around the accident scene, while Coop moved his vehicle so that the headlights and bright searchlights on the roof bar helped illuminate the scene, then joined Weber and Tommy Frost next to the wrecked car.

"What've we got?" Cooper asked.

"Pretty severe head laceration," Weber told him, "We need to stop the bleeding."

"I've got just the thing," Coop said, flipping open the first aid kit he carried in his patrol unit. "Here, use this," he said, handing Weber a sanitary napkin.

"But that's ….."

"Yes ma'am," Coop told the woman's friend, "it's a feminine hygiene product. But when it comes to a bad cut like this it does the job better than any gauze pads we carry."

"Check her out, Coop." Weber told the deputy. "She's got a lot of blood on her but she says it's just from her friend. But I want to be sure." Weber knew that in the adrenaline-drenched confusion of a major accident or catastrophe, victims often times did not realize that they had been injured because they were focused on the torn and twisted bodies of the people around them.

Turning his attention back to the woman on the ground, Weber continued to press the sanitary pad against her forehead to staunch the flow of blood. "What's her name?"

"Huh?" One of the men asked in confusion.

"Her name!" Weber asked again. "What's her name?"

"Oh. It's Jill. Jill Walker."

Weber wasn't sure if the man was impaired by drugs or alcohol, though he didn't smell anything, and he knew that it could just be the after effects of the accident that left him seeming dazed. Either way, he didn't have time to worry about it right at that moment.

"Jill? Jill, can you hear me? Jill, I need you to open your eyes, okay honey?"

There was a slight moan from the woman and her eyelids fluttered for a brief moment, but remained closed.

"Stay with us, Jill," Weber told her. "Help's on the way."

As he finished speaking, help did arrive, in the form of Big Lake's ambulance. Paramedics Rusty Heinz and Pat Price wasted no time coming to the woman's aid and Weber moved aside to let the professionals do their job.

"Okay, run it down for me," Weber told Tommy.

"I really don't know yet," Tommy said. "I just had time to put out flares when you showed up."

"Who was driving?" Weber asked the two men, who seemed transfixed by all the blood splashed in front of them. When neither responded, Weber raised his voice, "Hey! Wake up guys. Who was driving?"

"Uh, I was," said one of them, who Weber estimated to be in his early 20s. The man had curly black hair and just a wisp of a mustache on his upper lip.

"And what's your name, sir?" Weber asked.

"Brandon. Brandon Whitehead," the young man told him.

"Brandon, I'm Sheriff Weber and this is Deputy Frost. He's going to ask you some questions about the accident, okay?"

"Am I in trouble?" Brandon asked.

"I don't know," Weber told him. "Were you drinking or using any kind of controlled substance?"

"No sir!"

"You go with the deputy and he'll take your statement and we'll see what this is all about, okay?"

Brandon nodded and Tommy led him back to his department issued pickup truck, where they crawled inside be to out of the snow.

"And what's your name, sir," Weber asked the other man.

"Donald. Ahh they call me Donny. Donny Fortner."

"All right, Donny, let's you and me go sit in my vehicle and get out of this snow. Coop? Is that young lady going to be alright?"

"She's fine, Sheriff. Just pretty shaken up and worried about her friend here."

"Okay, why don't you take her up to your unit and get her out of the cold and see if you can help her clean up a bit. Is that okay with you, Miss….?"

"Lark," the young woman told him, her teeth chattering from both the cold and the adrenaline coursing through her body. "Tracy Lark."

"Okay, Tracy. Let's have you go with Deputy Cooper."

"I can't leave my friend," Tracy said. "She needs me!"

"She's going to be just fine," Pat Price assured her. "She's started to come around now and we're going to take her to the hospital to be checked out. I know this looks bad, but head wounds always bleed a lot. She'll be okay, I promise."

Tracy reluctantly allowed herself to be led away, looking back over her shoulder at her friend as Coop led her out of the ditch.

* * *

Just under an hour later, Weber, Coop, and Nate Sawyers, the Highway Patrol officer who worked the section around Big Lake, stood together watching as Randy Laird winched the Mitsubishi onto its wheels and pulled it out of the ditch with his tow truck.

"I always wonder how anybody can walk away from a wreck like that in one piece," Coop said.

"Chalk it up to outstanding car design," Weber said. "The girl who was injured had just unhooked her seat belt to lean over the back seat and get something out of the cargo compartment or she might not have got banged up either."

"She going to be okay?" Nate asked as he sipped from a steaming thermos cup of coffee.

"She'll need some stitches and will have a nasty headache for a little bit, but she lucked out," Weber told him.

"Straight stretch of road, no sign of what caused it. Any ideas?"

"The driver blew clean on a breathalyzer," Weber replied. "He didn't appear to be on anything and they all seemed like good kids. I think it was just a combination of speed and poor road conditions. Tommy cited him for failure to control his vehicle."

"Look at this circus," Coop said incredulously, as an SUV nearly rear-ended another vehicle that had slowed down to gawk at the wrecked car on the tow truck's hook. "Where are all these people coming from?"

"Tucson, Phoenix. They flock out of the desert at the first big snowfall," Weber told him. "And this is only Tuesday. Imagine what it's like on a weekend with fresh snow."

"Well, you boys have fun," Nate said as he threw the dregs of his coffee into the snow. "I've got crime to fight and traffic citations to write."

They watched as Nate got in his car and headed east down the mountain toward the Indian casino at Hon-Dah and the merged towns of Pinetop-Lakeside beyond.

"We've about got this cleared up," Coop said. "Why don't you go ahead and take off, Sheriff."

"Oh, so you're giving the orders around here now?" Weber asked with a smile.

"No sir. Just brown nosing the boss," Coop assured him.

"Well, with that attitude you're gonna go far," Weber chuckled. "I guess I'll get out from underfoot and let you professionals get back to work."

Coop nodded, then stepped forward and slapped the hood of a Jeep that had come to a near stop to see what all of the police activity was about. "Wake up! Keep moving. Nothing to see here."

***

It was after 8 p.m. by the time Weber made it back to the Sheriff's Office and he decided to wait until the next day to talk to Lenny Dewitt, Jake Gibbons, and Emma Moyer about the shots fired during the hunt that day.

Kate Copley was on dispatch duty and gave him a wave as he stopped inside the door and stomped snow off his boots.

"The radio sounds busy," Weber observed.

"A couple of fender benders, but nothing too serious," Kate said. "Dolan and Buz stayed on duty long enough to handle them, and Chad's on call to backup Archer and Dan if they need anything. A lady over on Sunset Lane called to say some kids were throwing snowballs at her house. Aside from that, not much happening."

Tommy Frost looked up from the desk where he was finishing his report on the accident out on the highway. "I'm about done with this, then I thought I'd run by the medical center and see how Miss Walker is doing. After that I'll come back here and hang around if you need anything."

"No need to," Weber told him. "Where are the other three from the accident?"

"They're at the hospital with her," Tommy said. "They have reservations at the ski resort and I imagine they'll pick them up with the shuttle van when she's released. Unless they keep her overnight for evaluation."

Big Lake's small medical center only had a dozen patient rooms so Weber knew that unless the young woman's head injury raised fears of a concussion, she would probably be released.

"Didn't you get off duty at six? Go on home and take it easy."

"Really, it's no problem. I don't mind hanging out here. With this snow and all the skiers headed up this way, it could get busy."

"Why are you avoiding going home, Deputy?"

The young deputy's face colored and he said, "I'm not, I just…"

"Is Tami Gaylord still stalking you, Tommy?"

Tommy's face grew even redder and he said, "I have to tell you, Sheriff, that lady scares me."

"Well you should be scared, son! She's twice your size and insatiable!"

Usually reserved and immune to the teasing that went on in the office, Kate couldn't help snorting from the dispatch desk, turning Tommy's face a deeper shade of crimson.

"What am I going to do, Jimmy? I stop for lunch and she shows up at my table. I go home and she's there parked in the driveway. Or else she's left a bunch of messages on my voice mail, always wanting me to come by and fix something for her."

Tami Gaylord was the large, heavily made-up owner of a shop that sold overpriced Native American art and chainsaw woodcarvings to gullible tourists. Overly dramatic in everything she did and given to hysterics at the drop of a hat, Tami had worked her way through four or five husbands, who all seemed to be more than happy to give her a large financial settlement and escape within months after saying "I do." A couple of months earlier she had set her sights on the handsome young blonde deputy and had been pursuing him ever since, never mind their more than twenty year age difference.

"Have you just told her you're not interested?"

"I did! Then she did this thing where she leaned in close to my face and kind of ran the tip of her tongue over her lips and promised me that I would be before too long! And honest, Jimmy, I really don't want to be!"

Kate lost total control, erupting into roars of laughter and pounding her fist onto her desktop. Weber couldn't help himself and gave in too, making the poor deputy's condition even worse.

Finally, Weber put his arm around the young man's shoulder and squeezed him affectionately. "I guess it's just your cross to bear. That's the price you have to pay for being such a good looking hunk."

More laughter from the dispatch desk followed Weber as he gave Tommy's shoulder another squeeze and headed for the door.

Chapter 5

The snow continued to fall throughout the night, a strong wind whipping it into a frenzy that rattled the doors and windows in Weber's cabin and left deep drifts across the countryside. The silence after the storm woke him up the next morning and he eased out of bed, careful not to wake Robyn as she slept beside him. He padded across the floor to the bedroom door and into the living room, where the digital thermometer on his window told him the outside temperature was 24°.

Peering outside, everything was cloaked in white. Weber spooned ground coffee into the filter in the basket of the automatic coffeemaker, filled it with water, and while it was brewing he slipped back into bed and spooned Robyn. She moaned softly in her sleep and moved against him.

Weber kissed her shoulder, drawing another soft moan, and watched as her eyelids fluttered open. "I love you."

"I love you," Robyn said. "Do we have to get up? It feels cold."

"We don't have to get up," he told her. "And I know a good way to warm things up."

"I bet you do. But eventually we'll still have to get up and it will still be cold. Then what?"

"Let's cross that bridge when we come to it," Weber said. "In the meantime…."

Robyn remained on her side and pushed herself against him. "Yes, in the meantime…."

***

An hour later Robyn was in the shower when the telephone rang. "Jimmy? Can you run by Emma Moyer's place on your way in? I got a call from Richard MacEwen. He's down in Tucson and said he hasn't been able to reach her since Monday night and he's getting worried about her."

"The phones are probably out again, with this storm," Weber told her.

"Probably so. You know how it is, if a dog pees on the ground in Show Low, the phones go out somewhere between Lakeside and here."

"Did he try Emma's cell phone?"

"You know Emma wouldn't have one of those," Mary said. "She's still got her panties in a twist over the new towers."

Emma Moyer, a thin, red-haired woman with a passion for causes, was Big Lake's resident environmental activist. Some people complained that she was anti-everything, leading protests against the summer cabins that wealthy residents of the desert communities to the south were building on the mountains that towered over the small town, against the building of the ski resort, against the town's new cell phone towers, and this time of year, against the deer and elk hunts that brought hunters from near and far. Though Emma was often a thorn in his side, Weber respected the woman for her commitment to what she believed in, even if he sometimes considered those strong beliefs misguided.

"I need to talk to her about that nonsense with Jake and his hunters yesterday," Weber told her. "I'll stop by her place on my way in. What else is going on this morning?"

"The usual after a storm like this. Lots of power lines down, some minor traffic accidents but no injuries, and schools are closed. The snowplows are all out. Oh, and David Kinter collapsed when he was shoveling out his driveway. Looks like a heart attack. The ambulance transporting him to the hospital in Show Low slid off the road and had to be pulled out. Nobody injured and it looks like David is going to be all right."

Weber leaned over the kitchen sink, wiping fog from the window glass as he looked outside. It was still snowing, but at least the wind had died down. The big old oak stump in the yard he used to split firewood on was buried under the snow. The stump was over two feet tall.

"How deep is it out there?"

"We've got about thirty inches at our place, and pretty close to that in town. The good news is that the DOT closed down both highways, over the Rim from Payson and north of the Canyon, so at least for a while whoever's here is here but we won't have that many more skiers coming up and getting in trouble, which should help our workload."

U.S. Highway 60 wound its way down and back up out of the Salt River Canyon between Globe and Show Low, and State Route 260 crossed the Mogollon Rim between Payson and Show Low. They were the main routes travelers took to the White Mountains from the desert cities to the south, and both could be extremely hazardous in bad weather. Knowing how vital tourist dollars from Phoenix and Tucson were to the small towns in the mountains, Weber knew it was a dangerous storm for the State Department of Transportation to take such action. And while fewer flatlanders meant fewer traffic accidents and other problems for the Sheriff's Office, it also meant a loss of business for the ski resort, motels, and other businesses that depended on those tourist dollars.

Weber rang off after promising to check on Emma Moyer on his way into the office as Robyn came into the kitchen dressed in jeans and a maroon wool cable knit sweater. She kissed him and poured coffee, asking over her shoulder, "Was that your girlfriend on the phone?"

"It was Mary, giving me a heads up on the day and asking me to stop by and check on Emma Moyer on my way in."

Robyn scowled at the sound of Emma's name, remembering the time a few months ago when the woman had organized a sit-in on the highway coming into town while Robyn was directing traffic around construction equipment for the cell tower project. "What's Emma done this time? Blocking the roads so the plows can't clear all of this natural snow?"

"Oh, Emma's got her faults, but she means well," Weber said. "She just goes about things wrong sometimes. But I think her heart's in the right place."

"Her heart may be in the right place," Robyn agreed as she put bread in the toaster. "But I think sometimes her head's up her butt!"

"Well, that may be. But Richard's down in Tucson and can't get her on the phone. He's worried and asked us to check on her."

"Richard!" Robyn said, with another scowl. "They make a perfect pair. Both airheads. She probably can't find the phone buried under all of those tree hugger fliers and propaganda she's always posting around town."

"Well, everybody can't be as perfect as you and me," Weber chuckled, then came up behind Robyn and wrapped her in a hug, kissing her neck. She let out a soft sigh, then turned and pushed him away.

"No you don't. You've got damsels in distress to rescue, and it's my day off and I intend to spend it reading a good book, feeding the woodstove, and listening to music."

"You'd send a man out in this weather while you stay all nice and warm here and read some trashy romance novel?" Weber protested. "I swear woman, your heart's as cold as that blizzard outside the door!"

Robyn smirked at him but didn't relent. "Maybe all that cold will take your mind off other things. Get the blood flowing to the rest of your body, where it's needed."

"But…but… haven't you ever heard of shrinkage? A man could suffer permanent damage out there in this weather!"

"Oh, poor baby," Robyn cooed, wrapping her arms around his neck and looking at him with a twinkle in her almond shaped brown eyes. "But think about this. While you're out there keeping the world safe for democracy, you never know what kind of tips I may find in one of those trashy romance novels. It could be in your best interest, you know?"

"Oh, you're bad!" Weber told her.

"Yes I am. In fact I'm very bad. It comes from reading so much. Now you, get to work! I have research to do."

Knowing further protest would not do him any good, Weber pulled on his heavy Carhartt coat, picked up his Stetson, and gave Robyn a kiss before opening the front door and going out into the storm.

***

Scraping snow off the windshield and back window of his Explorer as it warmed up, Weber wondered what life would be like as a lawman in someplace nice and warm like the Florida Keys or Tahiti. He climbed inside the SUV, grateful for the heater that blasted warm air out of the vents, pushed the button on the dash for four wheel drive, and backed out onto the road.

The snowplows had not made it to his road yet, focusing first on the main roads and streets in town, and nothing moved as he broke trail toward town. Smoke plumed from chimneys as he passed houses and cabins, the lake water dark and forbidding on the other side of the road, and Weber felt like he was in a world all of his own.

At 9,000 feet elevation, the town of Big Lake, Arizona sits, appropriately enough, along the shore of Big Lake, a three mile long body of deep, cold mountain water teeming with fighting trout that drew anglers from across the southwest. Once a sleepy little town that entertained a few fishermen who jealousy guarded their secret getaway, things had changed in the last few years as it was discovered by tourists from Phoenix and Tucson, quickly becoming a popular summer getaway for desert dwellers.

Suddenly hundreds of small cabins, as well as expensive custom homes, began springing up on the sides of the mountains that loomed over the town. Big Lake was changing fast, much to the consternation of long time residents who longed for the good old days before the upper crust of the desert cities to the south built their weekend homes and changed the face of the community forever.

These days, Big Lake's year round population of 4,000 tripled in summer as those weekend homes of part time residents and the area's numerous motels, lodges and tourist cabins filled up.

Cat Mountain Ski Resort brought even more tourists, who rushed to the slopes after every snowfall, their cars and sport utility vehicles carrying ski racks crowding the Main Street and the highway into town.

As he got closer to town he started to see more activity. The road had been plowed, but new snow had left another inch or so on top. Mike King stopped shoveling his driveway and waved as Weber drove slowly past. A little further on he came across a car that had slid off the road. Two teenaged boys were pushing it from the front as a girl sat behind the wheel and gunned the engine. Another girl waved from the back seat. Weber stopped and put on his roof lights.

"You guys okay? Need any help?"

"We've about got it, Sheriff," Adam Miller told him. One night the previous summer Weber had caught Adam parked with his girlfriend on a back road, doing his best to convince her that yes, a guy really could die of blue balls if he didn't get some relief. He remembered his own days as a high school junior trying to convince Kathy Pickney of the very same thing in the front seat of his old Chevy pickup truck. The sheriff had checked to be sure the young lady was all right and didn't feel threatened, relieved Adam of the two bottles of beer he had snuck out of his house, given him a quick warning on underage drinking and responsibility for his actions, and left them alone.

Apparently Adam had not died after all and the same girl was behind the wheel of his car. Weber got out of the Explorer and waded through the snow to the front of the car and helped the boys push. They managed to get the car moving and the girl backed it out onto the road.

"Thanks, Sheriff," Adam said, and Weber shook hands with both boys, tipped his hat to their girlfriends, and listened to them giggle.

"Where you guys headed?"

"Just out looking at all the snow," the other boy said. Weber knew his face from around, but couldn't remember his name. Neil or Nick, something like that. Usually the good kids were just familiar faces, while the troublemakers stood out from the crowd and got remembered.

"Well, be careful, and stay off the back roads until they're cleared. I'd hate to have you get lost and have to survive on melted snow and icicles until we could find you."

The boys nodded in understanding, the girls giggled again, and Weber got back in his Explorer and drove away.

Emma Moyer lived in a small cottage three blocks off Main Street, and though the road had been plowed, a deep bank of drifted and plowed snow blocked the driveway. Weber noted that Emma's car wasn't in the driveway as he left his unit in the street and waded through more snow to her porch. The house looked dark and nobody responded when he knocked.

"Emma? Emma, are you in there?" He rattled the doorknob and heard a small dog bark inside, but nothing else. As he walked back down the porch steps, a mound of snow broke loose from the roof and hit him on the head, knocking his hat off. Weber cursed as part of it found its way inside the back of his coat collar.

Stepping as high as he could, Weber made his way along the side of the house to the back and tried that door, which was also locked. The dog barked again when he knocked.

He went back to the front of the small house and trudged through the snow to the one next door. Celinda Zehnacker answered his knock and when she opened the door Weber could smell freshly baked cookies. His mouth watered, reminding him that he had not had breakfast.

"What brings you out in this mess, Jimmy?"

Celinda was a pretty woman, with friendly blue eyes and a smile that never seemed to leave her face. Weber knew that three years before, she had survived a bad bout of breast cancer that had nearly taken her life but couldn't destroy her spirit.

"Well, Celinda, I woke up this morning and smelled cookies baking, and my nose just led me right here."

"You've got an answer for everything, don't you, Jim Weber? Get inside out of the cold."

"Well, I do try," Weber admitted with a smile.

"Get yourself in here, then. I think the first batch has cooled down enough to eat."

"I'd love to," Weber told her, "but I need to get over to the office. I was actually wondering if you've seen Emma Moyer around yesterday or today. Her gentleman friend is down in Tucson and couldn't reach her by phone, so I came by to check up on her."

"The world will survive for five minutes without you. Besides, I get cold too easy any more."

"Sorry," Weber said, stomping snow off his boots and brushing his jeans and coat clear before stepping inside and closing the door behind himself. Celinda led him through a tidy living room and into the kitchen. Warm, deliciously scented air washed over him as he took a seat at the chair Celinda indicated.

She poured coffee for him, then sat a plate with three warm cookies in front of him. "I love to cook and bake, but I can't eat all of these and it doesn't look like I can make it into town this morning, so do me a favor and eat up, okay?"

Weber bit into a cookie and moaned with pleasure.

"Delicious."

Celinda smiled as she sat down across the table and watched him eat.

Weber finished the first cookie, then said, "I think I'm in love."

"You are. But not with me," Celinda told him. "You just want me for my cookies. That pretty deputy of yours owns your heart."

Weber blushed and said, "Yeah, that's true."

"I'm jealous," Celinda pouted.

"Oh darling, you and me? That would be almost incestuous, wouldn't it?"

Celinda didn't reply, just looked at him. Weber had known Celinda since she and his younger sister Debbie were schoolgirls. He had watched her grow up, and being older, had tried to ignore her and the rest of the girls who seemed to orbit around his beautiful sister. More than once he had been made to feel uncomfortable by their sudden silence if he passed by them and the laughter that erupted behind him in his path. But that was a long time ago, and as an adult he considered Celinda to be a beautiful, intelligent woman, and a friend. So he could not explain why he suddenly felt uncomfortable in her presence.

"Anyway, back to Emma. Have you seen her?"

"No, but then, we don't get along well so I'm not sure I'd notice if she was there anyway."

"You not get along with somebody?" Weber asked. He had never known her to have a bad word about anyone. Not even for her husband, who had left her after her mastectomy because he couldn't cope with what he saw as less of a woman. Weber had been tempted to hunt the jerk down and tell him that Celinda was still one hundred percent woman, and a thousand percent more than he deserved.

"Oh, I probably shouldn't say anything. But during my cancer, Emma kept trying to get me to take all kinds of natural remedies that she was sure would be better than the chemo and radiation. When I didn't follow her regime, she went off on me a couple of times. You know how she can get. I'm afraid she caught me once on a really bad day, right after Doug left, and I just wasn't up to it. She came over and started in on me about all of the poisons I was putting into my body and how the radiation could cause even more cancer down the road someday. I'm not proud to tell you that I lost it. I called her a nosey, meddling bitch and told her to mind her own business and to get out and stay out. We haven't spoken since."

"Do you mind?" Weber asked, getting up and crossing to the telephone that hung on the wall. He lifted the receiver and heard a dial tone.

"The phone's been working," Celinda said. "I talked to my mom last night and again this morning. She worries about me down there in Green Valley, when the news talks about storms up here. I keep telling her that she and Daddy never froze to death in all their years up here, and I won't either."

"How's she doing down there?" Weber asked.

"Oh, she's fine," Celinda assured him. "She had it rough after we lost Daddy, but she got past that. She's busy with her bridge club, taking water aerobics, and she's even taken up painting. She doesn't have a bit of talent, bless her heart, but she sure can slap paint on canvas!"

Weber finished the last of his cookies and thanked her for her hospitality, and said he needed to get back to work. Celinda followed him to the door and hugged him tightly. "Thanks for stopping in, Jimmy. I get lonely sometimes."

Weber held her for a moment longer and then broke the embrace, but Celinda held both of his hands.

"I'm not that silly little girl who hung out with Debbie anymore. I'm all grown up now, Jimmy, and I'm all woman, even if I have lost a couple of parts along the way. Robyn's a lucky lady, but if she ever breaks your heart, you come see me, okay?"

"You can count on it," he told her.

Celinda leaned in and kissed his lips quickly, then pulled away.

Weber thought he saw a tear in her eye as he turned toward the door. He walked down her driveway to his Explorer, looking back at the house as he climbed inside. He could see Celinda standing in front of the window watching him. He waved, then started the engine and drove away.

***

The snow had finally stopped as Weber drove by Richard MacEwen's cabin on Firefly Lane, on the chance that Emma was there, but the driveway was empty except for a deep cover of snow and the cabin was dark and empty. As he approached the corner at Arrowhead Road, three huge snowballs splattered across his windshield, obscuring his vision.

Weber stopped the Explorer and jumped out just in time to see a young boy run around the back of an empty summer cabin. He got back behind the wheel, drove to the end of the block and quickly turned left onto Sunset Lane just as three boys ran out into the street directly behind where Weber had seen the fleeing boy. They skidded to a stop when he put on his overhead lights, not sure what to do next. Weber got out of the Explorer and ordered, "Get over here!"

Heads down, the boys slowly approached him.

"What are your names?"

One of the boys mumbled something and Weber said, "Speak up. And look at me, all of you."

They reluctantly raised their faces and the first one said, "I'm Danny Coleson and this is my brother Curtis."

"And who are you?" Weber asked the third boy.

"Myron Bock."

"You guys have been throwing a lot of snowballs around here, haven't you?"

None of them answered, and Weber said, "We can talk here or I can take you all to jail and we'll talk there. What's it going to be?"

"We're sorry," Danny said. "We were just goofing off."

"Do you boys realize that you could have caused an accident? How would you feel about that?"

"We're sorry," Danny repeated.

An elderly woman had come out onto her porch to watch the encounter and called to Weber. "I think those are the ones who have been throwing snowballs at my house yesterday and this morning. I called the Sheriff's Office yesterday, but nobody came by."

"We've been pretty busy, what with the storm and all," Weber told her. "Was there any damage done?"

"No," the woman said, "but my fur kid, Buster, has been going nuts every time they come by and bombard my place."

Weber assumed that Buster, her "fur kid," was the yappy little dog that was creating such a ruckus inside the house that he could hear it out in the middle of the street though her door was closed.

"Did you kids do that?" he asked the three boys.

Myron nodded.

"Okay, we have two choices here," Weber told them. "I can take you to jail and call your parents to come and get you. Would you like me to do that?"

Danny, who looked to be about ten or eleven and was the spokesman for the trio, said, "No sir. My Dad would give us a whuppin' for sure."

"Mine too," Myron said.

"Okay, how about this then?" Weber turned back toward the woman on the porch. "Do you have any snow shovels?"

"I've got two right here on the porch. My grandson is supposed to come over after he gets off work to shovel the driveway."

"Well, these here boys need to perform some community service," Weber told her. "How about they do that and give your grandson a break?"

"Well, I don't know. What if they run off as soon as you leave?"

"Oh, they're not going to do that," Weber assured her. "They don't want me hunting them and their parents down. Do you boys?"

All three quickly shook their heads.

"Okay, now go up there and apologize to that lady and then get busy. And do a good job! Don't make me come back out here and hunt you down."

Relieved to be spared their parents wrath, the boys went to do their penance.

Chapter 6

"Where have you been?" Mary Caitlin asked when Weber walked into the Sheriff's Office. "I was just getting ready to send a search team out after you."

"Looks like he's been out building an igloo," Chad said, noting the snow clinging to Weber's coat and pants.

"Just out there being the face of the Big Lake Sheriff's Office and spreading joy and goodwill among the community since you slackers are hiding out here where it's nice and warm," Weber told him.

"Hey, I'm an old man!" Chad said. "I leave that stuff to the young bucks."

"And what's your excuse?" Weber asked Archer, who sat at a desk studying an Egg McMuffin as if it held the key to the secrets of the Holy Grail. Archer ignored him and continued to ponder his breakfast sandwich.

"Was Emma home?" Mary asked, handing Weber a cup of coffee and a stack of pink telephone message slips.

"No, and it doesn't look like she has been for awhile. Her car wasn't there and the driveway was snowed in. I tried the front and back doors. All I heard was a dog barking. And I checked with her neighbor, Celinda Zehnacker. She said she hasn't seen her and Celinda's phone is working."

"How's Celinda doing?" Mary asked. "She's had a rough time the last couple of years."

"She's a strong woman," Weber said. "She sure deserves better than she's had."

Weber started to throw the stack of telephone slips away but stopped when Mary sent him a stern look and went through the motions of looking at them as he went into his private office. Once out of her sight, he deposited them in the wastebasket next to his desk and settled into his chair.

"Caught you!" Mary said, bursting into the room. "Jim Weber, why do I even bother taking messages for you when you don't even look at them?"

"It's always been a mystery to me," Weber said. "I would think you could find better things to do with your time."

Mary didn't see the humor in his response and retrieved the messages from the trash and spread them out on his desk.

"Darn you, Jimmy! Did you ever stop to think that some of these might be important?"

"No. Because they're not," Weber told her. "If something was important you'd tell me, not write a message."

It was an ongoing struggle between them, and if Weber had to be honest, he probably ignored the messages as much to get under Mary's skin as he did from any lack of interest in them on his part. But to appease her, he gave the messages a cursory look.

There were three from Mayor Wingate reporting that citizens had complained to him about snowplows either not getting to their street fast enough, or else covering their driveway entrance when they plowed the street. Weber wasn't sure if he was supposed to hunt the drivers down and give them tickets, or call their supervisor and relay the mayor's complaints. A Beatrice Lansford on Sunset Lane had called to report boys throwing snowballs at her house, and Weber had already solved that problem. There were two messages from Richard MacEwen calling about Emma Moyer, and Weber set them aside to call him back. Hazel Fuller had reported a suspicious car stuck in a snow bank off Rainbow Lane and was concerned that it might be some sort of front for a prostitution operation. The final message was from Weber's best friend and sometimes roommate, FBI agent Larry Parks, warning the sheriff that he was headed back to Big Lake after working a special assignment out of the Yuma office. Parks advised Weber to stock up on ribeye steaks, beer, and junk food, and to alert the town's single women to be on standby.

"Well, the virtue of the community's womenfolk are safe until DOT opens the road and Parks can get here," Weber said. "I'll call Richard MacEwen and see if he has any idea where else Emma may have wandered off to. As for Hazel and the mayor...." He returned those messages back to the waste basket.

Mary considered getting Weber to actually look at the messages and agree to respond to at least one of them a major victory, and she left his office happy with her success.

Weber called Richard MacEwen's number in Tucson and a woman

answered. He identified himself and a moment later MacEwen came on the line.

Weber told him there was no one at Emma's house, and asked where else she might be located.

"If she's not home, she has to be out disrupting the hunters," MacEwen replied. "Emma has vowed to stop the trophy hunt this year."

Weber wanted to tell him that Emma's method of doing so was both dangerous and illegal, but instead said, "I don't think anybody's out in the field in this weather. And it doesn't look like she was home overnight."

"She had to have been there," MacEwen said. "She's got a dog and three cats that need fed and taken care of. Emma cares more about those animals than she does me. There's no way she left them alone overnight."

"Who else might have seen her?" Weber asked. "I know there's a group of you who are all into the same things. Maybe one of them?"

"Maybe, but I doubt it. Emma can be…. abrasive at times. Lately she'd alienated some of the people we've worked with in the past."

"Alienated? How so?"

He waited while MacEwen seemed to think of the best way to reply, and then the man said, "Sheriff, Emma has always been passionate about the things she believes in, but lately she's been… extreme. If everybody doesn't feel as strongly and isn't ready to take action, she kind of turns on them. She found out Peter Blankenship bought a cell phone and jumped all over him at the grocery store. She wanted to blockade the entrance to the gun shop to try and keep the hunters from buying equipment there, and when Jolene Brighton wouldn't come with her, she screamed at her and told her she was an accessory to the slaughter of our wildlife. But she's got so darned many causes that… well, I'll be honest with you, I'm burned out trying to keep up with all of them. I think a lot of people are. And that just made Emma even more angry. She felt betrayed anytime someone wouldn't go along with her latest plan or protest."

"Okay, well she's not home and I don't think she has been anytime lately. Give me some names so I can start checking around. It's worth a shot."

MacEwen gave him the names of a dozen or so people who had been active in Emma's various causes, and Weber told him he'd be in contact.

"Should I come back up there to help look for her?" MacEwen

asked.

"You couldn't get through," Weber told him. "The road's closed at the Salt River Canyon. Just sit tight for now, okay?"

He hung up after promising again to let the man know as soon as he located Emma.

***

"Emma's always been out there in far left field," Chad Summers said an hour later, after he and Mary had completed the last of the telephone calls to the people on Richard MacEwen's list. "But she does seem to have gone over the edge, from what I'm hearing."

"How so?" Weber asked.

"Everybody said pretty much the same thing. That they had had a falling out with her recently. Each time, it looks like they made her mad because they wouldn't or couldn't drop whatever they were doing and go save the trees or the animals or stop some project or another that she was against. I guess a few times it got pretty ugly. Kay Shadlee said Emma called her a "worthless piece of shit" because she wouldn't go with her a few weeks ago to protest outside the Baptist church to make them stop ringing their bell on Sunday morning because it was noise pollution."

"So nobody's seen her?"

"None that I spoke to," Mary said.

"Doesn't she have a sister that lives in Show Low?" Weber asked.

"Stepsister," Mary corrected. "Leslie. She was born after Emma's mom and dad got divorced and he married a woman over there."

Mary, the wife of Weber's predecessor in the Sheriff's Office and the longtime office manager, had an almost encyclopedic knowledge of what seemed to be everybody in town. She knew who was married to who, their often complex family lineage, who had been in trouble with the law in the past, and who was struggling to get by in the town's often shaky economy.

"See if you can find me a number for her," Weber said, then turned to Archer, who was snoring at his desk. "And somebody wake him up, will you? He's a disgrace sitting there like that."

"Yeah, but at least he's not breaking anything or getting into trouble," Chad said. "That's about the best contribution he can make to this place."

***

"We don't talk much," Leslie Ungren told Weber, "We're sisters, but Emma and I have never been close. I've tried, but she's hard to get along with. Actually, she's a witch, just like her mother was. That woman put my poor dad through hell until he finally couldn't take it anymore and left her. Then she harassed him and my mom until the day he died."

"So you haven't spoken to her lately? Or have any idea where she might be?"

"No. Like I said, we don't get along well. The last time I saw her was last summer. We ran into each other at the WalMart here in Show Low and she went off on me when she saw that I had chicken in my grocery basket. Ranting and raving about how animals were not put on this earth to be raised for slaughter. Typical Emma."

Weber ended the call with a new look into Emma's family dynamics but no better idea of where she might be. He was contemplating putting out an All Points Bulletin for her, but under state law he had no cause to. An adult was allowed to come and go as they pleased, or not to come and go as they pleased, as long as they did not present a danger to themselves or anyone else. Before he could decide his next step, Mary came into his office with news of another problem.

"Buz and Dolan just responded to the Mountain Mist Motel. It sounds like Jake Gibbons and his brother Sam are having an altercation with that gentleman we thought went missing yesterday. I thought I'd give you a heads up."

"Thanks, Mary. Do I need to get over there?"

"Probably. Patricia in the motel office called it in and said they were about to come to blows."

Weber knew that his deputies were experienced enough to handle anything that came up, but he still needed to talk to Lenny Dewitt about the incident the day before. On his way out of the office, he stopped to shake Archer awake.

"The town isn't paying you to sleep on the job," Archer. "Get a move on."

"What do you want me to do, Sheriff? It's cold outside."

It may have been cold outside, but Weber felt himself getting hot under the collar. For the thousandth time, he silently cursed Chet Wingate for foisting his ne'er-do-well son off on the Sheriff's Office.

"Get in your car and drive out to the Y, then follow the highway back to the T. Look for Emma Moyer. She drives a white Prius. One of those hybrid cars. If you don't see her there, keep driving around looking. And if you see anything else, somebody stuck or someone who slid off the road, stop to check on them and call it in."

"But it's cold outside," Archer repeated, this time with a whine in his voice.

"Archer, you wanted to be a deputy. This is what deputies do. Just like it says on the door of your unit, To Protect and To Serve. Now get out there and serve, damn it!"

The main highway bypasses Big Lake, while the business route branches off in a Y formation on the south side and makes a loop through town before connecting with the highway again in a T intersection on the north side. Weber had no reason to believe that Emma Moyer would be found anywhere along the route, but at least Archer would look like he was doing something productive. Assuming he didn't get lost or stuck in the snow himself.

***

By the time Weber drove the five blocks to the motel, Buz and Dolan had defused the situation and had the Gibbons brothers separated from Lenny Dewitt, while his two sons and son-in-law looked on. But Weber's appearance seemed to rekindle Lenny's wrath.

Dolan walked up to his Explorer and Weber asked, "What have we got?"

"What we've got is a loudmouth who likes to throw his weight around to get his way, and two stubborn guys who won't back down an inch," Dolan told him. "Mr. Dewitt there wants to go hunting and Jake Gibbons refuses to take him."

Before Dolan could continue, Lenny Dewitt stomped over and pointed a finger in Weber's face. "Are you the law around here?"

"I'm Sheriff Weber. Are you Mr. Dewitt?"

"You're damned right I am, and I want that asshole arrested," Lenny said, pointing at Jake.

"Well, Mr. Dewitt, how about you calm down, get your finger out of my face, stop calling people names, and then we'll talk about it, okay?"

"Listen you....!"

Lenny never got to finish his sentence, because Weber reached up and grabbed the offending finger, which the man had poked him in the face with, and bent it backward. Lenny howled and sank to his knees as Weber kept just enough pressure up to deliver a painful message without breaking anything. He held the finger in his right hand, while his left grasped Lenny's wrist.

"I asked you to calm down and get your finger out of my face, sir. Do you understand me now?"

"Let go! Owww!"

"Again sir. Do you understand me?"

"Yeah! Let go!"

Weber released him and stepped backward, allowing Lenny to get back to his feet. His sons, not used to seeing anyone stand up to their father, stared at the confrontation with mouths agape.

"I'll sue your ass for everything you've got," Lenny said once he had recovered his breath. "You can't put your hands on me like that. I've got rights!"

"Yes sir, you do," Weber told him. "And I'm about to put you in handcuffs and read them to you."

"For what? I didn't do nothing!"

"We'll start with disturbing the peace," Weber told him. "Then I'll add failure to comply with a lawful order. And since you touched me, we'll top it off with aggravated assault on a police officer, which is a Class 3 felony here in Arizona. A Class 3 felony can get you five to fifteen years in prison. Do you really want to continue this conversation? Or should we just calm down and start over. It's your choice."

Lenny Dewitt was born mad at the world and developed into a classic bully. He had learned at a young age that most people were afraid of confrontation and would rather give in to whatever he demanded than to stand up to him. That knowledge had carried him from his grade school playground through high school and into his professional life. And the more he got away with, the more confident he had become that it was his right to demand what he wanted and get it. Nobody had ever been willing to risk what would happen if they said no to Lenny Dewitt. Not his classmates, not his overworked and underpaid teachers, not his wife, his children, his first employer, and not the people who worked for him when he took over the janitorial supply business a few years later. Now at age 51, in less than 24 hours two different men had not only stood up to him, but had backed Lenny down. He didn't like it, but he didn't know what he could do about it. And that made him even angrier.

"Start from the top and run it down for me," Weber told Dolan.

"Apparently Mr. Dewitt paid the Gibbon's brother for a six day guided hunt. They were out two days so far. The first day, one of his sons took a nice buck while hunting with Sam. Yesterday, Mr. Dewitt and his son-in-law were out with Jake and his sons were with Sam. The son-in-law was getting ready to shoot a buck when Emma Moyer jumped out of the bushes, firing a gun in the air and scaring it off. That's when Mr. Dewitt fired a shot in her direction and Jake grabbed the gun away from him."

"Yeah, I know all of that," Weber said. "What happened today?"

"Apparently Mr. Dewitt wanted to go out again this morning and Jake refused. They got into a pissing match that got pretty ugly and the lady who runs the place called us. We separated them and you showed up. You know the rest."

"Okay, bring them all over here," Weber said, and waited while the Gibbons brothers joined them.

"It's cold out here and we've got more snow headed our way," Weber said. "Jake, Mr. Dewitt here wants to go hunting and you won't take him, is that right?"

"That's right," Jake told him. "After yesterday, I want nothing to do with him. Besides, nobody in his right mind would be out in this weather anyway. It's too dangerous up in those mountains, Sheriff."

"Okay, Mr. Dewitt. What do you want?"

"I want the hunt I paid for. This bastard is trying to cheat me out of $10,000!"

"I offered to refund $2,500," Jake said. "That's what we charged them for the entire party of four. One of them already got his buck, and the other two are welcome to finish their hunt as soon as it's safe to go back out. But I don't trust him and I won't take him back out."

"Well, Mr. Dewitt, that sounds fair to me. If the man doesn't want to take you out, I can't force him to. It sounds like a civil matter to me, and I'm no judge."

"You're not a lot of things," Lenny said. "We came here for a six day hunt and I want what I paid for. Or else I want a full refund. We don't need these bozos to find a damn deer."

Weber wanted to tell him that if it were that easy to locate a trophy buck, skilled guides like Jake and Sam would be out of business. He also wanted to tell him that the mountains were dangerous to inexperienced people even in good weather, and that the odds were that the only thing dying up there might be Lenny Dewitt himself or one of his party if they ran out of luck in this kind of weather. But he knew he would be wasting his breath. So instead, he walked over to where Lenny's sons and Brad stood shivering in the cold.

"Do you guys want to finish your hunt with Jake and Sam?"

Richey, having already harvested his buck, was just along for the ride, but Chuck shuffled his feet, not wanting to give up the hunt of a lifetime but afraid to further enrage his father. Brad would have been more than happy to just go home and forget the whole miserable experience.

"I'll take him."

"What? No Sam. We're not going to give in to this guy!"

"I said I'll take him," Sam Gibbons said again, then turned to his brother. "We need the money, Jake. It's too late to book another hunt and we've got a long winter ahead of us. You take Brad back out, and I'll take Lenny and Chuck. But we're not going out until the storm breaks. It's just too dangerous and the deer will be holing up under cover so we won't be able to find them anyway. Is that okay with you, Lenny? Another day or so and things will start to clear up. We should be able to fill all three of your tags by the time you have to fly home."

Lenny didn't like it, and Jake was glowering at his twin, but it seemed like the best solution for everybody. Finally, Lenny shrugged and nodded.

"Good, it's settled. Now, Mr. Dewitt, you and I need to talk about that stunt you pulled yesterday up on the mountain. I haven't decided yet whether to charge you with attempted murder or not."

"That crazy woman shot at us first! I wasn't shooting at her, I was just trying to scare her off."

Weber didn't think Lenny had actually tried to shoot Emma Moyer instead of just scaring her, and unless she decided to file charges against him, he knew he couldn't make a case that would hold up in court anyway. Whenever she showed up. But he didn't like men like Lenny Dewitt, who were quick to explode and bullied their way through life.

"Well, once I talk to Emma, we'll revisit this issue. But I'm warning you right now, you're skating on very thin ice. I don't know how they do things back in Pennsylvania where you come from, but around here that kind of nonsense can get you in trouble real quick."

"Emma's a damn catastrophe waiting to happen," Sam said. "She's always poking her nose in where it's not welcome, raising a ruckus about something or other. I have to be honest Sheriff, it wouldn't surprise me at all if someone does shoot her when she pops up out of nowhere shooting that damn gun of hers. Who knows if she's firing blanks or real bullets? She needs to be locked up somewhere in a padded room."

Weber couldn't disagree, and he wasn't sure if he wouldn't have instinctively fired back at somebody in the same situation. When he did locate Emma, he fully intended to turn the matter over to the Game and Fish Department and suggest that she be prosecuted under state law prohibiting harassing licensed hunters or interfering with a hunt.

"She started with us over a month ago," Sam continued. "Came out to the ranch raising hell about us booking hunts. We took a couple of archery hunters out two weeks ago and she was following us around blowing one of those canned emergency air horns like they use on boats every time we got out of the trucks. Then she showed up at the gun shop the other day and started a hassle when we took these guys in to pick up their ammunition. Old Matt, who runs the place, looked like he was about to strangle her."

With the problem at the motel over, Weber drove away, resolved to find Emma and try to rein her in before her actions led to a dangerous retaliation. Lenny Dewitt wasn't the only hothead with a rifle tramping through the mountains in search of a trophy buck.

Chapter 7

The storm had been stalled for almost four hours but it regained power in the afternoon and the wind picked up again. Weber had been restless and cranky all afternoon, finding himself snapping at Mary when she brought him a stack of reports to review and unable to concentrate when she left them on his desk and stalked out of his office.

Finally giving up on accomplishing anything worthwhile, he pulled on his coat and left the office. A pickup truck moved slowly down Main Street, tire chains clinking as it went by. Weber used the windshield wipers to clear away two inches of new snow while the Explorer warmed up, then drove past Emma Moyer's house again. The driveway was still empty and there were no fresh tracks in the snow.

Turning the SUV back toward the office, Weber called Mary on his radio and asked if Chad was still there. When she confirmed that he was, Weber asked her to tell him to meet him in the parking lot.

"What's up?" Chad asked as he climbed into the passenger side of Weber's vehicle.

"I want to drive up that Forest Service road Jake Gibbons was hunting off of yesterday," Weber said. "That's the last place Emma Moyer was seen. I'm worried she may have gotten herself stuck or something and is stranded in this storm."

"We can try," Chad said, "but let's swing by my house on the way and take my pickup instead of one of the department vehicles. It's got better clearance. Even then, it's going to be iffy, Jimmy. That road's not very good in the best of times, and in this mess we may not be able to get anywhere."

"Well, let's try anyway," Weber said. "I've just got a bad feeling about all of this."

***

Windshield wipers working overtime and heater blasting way, Chad's Ford pickup crawled its way forward through the deep snow in low range four wheel drive, all four tires digging for traction. But two miles off the paved road they lumbered to a stop and Weber felt the tires spin. Chad worked the clutch and transmission, rocking the truck back and forth and managing to get it moving forward again for a few yards before they couldn't go any further.

"That's it, Jimmy, sorry. Nothing short of a snowcat or a snowmobile is going to get up this road anytime soon. And it's too late in the day to find anything, even if we had one."

Chad was right. For the last fifteen minutes they had been driving in near whiteout conditions, and it was already getting dark. Getting themselves stuck on a remote road in the middle of a blizzard wasn't going to do anybody any good.

"Well, we tried," Weber said. "We'll give it another shot tomorrow morning if this damn storm ever lets up. Can you get us back out of here?"

"I hope so," Chad said. "I've got some emergency food and water behind the seat, but no offense, I'd much rather snuggle up to MaryAnn tonight instead of you."

Working carefully, Chad managed to get the four wheel drive truck turned around in a series of maneuvers on the rough road and they started back to town.

"Do you think she's really up there, Jimmy?"

"Who knows? She could be. We can't find her in town, she's not at home, and nobody has seen her. But for all we know she could be down in Phoenix or over in Albuquerque, or anyplace. It's not against the law to just take off without giving anybody any notice."

"Well, assuming that she is okay and has just gone off on one of her many causes, you can bet that if you put out an APB on her and she does get pulled over someplace, there'll be hell to pay. She'll be calling the ACLU and standing in front of the Sheriff's Office with a protest sign saying you violated her civil liberties."

Weber didn't disagree with Chad. Knowing Emma, that's exactly what would happen. But as they made their way slowly back to town, he couldn't help but worry that Emma was indeed in trouble further up the mountain.

***

Weber pulled out of Chad's driveway and drove back to the Sheriff's

Office, still mulling over Emma's disappearance. Most of the businesses had closed early due to the storm and the streets were almost deserted. Only the Cattlemen's Saloon was open, a couple of cars and a single pickup in the parking lot.

Paul Lewis was standing in the middle of Main Street taking a photograph of what looked like a snow covered ghost town. Weber stopped beside him and lowered his window.

"Hey mister, don't you know you're creating a traffic hazard? I should run you in."

The owner/editor of the weekly Big Lake Herald newspaper, a roly-poly, good humored little man, took another picture, then tucked his camera away inside his coat to protect it.

"Really? Is it warm inside your jail, Sheriff? Will you feed me? Do I get conjugal visits? Because if you do, put the handcuffs on me, I'm ready to go."

Weber laughed at his boyhood friend and said, "I don't know if we could feed you on our budget. Might have to just slap you with a big old fine instead."

"And what are you doing on this fine afternoon?" Paul asked.

"Well, I was trying to find Emma Moyer. She seems to have gone missing."

"Why would anyone want to find her? That woman's always underfoot somewhere raising hell about something. If she's not here bothering us, she's off someplace making someone else's life miserable. Better them than us."

"Probably so," Weber said. "Emma does seem to keep busy trying to save the world."

"Even if the world doesn't want or need saving," Paul agreed. "Anyway, I've got a newspaper to run, and now that I've got my front page picture, I'd better get at it. You stay out of trouble, Jimmy. But if you can't do that, at least let me know what you're up to, okay? I need something new to write about."

Weber flipped some snow that had accumulated on his side view mirror at his friend, closed the window and pulled across the street into the parking lot of the Sheriff's Office. Mary Caitlin was warming her Jeep Cherokee up and using a straw broom to clear a high mound of snow off the hood and windshield.

"You going to be able to get home okay?" Weber asked, taking the broom from her and finishing the job.

"I've got four wheel drive and was driving in this crap long before you were born," she told him. "I can manage."

"Mary, I'm sorry about this afternoon. I just can't shake the feeling that something is wrong about Emma going missing like this."

"Well I didn't lose her," Mary said, still stung by Weber's sharp words earlier.

"I know. I'm sorry. What else can I say?"

Mary had known Weber since the day he was born, and had known his mother and father before. She knew that he was a good-hearted man with a great sense of duty. But she also knew that one of his biggest faults was that he sometimes cared too much and quickly grew frustrated when he couldn't fix everything. In his own way, he was very much like Emma Moyer.

"She'll turn up, Jimmy. For all her faults, Emma grew up in these mountains and she knows how bad a storm like this can be."

Weber didn't want to push the issue, so he just said, "You're probably right. You be careful going home, okay?"

Mary smiled at him and got into her Jeep and Weber watched her drive away, feeling better that they had mended their fences but still troubled by Emma Moyer's disappearance.

Chapter 8

As happens often in the high country, the blizzard blew itself out overnight and the sun was shining brightly the next morning. Weber put sunglasses on when he left his cabin to ward off the glare from the snow. It was still cold and he had to use four wheel drive to maintain traction on the snow covered roads.

Emma Moyer's cabin looked just as empty as it had the day before, but he stopped and tried the doors anyway. The dog barked at him but nobody answered his knock. Weber dug his cell phone out of his coat pocket and called Richard MacEwen's number in Tucson.

"Something's wrong," he said when Weber told him that there was still no sign of Emma. "There is no way on earth she would leave those animals alone that long. Anytime she was going to be away overnight, she either arranged for somebody to come and feed them or she boarded them at the veterinarian over in Lakeside."

"Well she didn't do either one this time," Weber said. "I need to get inside the house. Does Emma have a key stashed somewhere?"

"On the front porch," MacEwen told him. "There's an old fashioned metal milk can. Lift the lid and it's inside the top."

There's nothing like making it easy for a burglar to get in, Weber thought as he retrieved the key and let himself inside Emma's small cottage. He knew he was technically breaking the law by entering the house without permission or probable cause that Emma was inside and in danger, but the only protest came from the small white terrier that barked furiously at Weber's intrusion. Two cats, a yellow tabby and a gray longhaired breed Weber wasn't familiar with, greeted him with meows and rubbed against his legs. An ancient white and black cat looked up disinterestedly from the couch to see what all of the commotion was about, then went back to sleep.

Weber called Emma's name loudly twice, but the only response he got was more barking from the dog. Holding the phone to his ear, he went from room to room looking for Emma, but she wasn't there.

"Nobody here but the animals," Weber told MacEwen.

"I can't wait any longer, Sheriff. I'm headed back up there. Are the roads open yet?"

"They should be by the time you get to the Canyon," Weber told him. "But take your time and be careful, okay? You can't help Emma if you get in a wreck rushing to get here."

"I'm on my way." MacEwen told him.

The animals' bowls were all empty, so Weber gave them water, then poked around the kitchen and utility room until he found canned food and fed them. The dog stopped barking long enough to eat, but still watched the stranger in his house warily and growled whenever Weber got too close.

Knowing it wouldn't do him any good, and fully aware that there would be hell to pay if Emma returned and discovered him prowling through her house, Weber still gave the place a quick search for any clue to where Emma may have been. Her toiletries were all still in the bathroom, her dresser drawers were filled with underwear and other clothes, giving no indication that she had packed for a trip. He locked the house up and replaced the key, no closer to finding Emma than he had been.

***

With the storm past, life seemed to be getting back to normal as Big Lake began to dig out. The DOT had reopened the roads and by noon a steady stream of cars and SUVs filled with skiers and people coming to play in the snow made their way into town. Weber was eager to get back up the mountain to search for Emma but a rash of fender benders and a road rage incident involving two out of town drivers rushing to get to the ski slopes, kept all hands busy.

Weber bounced from incident to incident, helping his deputies with the heavy workload, all the while fretting about the missing woman. Finally, by mid-afternoon things had slowed down enough that he and Chad decided to try again, and this time they were able to slowly work their way up the mountain road. It was six miles to the trailhead where Jake Gibbons had parked during the hunt on Tuesday, and it took almost an hour to get there.

"Well, nobody's here," Chad said. "But Jake said they didn't see her car here. Let's keep going up the road. There are a couple more pullouts up there, but it gets worse every foot of the way. I can't imagine

Emma getting up there in her little rice burner even in good weather."

"She's a determined woman," Weber said. "She could be sitting up there right now waiting for us to show up."

"Well then, let's go see," Chad said, putting the truck in gear.

***

"Son-of-a-bitch! Maybe she did make it up here!"

They pulled into the last parking area on the road and looked at the huge mound of snow that could only be a car. Leaving the truck, they waded through the snow to the mound and wiped enough snow off to reveal Emma Moyer's Prius squatting low in the snow.

"Here's something interesting," Chad said, kneeling in the snow by the front of Emma's car. "She had a flat tire."

"It's a wonder that little thing made it up here at all," Weber said. "She was lucky she didn't tear the whole undercarriage off of it."

"I don't know if we could call her lucky," Weber said, "given the way things turned out."

"They're all flat," Chad told him as he worked his way around the car. "Look here."

Each tire had a slash in the sidewall.

"Nobody inside," Chad said, after fighting the snow to get the passenger side door open enough to look. "If she's been up here all along, this is gonna be bad, Jimmy."

A noise from inside the tree line soon let them know just how bad it was.

"Did you hear that?"

"Yeah, it came from over that way," Weber said.

They walked toward the sound and had only gone a few feet into the trees when they were confronted by a large black bear. Having lived all their lives in the mountains, Weber and Chad had encountered many bears over the years, and usually the bruins ran away at the first sign of men. But not this one. It had a reason to stand its ground. It looked up at them and growled menacingly as it stood guard over the corpse of Emma Moyer.

"Shit! Get out of here," Weber yelled, yanking his coat open and jerking his pistol out of its holster. The bear growled again and gnashed its bloodstained teeth at them.

"Can I kill it with my .45?" Weber asked.

"I don't know. Let's back off, I've got my rifle in the truck."

"We can't just leave her there," Weber said.

The bear decided the issue when it seized Emma's leg in its mouth and started to drag her away.

"No!" Weber yelled in horror, and fired two quick shots at the bear. It yelped in pain and dropped the woman's leg, but refused to retreat. Lowering its head, it regarded the men with hatred. Weber aimed carefully, his pistol's front sight centered between the bear's glaring eyes. They were no more than ten yards apart and Weber was an excellent shot. He knew he could hit the bear, but he wasn't sure if the 200 grain hollow point bullet would do the job. But he couldn't let it abuse Emma's body any more than it already had. The bear decided the issue for him, giving one last snarl before backing away and lumbering into the trees.

"Is it gone?" Weber asked.

"I don't know," Chad said. "Maybe. Or maybe it's just out of sight waiting for us to leave."

Weber had seen violent death before. In his years with the Sheriff's Office, and a stint as an Army MP before that, he had seen bodies mangled in car accidents, shootings, bar fights, and every other kind of mayhem known to mankind. Less than a year earlier. he had been forced to kill a young man in the line of duty. But the sight of Emma's body and the aftermath of what the bear had done to her was the stuff of nightmares.

"What now?" Weber asked.

"Hell, I don't know. You're the Sheriff, you tell me."

Weber was torn between moving Emma's body out of danger from the bear's return, and preserving the scene until a proper investigation could be done. Black bear attacks on humans were rare, and fatalities even more so, but they did happen. However, they were scavengers and if Emma had died in the storm or from an injury, the bear may have been lucky enough to find a free meal.

"Go get your rifle and bring it back, in case that damn bear comes back," Weber said. "Then get on the radio and call this in. Get us some help up here."

"That's not going to do any good," Chad said. "Even with four wheel drive, I don't know what department vehicles we have that can make it up here. We barely did in my truck. And we've only got a couple of hours of daylight left. So we either stand guard over her until tomorrow, or we carry her out. Which is it, Jimmy?"

"I'm not staying up here with that thing hiding in the bushes," Weber said. "Go ahead and call it in and let Mary know what's happening, and grab a camera so we can photograph the scene the best we can. But first bring me that rifle. That bear scares the hell out of me."

Moving as fast as he could in the deep snow, Chad retrieved the rifle from his truck, then went back to radio the news of Emma's death to the Sheriff's Office. Working the bolt to chamber a round, Weber cradled the Remington in one arm while he put a fresh magazine in his Colt. If the bear did come back, he wanted as much ammunition in both guns as he could get.

Chad returned with his digital camera and began photographing the scene from every angle, while Weber stood guard with the rifle, his heart jumping with every sound from the forest.

Emma lay on her back, her face gray and hard, the skin frozen. The butt of an old top-break Iver Johnson .38 revolver poked out of the snow nearby, where it had fallen from her pocket as the bear rolled her body over. Her chest and stomach were a mass of gore, and there were rips and tears in her clothes from where the bear had mauled her.

The light was fading as Chad finished recording the scene and they slid Emma's body onto a plastic tarp and carried it to the back of the truck. Both men were silent as they began the long ride back to town, each lost in their own thoughts.

***

Blue and red flashing lights greeted them when they reached the pavement, and two paramedics loaded Emma's body onto a stretcher and put her in the back of the ambulance.

"Go on home, Chad," Weber said. "You can write your report in the morning."

It was the first time either man had spoken since they had carried Emma out of the forest. Chad nodded and opened the door of his truck, then turned back to Weber.

"I'm getting too old for this shit, Jimmy."

"Me too, Chad. Me too."

Chad nodded, then got in his truck and drove away.

***

Coop drove Weber to the medical center, where Emma's body would get its first examination before being transported to Tucson for an autopsy. On the way, he pulled into the drive-through lane at McDonald's.

"Oh God, I can't eat, Coop," Weber protested.

"Your body needs fuel," Coop said. "And you're half frozen. Let's at least get some coffee into you."

Weber sipped the coffee and allowed it to start spreading warmth through his body, and was surprised to find that as he warmed up, the smell of the food inside the bag was making him ravenous. He realized that all he had eaten all day was a breakfast bagel, and wolfed down a box of Chicken McNuggets by the time Coop parked at the emergency entrance of the medical center.

Grim faced, Dolan Reed and Buz Carelton met them in the hallway leading back to the examination rooms.

"Jesus Christ, Jimmy! In twenty years on the job, I've never known of anybody being killed by a bear around here," Dolan said.

"Me either," Weber said.

"I thought bears hibernate in the winter," Coop said.

"Not around here," Buz told him. "I've seen them every month of the year."

As he spoke, the double doors behind them whooshed open again and Mark Santos, the Game and Fish officer assigned to their area, came in.

"How you doing, Jimmy?"

"It's been a rough day, Mark."

"So I hear."

Weber had a good working relationship with Santos, who took his job seriously and was as skilled as any law enforcement officer he knew, and he needed to be. While it was legal to carry a gun in Arizona, and a lot of people in the area did, Santos could pretty well expect anyone he encountered out in the field enforcing game laws to be armed.

"So tell me about this bear," the game warden said.

Just then the young intern on duty poked his head outside the exam room curtain, saw the lawmen, and walked up to them.

"The bear fed on her body, but that's not what killed her," he told them.

"She froze to death first?" Buz asked, grateful at least that Emma had been spared the horror of a bear attack.

"No, she was murdered."

Chapter 9

Emma was naked and laid out on her back on a stainless steel exam table. No matter how many times he saw a body in the same position, it offended Weber. He always felt it was one last invasion on the deceased's dignity.

"The bear, or maybe coyotes, tore up her leg there," the doctor told them, pointing at Emma's right leg, which was missing the lower part of the foot. "And he fed on the soft tissue of her abdomen. But this," he paused to roll Emma onto her left side, "is what killed her."

The bullet hole was in the center of her back, a few inches down from her shoulders.

"Damn it," Weber said. "I had no idea."

"You couldn't have known unless you undressed her. Have you seen enough?"

"Oh yeah," Weber told him. "More than enough."

The doctor eased Emma's body back down and a nurse pulled a sheet over her.

"The exit wound, if there was one, was masked by the bear's activity," the doctor told them.

"We'll need some pictures," Weber said, not relishing the task.

"I'll do it," Buz said, and went out to his department-issued truck to get his camera.

"Is there a way you can tell if the bullet is still inside of her?" Weber asked.

The doctor nodded. "We can do a couple of X-rays, but I'm pretty sure we won't find anything. She was a small woman and the hole looks like it came from a large caliber firearm. It's my guess that it passed completely through her body."

"A large caliber bullet could have made a large exit wound, which in turn allowed plenty of bleeding," Santos said. "The strong blood scent may be what drew the bear and any other scavengers to her,"

"Given what we know now, I'd say the bear found her body, maybe chased away some smaller scavengers, and was protecting its find when you showed up," Santos said. "That makes me feel good in that we don't have an aggressive animal out there."

"No, but we do have a wounded one," Weber said. "I know I hit it at least once with my .45. Maybe twice."

They both knew that an injured bear was just as dangerous as an aggressive one. Maybe more so. Weber felt bad about that and hoped that his shots had killed the animal and not left it in misery.

"Nothing we can do about it tonight," Santos said. "And you probably don't want me tramping all over your crime scene anyway. The best we can do is get out there in the morning before the hunters are out."

"Are we sure it was murder?" Dolan asked. "Is it possible it was a accident? Just a stray shot from a hunter?"

"Not with all four of her tires slashed like they were," Weber told him.

"Damn. Emma was a handful at times. But who'd have ever thought it would come to this?"

"Do you think the bear moved her very far?" Weber asked Santos. "We couldn't tell with all the snow that's fallen."

"Probably not," the game warden told him. "Bears are opportunists and pretty lazy. They will usually eat what they can, where they find it, and then stash what's left in a hole or under a deadfall, or try to cover it up nearby. The way you've described the scene, I'd bet the victim died within a very close proximity to where you found her. No more than a few yards, if that."

"Do you want to bunk at my place?" Weber asked. "It will save you from driving all the way home and then back over here again in the morning."

"Might as well," Santos said. "I appreciate the hospitality."

Weber's radio squawked and Judy asked if he was available. He replied in the affirmative and she asked him to call in on the telephone.

"Richard MacEwen's here," Judy told him when Weber called. "Do you want me to send him to the hospital or…?"

"Does he know yet?"

"No."

"Okay, I'll be there soon," Weber told her.

***

Richard MacEwen was a tall man with a mop of curly brown hair who wore a small gold hoop in one earlobe. Weber had not had many dealings with the man, but knew he had moved to Big Lake a few years before, worked as a letter carrier for the post office, and had been romantically involved with Emma for the last year or so. The sheriff wasn't sure if MacEwen was as ardent about the various causes the couple were always involved in or had simply found it easier to go along with whatever Emma wanted, just to be with her.

MacEwen looked haggard and his eyes were red rimmed. Weber wasn't sure if that was from fatigue, crying, or the faint odor of pot that lingered on the man's clothes.

"Let's go into my office," Weber suggested, and MacEwen followed him in and took the seat next to Weber's desk that the sheriff indicated.

"Coffee?"

"No thanks, I don't do caffeine."

"Mr. MacEwen, Richard, there's no easy way to tell you this. I sure wish there was. Emma's dead. We found her body up on Tomahawk Mountain this afternoon."

MacEwen's face trembled and he buried it in his hands as the tears started to flow. Giant sobs wracked his body. Weber laid a hand on the man's shoulder, trying to offer what comfort he could.

"My God! What happened to her?"

"I'm afraid she was murdered."

"What? No! No! I want to see her. Oh, Emma, noooo!"

The grieving man bent over in the chair and clutched his head in both hands, moaning. "Emma. Oh baby, no!"

Weber knew that there were no words he could offer to help the man deal with his loss, so he sat quietly waiting until MacEwen managed to somewhat compose himself. He looked at Weber with a tortured look on his face and asked, "Who did it? How did it happen? Why? I just can't believe it. Not Emma. I have to see her."

"We don't know who did it yet. I'm hoping you can help me figure that out."

"Can I see her? Please? I have to see her."

"Not now," Weber told him. "I'm sorry, but we have to have an autopsy done down in Tucson. I'll make arrangements at the medical center for you to see her before they have her transported in the morning."

He didn't want MacEwen to see Emma in her present state, and Weber wanted to be sure that when MacEwen was allowed to view the body, he or one of his deputies was there. Though it looked like he had been over 200 miles away in Tucson at the time of Emma's murder, and though Weber believed his grief was real, MacEwen was still Emma's boyfriend and that, by default, made him a possible suspect in her murder.

"Richard, do you have any idea who may have done this? Anyone who Emma had a problem with?"

"Emma had a problem with just about everybody," MacEwen said. "You knew her, Sheriff. You know how she was. Always ruffling feathers and stepping on toes."

Weber recalled his own interactions with Emma over the years. She had an abrasive personality and never hesitated to tell others what they were doing wrong, whether it was their choice in food, or their cars that used too much gasoline. A particular target had been the developers that had discovered Big Lake and were transforming the once quiet little mountain town into a playground for people from Phoenix, Tucson, and as far away as California.

"When we talked on the phone yesterday, you said that lately Emma had alienated a lot of people because she had become… what was the term you used? Extreme?"

MacEwen nodded. "I don't know what was going on with her, but yeah, it seemed like she'd become mad at the world. Even me, and I'm pretty easy to get along with. The last time I saw her we had a nasty argument."

Coop, sitting in a chair across from them, raised his eyebrows at Weber, sending a silent message. If the couple had quarreled, how bad had it been?

"What did you argue about?"

"She was mad that I was going down to Tucson to see my daughter. Monday was Carrie's ninth birthday, but Emma wanted me to stay to help her stop the hunters the Gibbons' brothers were taking out from killing their deer. She just couldn't understand how important it is for a little girl to have her dad there for her birthday. I guess because her own dad was never there for hers. She said birthdays come and go, but those deer needed protecting now!"

Weber recalled Leslie Ungren's comments about their father and his bad relationship with his ex-wife.

"You said you had a nasty argument. I'm sorry, but I have to ask…"

"No way!" MacEwen said loudly. "No! I'd never hurt Emma. You can give me a lie detector test or truth serum or whatever you want. I didn't do anything to her. I loved her!"

Weber believed him, and the man's story about being in Tucson during the time Emma was killed was easy enough to check out.

"Okay, sorry. I'm just doing my job."

"I understand," MacEwen said. "And really, Sheriff, do whatever you need to do to rule me out so you can concentrate on finding who did this to Emma. I'll take a lie detector test right now, or whatever you need me to do."

"Let's hold off on that for now. You said the argument was nasty. How so?"

"Like I said, lately Emma has been different. She was always active in her causes, but the last few weeks it was like she went way overboard. If somebody had to work and couldn't go with her to hang up signs, or to hold a protest, she acted like it was a personal insult to her. She'd scream and cuss them out, call them all kinds of names. It wasn't like her. And she had ramped up the number of things she was trying to stop. It used to be just the developers, then the hunters, but church bells? Really? I kept telling her she needed to slow down, because she couldn't save the entire world in a week."

Weber recalled Kay Shadlee's comment about Emma getting so upset when she wouldn't protest at the church with her.

"So when I told her I was going down to Tucson, it really set her off," MacEwen continued. "She said I was putting a silly birthday party over the lives of innocent animals. She just wouldn't listen to reason. She told me if I wasn't going to help her stop the slaughter, I might as well be pulling the trigger myself. She called me all kinds of terrible names. It hurt me. But lately she's been acting so crazy, I don't know. Sometimes it was like she was possessed or something."

"Why the Gibbon's brothers?" he asked. "There are hunters all over the mountains, why did she single them out?"

"Emma hated hunting. She was a vegan and believed animals were not put on this earth to be eaten. Or even saddled and ridden. But as much as she hated the thought of hunters killing wildlife, she also understood that for a lot of people up here, they need the meat to feed their families. The Gibbons' take out trophy hunters who don't care about the meat. All they want is a big rack to hang on their wall. To her, that was obscene."

"Did she tell you how she planned to stop the hunt?"

MacEwen shrugged his shoulders. "I guess she was going to try to block them somehow. Maybe park her car across the road so they couldn't get up the mountain."

"You didn't know anything about her shooting the gun off to scare the deer away?"

"Gun? No way! Emma hated guns."

Coop handed him the clear plastic evidence bag holding the revolver they had found next to Emma's body. "Have you ever seen this before?"

"Never. Are you saying that Emma had this on her? I don't believe it."

"Jake Gibbons and the two hunters with him said she jumped up and started shooting it into the air to scare a trophy buck away."

"That's crazy even for Emma! Blowing horns, yelling, beating on pots and pans, rattling tin cans to scare the deer away? We've done it all. But a gun? No way!"

"Do you know anybody who might have wanted Emma dead?" Weber asked.

"It would be a long list, depending on who she's interfering with at the moment. Start with the Gibbons brothers. A couple dozen developers whose projects she was trying to stop. Every construction company she was trying to keep from building something. About a hundred deer hunters. The ski lodge. The cell phone company. I guess even the Baptist church."

***

"What do you think?" Weber asked Coop after they had finished the interview and made arrangements for Coop to take MacEwen to the medical center the next morning to view Emma's body before it was transported to Tucson. He knew that Coop would be sure that the man would only be allowed to view her head and shoulders, to protect him from seeing the damage she had suffered after her death. He also knew Coop would be watching MacEwen's reaction to seeing his girlfriend. Weber was convinced that MacEwen had no involvement in Emma's death, but then he never would have believed that his own kid sister would be sitting in prison convicted of the deaths of three people, including her own husband.

"I think I made a big mistake when I thought I was going to live out my golden years playing traffic cop in a quiet little small town," Coop told him, stretching.

"Having regrets already?"

Coop chuckled and shook his head. "Naaa… I'd get bored if you didn't throw a homicide or some other major case my way every once in a while. How many tickets could a guy write, anyway?"

"My gut reaction is that the boyfriend didn't do it," Weber said.

Coop nodded in agreement. "It's not going to be hard to confirm that he was in Tucson. But it sure sounds like we won't have any problem coming up with plenty of other suspects."

"What about Lenny Dewitt?"

"Well, we know he shot at her once, but she was still alive when Jake and his hunters left her there on the mountain. Did he go back and find her? We can't account for his whereabouts once he disappeared from the parking area. Do you want to go roust him?"

"Yeah, what the hell? It's late and it's cold, why should we be the only two miserable guys in town?"

***

Chuck Dewitt opened the motel room door and Lenny grunted in his sleep from one of the twin beds in the small room at the sudden blast of cold air.

"We need to talk to your father," Weber said, and Chuck stepped aside to let them into the room. "Good luck."

The strong smell of cigarette smoke and alcohol hung heavy in the room's stale air. Weber called Lenny's name twice, but all he got in return was a snore.

"He's been hitting it pretty hard all day long," Chuck said. "He's been asleep an hour or so and there aint' a thing that's gonna wake him up before morning."

Weber shook Lenny's shoulder, shook it again harder, and called his name several times. The man scowled in his sleep and rolled over on his other side with a fart. Weber had dealt with enough drunks in his time to know that Chuck was right and gave up.

"What's going on?" Chuck asked. "It's late and I was just going to turn in, too. We've got to be up early to go hunting."

Weber didn't want to reveal anything, so he just told Chuck he'd check back the next day and the two lawmen left.

Back outside, Coop asked, "Now what?"

"We need the road up to Tomahawk Mountain blocked so nobody

goes up there tomorrow morning before we do. I'm going to get that set up, then I need to get hold of the Gibbons' brothers and tell them I need to talk to them and their hunters tomorrow. And then…"

"I'm on duty until midnight. How about you get some rest, Boss? I can handle all of that."

"No need," Weber said. "It's my job. I can…"

"Sheriff, I spent a lot of years running criminal investigations. I can handle it, okay?"

Weber looked at his watch. It was almost 10 PM and he felt tired to the very depths of his soul. He nodded and said, "Thanks, Coop. I'll see you at the office at 6 AM."

Driving home, Weber tried to shut out the memories of the horrible discovery of Emma with the bear, and the sight of her naked, abused body in the hospital exam room. While he couldn't erase them, he managed to push them into the dark corners of his mind where so many other terrible visions lurked.

Chapter 10

"I go away for a month and you move somebody else in?" Larry Parks said, feigning a look of pain as Weber sat bleary eyed at his kitchen table the next morning, scalding his tongue with coffee in an attempt to wake up.

"It's not what you think," Mark Santos said as he buttered a slice of toast. "It was just a sleepover."

"Uh huh. And I've got some swamp land in Florida I want to sell you, too."

"How was Yuma?" Weber asked.

"Warmer than here," Parks told him. "But I missed Dogpatch. You people are a lot nicer than those big city folks."

"I don't think Yuma qualifies as a big city, does it?" Santos asked.

"Parks grew up in Armpit, Oklahoma," Weber told him. "There were only nine people, two hogs, and a chicken living within a hundred miles. To him, anything's a big city."

"You keep quiet and eat your toast, you home wrecker," Parks told Santos, then turned to Weber. "So tell me about your murder case."

Weber brought the FBI agent up to speed, then asked, "Do you want to play?"

"Well, it's either that or sit around here watching the snow melt. That's National Forest land, isn't it? Sure, the full force of the Federal Bureau of Investigation is at your disposal, Sheriff."

"Does he ever shut up?" Santos asked. "It's not even daylight yet and he's chattering away like a squirrel on meth."

"The only time he's not talking is when he's eating," Weber said. "And half the time he talks with his mouth full."

"That reminds me, I'm hungry," Parks said, snatching the toast from Santos' hand and stuffing it in his mouth as he headed for the bathroom. "Hurry up, ladies, we've got work to do and crimes to solve."

***

"Anything new?" Weber asked Coop as he unrolled a topographic map of Tomahawk Mountain on a desk.

"The doctor from the medical center called and said the X-rays didn't show a bullet in Emma Moyer's body, so it's a pretty safe bet it passed right though her. I stationed a deputy at the road up the mountain to keep anyone from using it, and I called the Highway Department. They have a big four wheel drive truck with a plow that's standing by to try to clear that road if you need it."

"Good work, Deputy. Did you get any sleep?"

"I sacked out on the couch in your office for a few hours."

"Go home and get some rest," Weber told him.

Coop shook his head and said, "I'm fine. I've always been able to get by on four or five hours."

They were interrupted when the door flew open and Lenny Dewitt stormed inside, followed by Sam Gibbons. Jake Gibbons and the rest of their hunting party followed.

"What the hell is this bullshit? First these so-called guides say we can't hunt because of that damned storm, and now that the storm's over they're saying you won't let us go out!"

"We need to talk," Weber said.

"No, I need to go kill the deer I came here to kill! We've got three tags left and I'm not leaving here until they're filled. I don't know what kind of scam you guys have worked up here, but I am going to get what I paid for."

"Calm down, you'll have plenty of time to finish your hunt," Weber told him. "But first…."

"Stick your but first where the sun don't shine," Lenny said. "We're out of here!"

Weber hadn't liked Lenny Dewitt even before he met the man, and with every minute and every word, he liked him less.

"Okay, I tried to be reasonable, but you don't like that. So how about this, then? You're under arrest for aggravated assault against Emma Moyer."

"What? That crazy, tree hugging bitch? I never touched her!"

"No, you shot at her with a rifle, in front of two witnesses. Deputy Carelton, handcuff this man, please."

Buz Carelton, who had earned his nickname back in high school for his skinny neck and hawk-like nose, pulled the protesting Lenny's arms behind his back and snapped handcuffs in place, then read him his

Miranda rights.

"She shot at us first," Lenny yelled, "Why isn't she under arrest too?"

"Because she's dead," Weber told him. "And that doesn't look good for you, does it?"

"Emma's dead?" Jake Gibbons asked in disbelief.

"We found her body up on the mountain yesterday, not too far from where you had your run-in with her," Weber told him. "She had been shot in the back."

"Sheriff, I don't like the man, but I really don't think he was trying to hit Emma," Jake said. "And he didn't. I saw the bullet hit the ground near her. It was a dumb ass stunt, but she was still standing there yelling at us when we left."

"That could be," Weber said. "But you also reported him missing once you got back to the trailhead, and there's a big piece of time that can't be accounted for before he turned up at the motel. Emma was found less than a mile away. He could have easily hiked up there and shot her."

"I didn't!" Lenny protested, suddenly aware of just how serious his situation had become. "I told you, I got a ride from a couple of other hunters and we stopped and had a couple of drinks on the way back to my motel."

"Do you have those guys' names?" Weber asked him.

"Hell no, they were just guys out hunting. We didn't get to be best buddies or anything. They gave me a ride and I bought them some beers."

"That's not much of an alibi," Weber said. "Where did you have those drinks you're talking about?"

"I don't know. Some bar."

"There's lot of bars in Arizona," Weber said.

Lenny shook his head, trying to clear it from the booze he had consumed the night before and this morning's sudden turn of events. He was a man used to getting his way, who never had to explain his actions or account for his whereabouts. He knew he was in uncharted territory and he didn't like it.

"It was a run down dump, the first one we came to once we got back on the paved road. I remember it was real dark inside."

Weber knew the place Lenny described all too well. The Antler Inn was a square, cinder block building two miles outside of Big Lake, and a regular trouble spot. His deputies responded to trouble calls there on a regular basis to break up fights among the patrons, which included a rough crowd of cowboys, loggers, bikers, and tourists who strayed away from the cleaner, more respectable watering holes in town.

"Until we can prove your story, you're not going anywhere," he told Lenny.

"I want a lawyer."

"No problem. I'll make sure you have access to a telephone to find one. Book him and lock him up, Buz."

While Buz led Lenny down the hallway to the booking room and cells, Richey Dewitt said, "This is crazy. My dad didn't kill anybody!"

"Well, at this point he's all I've got," Weber said. "Jake, I need statements from you and whoever else was there with you when you guys had your confrontation with Emma."

"That was me," Brad Gleason said. "I'm Lenny's son-in-law."

"How about you three?" Weber asked, and Sam Gibbons shook his head.

"We were on the other side of the mountain, came up the old fire trail that starts behind that old closed up gas station on Crayter Road. Richey here got his buck mid-morning and we spent most of the day getting it out and back to town. By then the storm was coming in, so I dropped them off at the motel and started back home when Jake called me on the radio and said Lenny was missing."

Weber had Coop interview Jake while Buz took Brad's statement. When they were done, both accounts of the confrontation with Emma Moyer were basically the same, and no different than the story Weber had heard before.

Weber sent the guides and their hunters away, telling them that they were free to hunt the backside of Tomahawk Mountain, but that the front slope was now a crime scene. It looked like all thoughts of the hunt were gone, as Lenny's sons and Brad turned their attention to finding him legal representation.

At 8:30, while the snowplow was trying to open the Forest Service road up the mountain, Weber called Leslie Ungren to inform her of her half-sister's death. She didn't seem to show any emotion, simply asking him what happened next. He told her that as Emma's next of kin, burial arrangements were her decision.

"Did she leave me any property or money?"

"I have no idea," Weber told her. "She owns a small house here, but

I don't know anything about her financial situation or any will she may have had."

"Knowing Emma, she left anything she did have to try to save the rainforest or some other stupid cause of hers. I wanted nothing to do with her when she was alive and I'm sure she didn't leave me anything, so the hell with her. You can throw her out with the trash."

With that she hung up, and Weber sat looking at the telephone for a moment, wondering what his own sister would have to say down at the women's prison in Perryville, if she was told he had been killed. Since Weber had been the one that exposed her crimes, he imagined it wouldn't have been as kind as Leslie's response.

***

The snowplow had done better than Weber expected, making it well over halfway up the rough road. Weber, Chad, and Parks were crammed into the cab of Chad's pickup, while Buz rode with Coop and Mark Santos' in his Game and Fish Department pickup, as they followed the trail of Chad's tire ruts from the day before through the snow.

"Doesn't look like anybody else has been here," Chad said when they arrived at the parking area.

Both Chad and Santos had rifles slung over their shoulders in case they encountered the wounded bear, but it didn't make an appearance. The spot where they had found Emma's body was trampled from the day before and there wasn't anything new to see.

"Any chance of finding the bullet that killed her?" Parks asked.

"Like looking for a needle in a haystack. Worse in all this snow," Weber said. "First we'd have to know where she was when she got shot, and where the shooter was standing. With all this snow, any tracks they made are long gone. Unless we see a fresh hole in a tree, but I doubt that."

They searched the area as carefully as they could in the snow, hoping to find any clues, possibly the spent cartridge case from the bullet that killed Emma or the bullet itself, but there was nothing to be found.

Finally, after two hours they gave up, and Santos said, "I need to find that bear and put it down." They all knew a wounded bear was not only a potential danger, but that depending on how badly injured it was, it might also linger in pain for days.

Weber still felt bad about wounding the animal and then leaving it to suffer, although he knew there was nothing else he could have done under the circumstances. Though there was no blood trail to follow, they tracked the bear's paw prints in the snow for thirty minutes before they came upon it under a rock outcropping. The animal was stiff, indicating that it had been dead for several hours,

After measuring and photographing the animal, they tied its front and back legs together, then found a sturdy length of tree limb and slid it between those trussed legs and took turns carrying it back to the parking area, one man on each end. The bear weighed close to 400 pounds, and it was slow going in the rough, snow-covered terrain. They were all breathing hard by the time the dead animal was loaded into the back of Santos' truck.

They made their way back down off the mountain and stopped at the Sheriff's Office.

"I'll let you know what the results of the necropsy are," Santos said, as Paul Lewis took photographs of the bear for the newspaper.

Weber thanked him for his help, and watched as Santos drove out of the parking lot and back toward Pinetop, 40 miles to the east.

"Now what?" Buz asked.

"Now we go find ourselves a killer," Weber told him.

Chapter 11

It didn't take long to realize that Emma had left them a long line of potential suspects. While Weber had always considered her a bit of a wacko, even eccentric, there were plenty of people who had a much harsher opinion.

"Emma Moyer cost us hundreds of thousands of dollars and set back our opening an entire season with her lawsuits, injunctions, and protests," said Ashley Knott at the ski lodge. "I hate to sound cold and callous, but I have to admit that I'm relieved we won't have to deal with her anymore."

"Good riddance! That dizzy bitch was always causing us trouble," construction company owner Bill Stevens told Weber. "Whenever we started prepping a new building site, she'd file motions in court to try to make us stop and then she and her pals would show up with their signs, raising hell!"

"She won't be missed," said Wayne Duncan, who ran the paving company that created most of Big Lake's parking lots. "For a little old gal, she sure had a lot of spite in her. I sometimes wondered if she really cared about all of that nonsense she was always getting so riled up about or if she just liked raising hell for its own sake."

"Emma!" Lillian Neafie at Meadowlark Realty spoke the dead woman's name as if it left a bitter taste in her mouth. "Do you have any idea how many times she and her crew of dingbats would show up at an open house or model home showing waving their protest signs? Potential buyers would take one look and turn right around and go the other way!"

The best comment Weber heard about her passing was from Robert Goldhatch, minister of the New Hope Baptist Church, whose church bells Emma had protested, who said, "Well, she's God's problem now."

Even among Emma's former friends, those who had been active in her various protest movements, there seemed to be little love lost.

"Emma and I used to be very close," Jolene Brighton told the sheriff. "But it just got harder and harder to keep up with her. It was church bells one day, hunters the next day, and some new building project the next. I've got two kids and a husband to take care of, but if I wouldn't just drop everything and come running when she called, she'd start screaming at me over the phone. I finally stopped answering when I saw it was her number calling."

"I wish I'd have never met her," Peter Blankenship said. "Melissa and I used to support her but she just became more and more erratic the last few months and we realized she wasn't just on a mission to save the forest, she had gone way over the edge. When we started to draw back, she began almost stalking us. She came by the house and stood in the yard screaming at us, she accosted us in stores and restaurants. It was like we had become one of her targets."

***

It was mid-afternoon and Parks had been complaining about starvation for two hours before Weber finally took a break from his telephone calls to Emma's enemies and few friends, and they adjourned to the Wagon Wheel Restaurant for a late lunch.

Noting the jeans and heavy coats Weber and Chad wore instead of their uniforms, Susie Odell asked, "Been hunting?" as she showed them to a table.

"Not for anything we wanted to find," Weber told her.

"So, do you have any news for me on Lenny Dewitt's claim that he was drinking at the Antler Inn?" Weber asked Tommy Frost, and the young deputy shook his head.

"You know how Margo is. First I had to listen to her complain about how we're always hassling her, and then after listening to all that, all she said was that it was real busy Tuesday afternoon with all the hunters mixed in with the regulars and she didn't recognize his picture."

Margo Prestwick, the owner of the Antler Inn, was a crude, heavyset blonde with a bad attitude who presided over her rough clientele with a foul mouth and dire threats of what she would do if they got too far out of line. Though, at the Antler Inn, standards of behavior were so low that Weber wasn't sure just how bad someone would have to act before they stepped over the line with Margo.

The bell over the front door chimed and Charles Gelman stepped inside, blowing on his hands to warm them. Weber made eye contact and waved him over. Charles, who owned the BookCellar, was a tall, handsome man of about 50, with short, sandy brown hair, with a trim mustache and beard.

"Pull up a chair and join us," Weber invited.

"What are you fine gentlemen up to on this cold winter's day?" Charles asked as he sat down.

"We've been looking into Emma Moyer's death," Weber told him. News travels fast in a small town, and he knew that most people in Big Lake were already well aware of the murder.

"A terrible thing," Charles said, nodding gratefully to Susie as she sat a cup of coffee in front of him. "I only met her a time or two but she seemed to be…. challenging, shall we say?"

"How so?"

"She came into the store once and asked me to hang a poster in the window that called the owners of those new cabins going up out by the T intersection rapists and pillagers. I didn't feel comfortable with that and declined, and she just went ballistic on me. She was screaming and telling me that I was just another newcomer here to bleed the mountain dry, who didn't care about Mother Earth."

"Sorry about that," Weber said, and Charles shook his head and laughed.

"Oh, she wasn't half as bad as Miss Fuller. Every week or so she comes into the store with a Magic Marker and starts going through books blacking out all of the profanity and sex scenes. And to her, the word "damn" is profane and even a kiss is sexual. I have to watch her like a hawk or she'll ruin half my inventory."

"Well there you have it, Charles," Parks said. "You're not really gay, you just attract the wrong kind of women. If we could find you a nice, mousey little bookworm instead of all of those lunatics your store attracts, you might just jump ship and come over to our side!"

Charles, who was comfortable with his sexuality and his friends, laughed heartily and slapped Parks on the back. "I'll be honest with you, Special Agent Parks, I've considered it, since the, err… pickings in my sphere of interest are a bit slim around here. But I know I just couldn't compete with all you handsome gentlemen. I'll tell you what though, if you ever decide to "jump ship," call me."

It took a lot to make Parks blush, but that did the trick, and the table erupted in laughter.

The bell over the door chimed again and Tommy said, "Oh Lord. How does she do it? Everywhere I go, she shows up."

"Speaking of lunatic women, isn't that your girlfriend?" Chad asked, and Tommy blushed even deeper than Parks had.

"Come on, guys, it's not funny," he said as he tried to shrink into his seat.

"What do we have here?" Charles asked. "A May-December romance?"

"More like a dangerous cougar who's found herself a tasty little bunny rabbit," Weber told him. "Tami's been stalking poor Tommy here for months now and won't take no for an answer. We may have to send him off to a seminary just to get him away from her."

"Trust me, I'd prefer a life of celibacy over having anything to do with that woman!" Tommy said, and added, "Oh no, here she comes. Shoot me, Sheriff! Please?"

The men tried to hide their delight at the young deputy's discomfort when Tami spotted him and called out in her best Southern diva impersonation, "Why Tommy Frost! Have you been avoiding me?"

She sashayed across the room to their table, as much as any woman her size and age could sashay, and stood with her hands on her hips leering at Tommy with bright red lips as he shrunk back in his chair trying to make himself invisible.

"Sheriff Weber, I just may have to register a complaint with the mayor's office. Why, every time I try to arrange a social engagement with this handsome devil he tells me you've got him working extra shifts. You really do need to allow him some free time. All work and no play, don't you know."

"Nice to see you, Tami," Weber told her. "I'm sorry, I didn't realize we were depriving young Tommy here of a social life. The good news is that since we hired those two new deputies, the schedule is clearing up a lot. In fact, I seem to remember that Deputy Frost has the entire weekend off, starting right now."

Tommy looked at his boss with horror, and both Parks and Chad had to stare at their coffee cups to avoid bursting into laughter at the panic in his eyes.

"Well, that's wonderful news!" Tami gushed. "Thank you, Sheriff. I do intend to see that this hardworking public servant is well rewarded for all that he does for our community."

"Did she say public or pubic?" Parks whispered to Chad, who had to bite the web of his hand to keep from laughing out loud, though he could not stifle the giggle that fought its way out.

But Tami didn't notice, her attention was focused entirely on Tommy, who seemed to have physically shrunk in the last few minutes. His ears were a deep crimson and he had the resigned look of a man headed for the gallows, but he made a last valiant attempt to escape his fate.

"Sheriff, I can't take any time off right now. Not with us right in the middle of a murder investigation. You need me."

"Oh, you kids run along and have fun," Parks told him. "Now that I'm back in town, I'll be happy to pick up the slack."

Chad snorted and tried to cover up by coughing violently into his hand.

"That settles it," Tami said. "Let's go by your house and you can change out of that uniform and into something more comfortable. Then we'll go to my place and I'll fix you a nice candlelit dinner. And from there… who knows?"

Even Weber had a hard time maintaining his composure when Tami did, indeed, slowly run her tongue over her upper lip. In some women it might have been sexy, but in this situation Weber couldn't help but think of a predator eyeing a fresh kill.

"Miz Gaylord, I just can't!"

"Oh yes you can, Tommy. Trust me, I'll show you everything you need to know."

Chad erupted in a new round of coughing and pounded the table with his fist, but everybody ignored him. The show was better across the table.

"No, I can't," Tommy protested. "Really, I can't!"

"Oh, I love it when a man plays hard to get," Tami said, running a finger with a red lacquered nail along Tommy's cheek. "And I just know the chase is going to be well worth it."

"No," Tommy said, shaking his head. "I don't want to hurt your feelings, Miz Gaylord, but I keep trying to tell you that…."

"What Tommy's been trying to tell you is that he's already in a relationship," Charles Gelman said, as he gently reached out and removed Tami's finger from the young deputy's cheek.

Tami stopped, her hand frozen in mid-air, and suddenly a look of understanding came across her face. "Oh my God! Do you mean…?"

"That's right," Charles said as he draped his arm affectionately across Tommy's shoulders and squeezed gently.

Parks spewed hot coffee across the menu he was hiding behind and Chad had to leave the table and rush to the men's room. But Tami didn't notice anything but the two men in front of her.

"Oh Tommy, I am so sorry! All this time you've been trying to tell me and I just didn't see it. I…"

"It's okay," Charles assured her. "When a young person first starts to realize that they are…"

Tami held up her hand and said, "Say no more. I have a nephew in the exact same situation. Confused, afraid, anxious. Oh, you poor boy!"

Weber and Parks both nodded sympathetically, while Charles just squeezed Tommy's shoulder reassuringly.

Tami lowered her face to within an inch of Tommy's and placed a tender palm upon his cheek as she said, "I just want you to know I only wish you much happiness," tears welling up in her thickly mascaraed eyes.

Tommy could only nod, and Tami straightened up and look at Charles, smiling through her tears as she said, "Be good to him."

"Oh, I will," Charles assured her. "We'll travel this road together at your own pace, won't we Tommy?"

Chad, on his way back to the table, heard that and did an abrupt about face and headed back for the men's room.

After Tami had departed, leaving the scent of honeysuckle in the air behind her, the table was quiet for a long moment, until finally Tommy said, "Charles, I don't know if I should thank you or what. I owe you, I guess."

"Oh, you'll thank me," Charles assured him. "The sheriff said you have the whole weekend off to do it in." And with that he ran his tongue over his lips.

This time, when Parks spewed his coffee, it made its way clear across the table to spray Weber, who was laughing too hard to even attempt to wipe it off.

***

At 4 p.m. Lenny Dewitt was arraigned in front of Judge Harold Ryman, with his hastily recruited attorney, Amy Karasik, a young woman who was under contract by the Town to represent criminal defendants who did not have legal counsel present.

Bob Bennett, the Town's attorney, presented the case against the defendant; that Lenny had fired a high-powered rifle at Emma Moyer on Tomahawk Mountain on Tuesday afternoon, in front of two witnesses, his son-in-law Brad Gleason and hunting guide Jake Gibbons.

Jake was a man more comfortable in the outdoors, whether it be working the small ranch he owned with his brother or guiding hunters in the mountains, than he would ever be inside, especially in a courtroom. Brad looked like a condemned man who knew he was in trouble no matter what he said; if he testified truthfully against the man who was both his employer and father-in-law, the rest of his life would become even more miserable, and if he lied, he was committing perjury and could be sent to prison.

Fortunately for both men, they would not be there long. When Judge Ryman asked Lenny how he pled to the charges against him, the defendant said, "Guilty, Your Honor."

"Does anybody have any comments before I pass sentence," the judge asked.

"Your Honor, while my client freely admits that his actions were wrong, this kind of behavior is not common for him. I would ask that the Court consider the fact that it was Ms. Moyer who first fired a gun, not once, not twice, but three times into the air. Mr. Dewitt is not a police officer, he has no military training, no experience with a situation like this. He is a 51 year old family man who owns a janitorial supply business back in Pennsylvania. He has no criminal record. He's never even had a traffic ticket before. He came here with his two sons and his son-in-law to hunt deer, not to be confronted by a fanatical woman who first accosted him at Matt's Sporting Goods on Friday when he went to purchase ammunition and then showed up again on the mountain shooting a gun! Was his response right? No, Your Honor. Was it dangerous, even foolhardy? Yes it was. Mr. Dewitt realizes that. He regrets his actions and he would only ask your understanding that it was a foolish, one time mistake that he will never make again."

Judge Ryman thought for a moment and then turned to Bennett. "Do you or Sheriff Weber have anything to add?"

"Yes, we do, Your Honor. While Ms. Moyer's actions were foolhardy, even dangerous, that doesn't give Mr. Dewitt the right to shoot at her."

"Self-defense, Your Honor," Amy interrupted, and the judge held up his hand to silence her.

"I don't believe Mr. Dewitt acted in self-defense," Bennett said.

"He acted in anger. Something he seems to do quite often."

Amy started to object, but the judge stopped her again. "The defendant has already pled guilty, we're not going to spend a lot of time debating the case after the fact. Anything else, Mr. Bennett?"

"As I'm sure you're aware, Your Honor, Emma Moyer was found dead on Tomahawk yesterday. She had been shot and…"

"Objection, Your Honor! My client has not been charged with Ms. Moyer's death and it has no relevance to this case."

"No relevance? Your client shot at her and he was one of the last people to see her alive."

"Enough," the judge said. "Mr. Bennett, are you charging the defendant with Ms. Moyer's death?"

"Not at this time, Your Honor. But we would like the Court to order Mr. Dewitt not to leave town until the investigation into her death is complete, or until he is ruled out as a suspect."

"Does your client have a problem with that, Counselor?"

The attorney and Dewitt put their heads together for a hurried conference and then she said, "My client has a business to run back in Pennsylvania, Your Honor. He can't stay here for months on end while the case lingers."

"He can if I sentence him to prison based upon his guilty plea," the judge told her. "I was considering a stiff fine, but if your client doesn't want to cooperate in Sheriff Weber's investigation, maybe I need to insure that he'll be available."

There was another quick exchange of whispers, then Amy said, "We understand, Your Honor. Mr. Dewitt will remain in Big Lake as long as necessary."

"Fine. Mr. Dewitt, while I support the right to self-defense under law, I don't believe you felt your life was in danger when you shot at Emma Moyer. And while she was wrong in her actions, two wrongs don't make a right. However, based upon your clean record and the fact that Ms. Moyer did initiate the confrontation, I'm going to give you a break. I'm reducing the charge down to misdemeanor assault, which will spare you a felony conviction, and I'm sentencing you to six months in jail and a $500 fine. However, if you keep out of trouble and cooperate with Sheriff Weber's investigation, I will suspend the jail time."

Lenny sighed in relief, and the judge gave him a stern look before continuing, "But let me assure you, Mr. Dewitt, that if you step over the line in any way, you'll spend the next six months behind bars. Is that understood?"

"Yes sir, Your Honor," Lenny said. "Thank you."

Judge Ryman rapped his gavel and said, "Court is adjourned. See my clerk to pay your fine."

"Well, he got off easy," Bennett said as he and Weber left the courtroom.

"If he wasn't such a jerk, he'd never have been in there in the first place," Weber replied as he buttoned his coat against the cold. "But instead of answering my questions, he wanted to throw his weight around."

"One of those guys who's his own worst enemy?"

"You got it. Maybe he learned a lesson."

"I doubt it," Bennett said. "His kind seldom do."

The attorney had no idea how prophetic his words would prove to be.

Chapter 12

How does one find the guilty party when there is a long list of potential suspects to choose from, but none that stand out from the crowd? Weber started with a whiteboard and an erasable marker, writing down the names of anybody he believed could possibly have been involved with Emma's murder. At the top of the list was Lenny Dewitt's name, followed by Richard MacEwen, then Jake and Sam Gibbons. The list went on to include Ashley Knott from the ski lodge, Bill Stevens, Wayne Duncan, Lillian Neafie, and over a dozen others who had lost time and money when Emma tried to stop their various building projects. He also included some of Emma's former allies whom she had alienated, including Peter and Melissa Blankenship, and Jolene Brighton. As an afterthought, Weber included the name of Emma's half-sister, Leslie Ungren. Even though they were estranged and Leslie had claimed she had not seen Emma in months, the fact that there was bad blood between them and that Leslie, as next of kin, stood to potentially benefit from Emma's estate, made her a suspect.

"Okay, talk to me," Weber told his assembled deputies. "Is there somebody I'm missing here? Or is there somebody who doesn't belong on the list?"

"You could add a hundred names more to the list, theoretically," Coop said. "In all my years investigating crimes, I don't think I've ever run across anybody so universally disliked. From the feedback we're getting, I'm beginning to think that the only person in this town who did like Emma was her boyfriend, Richard MacEwen."

"Okay, let's start with him," Weber said. "He said he was down in Tucson at the time of the murder. Have we corroborated that?"

"It couldn't have been him," Dolan said. "We estimate that Emma was killed sometime after the confrontation with Jake Gibbons and his hunters on Tuesday afternoon and Wednesday morning when MacEwen reported her missing. More likely, it was Tuesday, since once the storm hit somebody would have had a hard time getting up that mountain. MacEwen's ex-wife and a dozen family members all say he was at his daughter's birthday party Monday afternoon. His ex-wife says he spent the night with them, and that Tuesday morning they took their daughter to the Desert Museum and were there all day. He's got receipts for the museum tickets and a gasoline purchase made in Tucson on Tuesday morning. And his ex-wife said he was there again Tuesday and Wednesday nights, and left Thursday as soon as the roads were open up here. He's got credit card receipts from restaurants where they had dinner every night."

"Wait a minute, he spent how many days sleeping at his ex-wife's house?" Coop asked incredulously.

"Apparently they had an amicable divorce and she said she still considers him her best friend. I guess people are different down there in the big city."

Coop whistled and said, "I'd be afraid to fall asleep in the same state where my ex lives for fear that when I woke up I'd be an ex-man!"

"Okay, it looks like MacEwen's in the clear," Weber said as he drew a line through the man's name. "Next?"

"What about Lenny Dewitt?"

"Good question, Chad. We know he's a bully and likes to get his way, we know he shot at Emma earlier in the day, and we know that he disappeared for a couple of hours during the time when we estimate that she was shot. At this point, he's our best suspect. Were you able to turn up anything at all to back up his alibi about being picked up by a couple of hunters and drinking with them at the Antler Inn, Tommy?"

"Tommy's too busy being the mountain's official stud muffin to devote much time to police work these days," Buz teased, drawing laughter from the room and reddening Tommy's neck and ears.

Tommy ignored the ribbing and shook his head. "I've been out there three times now and haven't gotten anywhere. It's been busy, and when the storm hit it looks like all the hunters stayed in town and went drinking. Some of the regulars told me that there were a lot of strangers there drinking, but none of them could remember him from the pictures I showed them."

"We can't confirm his alibi," Weber said. "But can we prove he was the one that shot Emma? Can we timeline that?"

Chad looked at his notes and said, "We don't have exact times. Jake Gibbons said it was late afternoon when they loaded up the horses at the trailhead and that he realized Lenny was gone. He said he drove up and down the road several times, then dropped off Brad Gleason at the motel and came here to report him missing. Mary logged that in at 5:03 p.m. Tuesday. So let's say it was what, 3 or 3:30 when Lenny fell off the radar? And he called to say he was back at the motel just before 6, because that's when the call came in for that rollover traffic accident."

"So that gives him as much as three hours," Weber said. "Plenty of time to hike up the road to where Emma's car was parked, shoot her, and make it back to town."

"Is it?" Robyn asked, and every head turned in her direction. Robyn wasn't used to being the center of attention, and was not comfortable in the spotlight, but she pressed forward with her argument. "Lenny Dewitt is a middle aged man. He's in decent shape, but he's not a kid anymore. He'd have had to have hiked uphill a half mile or more in a snowstorm, shot Emma, and then hiked over six miles back to town. That part was all downhill, but still, at over 9,000 foot elevation, the air up here is pretty thin. I think it would be a challenge even for a younger man in better shape."

A couple of the deputies nodded their heads, well aware of the number of emergency calls they had responded to for out of town visitors with chest pains or shortness of breath that were caused by altitude sickness.

"And then we have the pure coincidence of it all. Let's say Mr. Dewitt did hike uphill instead of down. Why? And how did he just happen to get turned around and arrive at the parking area where we assume Emma was shot at the same time she was there? And then make a spur of the moment decision to shoot her. There was no way he could have planned it in advance since they didn't know she was going to be out there or where she had left her car."

Robyn had everyone's attention by then. Any experienced investigator will tell you that they don't believe in coincidences.

"But let's go out on a limb and assume he did," Robyn said. "He still had to hike all the way back down that road, undetected. Both Jake and Sam Gibbons were out there looking for him, and then Buz and Dolan came on scene. But none of them saw him. I don't know, it just doesn't add up to me."

"That makes a lot of sense," Parks agreed. "It's a long shot. But I still think we need to keep him on the list for now, at least. You did good, kid."

Robyn blushed but her smile showed she was obviously pleased with the compliment. Being the only female deputy in the department, and a rookie to boot, Robyn's position was further complicated by the fact that she and Weber were linked romantically, a tidy bit of gossip that had caused some unrest and set tongues to wagging all around town. Her fellow deputies and the administrative staff had shown overwhelming support for them when the mayor had tried to make it an issue before the Town Council, but it was still important to her that she prove she could pull her own weight and that she neither wanted nor received any special favors from the sheriff.

"What about Jake or Sam Gibbons?" Coop asked. "They seem to have been the most recently affected financially by Emma's activities. Could it have been one of them?"

"You'd have a hard time convincing me of that," Chad said. "I've known both of them all my life. Grew up with them and we went to school together. They're good men and I've never known either one to do anything the slightest bit wrong."

Dolan nodded in agreement. "Me either. I just don't see it."

Weber left the brothers' names on the board, under the anything's possible category, and moved on. By the time they got to the end of the list, they had managed to eliminate a couple of names of people who were known to be out of town when the murder took place, but they were no closer to homing in on a suspect than they had been when the meeting began.

With nothing else to do, he decided to hit the street and see what kind of information he could dig up.

Chapter 13

"I won't lie to you and say I wasn't tempted to bash that crazy woman's head in a time or two," Matt Wells told Weber as he stood behind the counter of his sporting goods store restocking boxes of ammunition on the shelf that took up most of one wall.

The shop was small, not much over 1,400 square feet, but it was filled with an impressive array of inventory that included fishing and archery equipment, hunting rifles and shotguns, three glass showcases of handguns, and racks stocked with holsters, and assorted accessories. If you needed the right gear for an outdoor expedition, Matt stocked it, and he had a large and loyal following of sportsmen from throughout the region.

"I heard she was in here creating a ruckus a few days ago," Weber said, as he admired a beautifully crafted 20 gauge Browning Citori over and under shotgun.

Wells took the gun back when Weber reluctantly handed it to him, saying, "I can make you a good deal on that, Sheriff. It'd make you a fine bird gun come quail season."

"Don't tempt me," Weber said. "I'm a poor but weak public servant."

"I've got it priced at $1,600, but I'd let you have it for $1,200 out the door."

"Wish I could," Weber said. "But the timing's just not right."

"You saving up for a wedding ring?" Wells teased, then chuckled at the sheriff's discomfort.

"So anyway, about Emma," Weber said, steering the subject away from his personal life. "What happened the other day?"

"Well, she was out there for a couple of days waving one of those protest signs of hers, something about slaughtering animals for sport," Wells said, pointing toward the parking lot. "I called your office, but Mary said that as long as she stayed on the curb and didn't step foot on my property, there was nothing you guys could do."

"Afraid so," Weber told him. "Freedom of speech and all that."

"I know," Wells said. "And I have to give her credit, she stood her ground right there when a couple of guys started hassling her. She didn't back down an inch."

Weber perked up at the mention of Emma being hassled. "What happened?"

"Oh, it was nothing," Wells said. "Most of it was more good spirited fun then anything. You know Ralph Tigthe, owns the saw shop?"

"I know Ralph," Weber said. "He's a good man,"

"Damn fine man," Wells agreed. "Anyway, he was in here looking at a new scope for his rifle and we got to commenting on Emma and all her causes, so he made up his own PETA sign."

"Peta?" Weber asked, not understanding.

"You know, that anti-hunting group, what is it, People for Ethical Treatment of Animals or some such? Anyway, old Ralph, he cuts a piece off a cardboard box and takes a red marker and makes his own PETA sign. But his says People Eating Tasty Animals!" Wells hooted at the memory, then said, "I have to give Emma credit though, she stood right there toe-to-toe with him and wouldn't back down an inch."

Weber had known Ralph Tigthe, the owner of Ralph's Power Products, for years and considered him a friend. Ralph was a big, good natured man with coal black hair and a bushy beard, who held his Levis up with wide red suspenders, and whose cheek always seemed to bulge with a wad of chewing tobacco. He could picture Ralph pulling a stunt like that, but didn't believe the man had a mean bone in his body.

"You said a couple of guys hassled Emma. Who else?"

"Can't tell you his name for sure. He's new in town, one of those real estate speculators that came here to get rich. Fat little guy, drives a red SUV of some kind." Wells, thought for a minute, then snapped his fingers. "Brian something. He's always got an ad in the paper with his face on it."

Though he was raised in Big Lake and knew most of the long time residents at least enough to nod to, Weber had a hard time keeping up with all of the newcomers and didn't know the man Wells referred to. But with the information he had, it wouldn't be too hard to find him.

"What did they fight about?"

"Who knows? He wasn't in here buying anything, he just stopped out front and they got into it. I was busy with a customer and just saw them through the window."

"What happened between Emma and those hunters the Gibbons

brothers brought in here?"

Wells' face darkened and his smile disappeared. "Now that one pissed me off! Those guys can check their hunting rifles as cargo with the airlines as long as they're inspected first and in proper cases. But they can't bring any ammunition with them, so Jake and Sam brought them in to get what they needed. Eight boxes of Winchester Super X 180 grain .308 ammo. That was a nice sale to start the day."

"Why so much ammo for four hunters?" Weber asked. "Were they planning to start a war?"

"It's always a good idea to sight in a rifle after it's been shipped," Wells told him. "Scopes can get fogged, sights knocked out of alignment."

"Makes sense," Weber said. "What happened with Emma?"

"She came barging in the door there, yelling for them to go back where they came from and screaming about how they were murderers. She warned them that she was going to stop them from killing any deer, no matter what it took."

"Then what happened?"

"It just got uglier. The older guy, I think he's the dad of the rest of the hunters, he was yelling back at Emma, and Jake was trying to calm everybody down. I'll tell you what Sheriff, I was afraid she was gonna pull that damn gun of hers out and shoot somebody, she was acting so crazy! If I knew how far over the line she could get, or what she planned to do with it, I'd have never sold it to her."

"Wait a minute. You sold Emma a gun?

"It was all on the up and up," Wells said, getting defensive. "I called it in, she passed the background check. I don't play games with the law. You can check my books anytime you want to."

"No, that's not what I meant," Weber reassured him. "Her boyfriend kept saying he couldn't see Emma with a gun. Did she say why she was buying it?"

"She said she had some deer getting into her garden and she wanted to scare them away, so she bought the gun and a box of blanks. In fact, I had to special order them for her. They're not something I usually carry."

"Matt, can I see the paperwork on that sale?"

"Sure can," he said squatting down to pull a thick three ring binder out from under the counter. "Like I said, I've got nothing to hide."

He thumbed through pages of 4473 forms the Federal Bureau of Alcohol, Tobacco and Firearms required of any firearm purchase. "Here it is," Wells said, turning the book so Weber could read the form.

The form reported that on August 5, Emma Mae Moyer had purchased a used .38 Iver Johnson revolver with a three inch barrel. Weber was very familiar with firearms of all kinds and knew that though they were ancient, the reliable and easy to use old handguns had been immensely popular at one time. Though they were overshadowed by newer, more powerful weapons with higher ammunition capacity years ago, there were probably still thousands sitting in nightstand drawers, gun safes, and vehicle glove compartments.

Since she had purchased the gun months ago, well before the hunting season arrived, it was obvious that Emma had been planning to disrupt the hunt well before she spooked Brad Gleason's deer on Tomahawk Mountain, Tuesday afternoon.

Weber closed the book and Wells returned it to its shelf. "Like I said, if I had known how crazy she could get I'd never have sold her the damn thing."

"You were telling me about her coming in here and jumping on your customers the other day," Weber prompted.

"Yeah, like I said, she was screaming like a banshee. And I don't mean she was just raising her voice. By the time it was done she was literally screaming, and that older fellow was right back in her face, calling her a fruitcake and a crazy bitch and warning her that if she got in his way she'd regret it."

"Regret it? What else did he say?"

"The usual crap you hear when two people go at it like that. He told her he didn't come all this way and spend a fortune to have some tree hugging maniac like her try to stop him."

"Matt, did he physically threaten her?"

"Oh, no, nothing like that, Sheriff. He just told her he had had a lot tougher people than her get in his way and they always learned not to screw with Larry Dewitt or whatever his name is."

"Then what happened?"

"I was just about to call 911, but then Jake Gibbons had enough and he just came up from behind and picked her up and carried her kicking and screaming out the door. They yelled at each other in the parking lot and he was pointing his finger in her face telling her to back off or he'd see her in jail. Anyway, I guess Emma finally had enough, or felt like she had made her point, and she took off."

Weber thanked Matt for his time and left, thinking that he needed to talk to Jake Gibbons and ask him why he had omitted that part of the incident with Emma when he told Weber about the encounter at the gun shop.

***

"Oh, it was all in good fun, but I'll tell you what, that little old gal didn't back down an inch," Ralph Tigthe told Weber as he put a piece of split wood in the old, square woodstove at his shop. He stood up and wiped his hands together, smiling at the memory. "She weren't no more than a popcorn fart in the wind, but she didn't take no bullshit from anybody. I had to admire her for that."

"I know you were just pulling her chain," Weber said, "but do you know of anybody who may have had it in for Emma? Who might have wanted her dead?"

"Oh, there'd be a long list, Jimmy. You know she had a lot of construction projects tied up with lawsuits, right? She was always getting them injunction orders to try to stop some new cabin going up, or to stop them from breaking ground for a resort or something."

"Anybody specific come to mind?"

"Well, I know that she had a big run in with Roger Wilson last week."

"Roger Wilson?"

"Yeah, you know him. The real estate guy."

Weber nodded, "What about him?"

"My wife's kid sister picks up some extra money cleaning offices to help ends meet, since that no 'count husband of hers ain't worth a damn. She told me about the whole thing."

Weber knew Susan Holman enough to say hello to, though her husband was more familiar. George Holman was a know-it-all that couldn't hold down a job, and his wife depended on whatever part time work she could pick up and the charity of her older sister to keep their two young children fed and clothed.

"What did she say?"

Ralph spit tobacco juice into a paper cup and wiped his mouth with the back of his hand before he continued. "It was late, after 8, and Wilson was in his office doing some paperwork when Emma came barging in and walked right across the carpet Susie had just vacuumed, tracking mud all over it. Susie about blew a gasket!"

Ralph paused to open the stove's cast iron door and poke at the fire, sending a shower of sparks upward. As hot as the fire was, it barely took the chill off the air inside the poorly insulated shop. Weber wanted to urge him to get back to the story, but he had known Ralph long enough to realize that he'd tell it in his own time and not a minute sooner.

"Anyway, she marches right past Susie to Wilson's private office there in the back and she commenced to tell him off about something and pretty soon they were both going at it. Susie said Emma was knocking papers off that man's desk and calling him every name under the sun. And Wilson weren't holding back either. He called Emma a bitch and a couple other names that Susie wouldn't repeat, and then she said he grabbed her and slammed her up agin' the wall right there in the office. She said that must have scared Emma, 'cause she went all stiff and never said another word. And then Susie said Wilson told her that if she didn't shut up and stay out of his business, he'd shut her up for good."

Ralph spit in the paper cup again and said, "Susie told me that Wilson looked over and saw her standing there, kinda in shock, and then he let go of Emma, and Susie said Emma got out of there real fast. Susie said she was kind of scared, and it must have showed on her face 'cause she said Wilson apologized to her for blowing his stack like that, and then he gave her a hundred dollar bill and said he was sorry Emma tracked all over her new cleaned carpet like that, and asked her to sweep it up again."

Roger Wilson owned High Country Realty, one of the most successful real estate agencies in the northern half of the state. He was rich, handsome, and word had it that he had political ambitions. His wife Laura was a stunning redhead who had spent time in Hollywood. The couple always seemed blissfully happy, and lived in a magnificent log home perched on the top of Saddleback Mountain with a commanding view of the valley and lake below. But Weber had been inside the Wilson home and knew what went on behind its closed doors. He thanked Ralph for the information, asked him for Susan Holman's address, and started to leave.

"I was real sad to hear about Emma, Jimmy. Real sad. Way back what seems like a hunnert years ago, Emma wasn't like that. Back in school she was 'bout the prettiest thing I'd ever seen. She wore that red hair a hers long, clear down to her butt. Oh, she was feisty, even back then. But me and her…," he looked around to be sure they were alone in the shop, "me and her, well, we was head over heels in love. Or at least we thought we were. But what do kids know about love? Oh, we figured out the physical part, that's easy enough."

Weber paused with his hand on the doorknob. "You and Emma?"

"Oh yeah. Now, I wouldn't say something about that to anybody while she was alive, and I know you'll keep it under your hat out of respect for the woman's memory. But we was each others' first. We both thought we'd have a life together, 'course that didn't happen. Emma went off to that college in California when we got out of high school, and I joined the Army and I guess we just drifted apart. By the time we both got back home, we was different people. Those things happen. I'd see her around town, and neither of us ever talked about the way things was between us way back when. But I'll tell you what, Jimmy, when you find out who killed Emma, I'd 'preciate it if you'd give me 'bout five minutes alone in a cell with him."

The big man opened the stove door again and poked at the fire, not because it needed poking, but because he didn't want Weber to see the tears that had welled up in his eyes.

Chapter 14

A young girl of about five, wearing her black hair in two pigtails that were tied with yellow ribbon with a matching yellow ribbon headband that sported two red feathers made from construction paper, opened the door of the dilapidated mobile home at Weber's knock. She smiled at the sheriff, a gap revealing two missing upper front teeth, and said "I'm Pokeyhanes! Who are you?"

Behind her, he could see a nineteen inch TV set playing a Disney movie that Weber remembered seeing advertisements for a couple of years earlier.

Weber squatted down to bring himself to eye level. "Well, if you're Pocahontas, can I be Captain John Smith?"

The girl giggled and shook her head. "No. 'Course not!"

"Why not?"

"Because you're too old! Captain John Smith is Pokeyhanes' boyfriend, you silly!"

"I'm old? Really? How old do you think I am?"

Pokeyhanes giggled again, and said, "I don't know. At least a zillion years old."

"Well, darling, I'll tell you what. Sometimes I feel that way."

"Then you can be Pokeyhanes' father, Chief Powhatan."

"Chief Powhatan it is," Weber agreed.

"Hey, get away from the door! You know you're not supposed to talk to strangers. He might be one of those child mowesters."

A slightly older boy, wearing a cape fashioned from a blue bath towel, tried to shove his sister aside, but Pokeyhanes held her ground.

"He's not a child mowester, Georgie! You dumbhead!"

"I'm not Georgie, I'm Batman!"

"Are not!"

"Are too! And he's a child mowester."

"He can't be a child mowester. They didn't have child mowesters in Pokeyhanes! He's Chief Powhatan."

"Will you kids keep it down, I'm trying to sleep here! And close the damn door, we ain't heating the outside. Susie, get off your butt and do something with them, will you?"

"Yes, George. Come on kids, quiet down, your daddy don't feel good." A harried looking Susan Holman walked into the living room carrying a green plastic laundry basket piled high with clothes. Seeing Weber at the door, she sat the basket down and crossed the room.

"Sheriff?"

"He's not a sheriff, Mama, he's Chief Powhatan."

"No he's not, he's a child mowester!"

"Come on, kids, get out of the way so the Sheriff can get in out of the cold."

She held the door open, revealing more of the living room. It was shabby, but except for a few toys scattered on the floor, it was tidy. George Holman, wearing a pair of worn gray sweat pants and a sleeveless tee shirt, lay on the couch.

He was an average looking man in his mid-thirties, medium build, medium brown hair, who wore a perpetual look of woe. The look was because George was convinced that he was smarter than the rest of the world, and even though he had spent much of his life sharing that knowledge, the world just didn't seem to get it and appreciate him. He could never hold a job, because the darned bosses were all jealous of him, and as soon as they realized just how smart George was they saw him as a threat and found some excuse to fire him. Lately he had been down with a bad back, no doubt from carrying the weight of the whole world upon his shoulders. Even so, he managed to sit up with an exaggerated groan when he saw Weber.

"Sorry, Sheriff, didn't see you there. Been in a lot of pain lately and just tryin' to get some relief."

"Sorry to hear that, George," Weber said. "Have you been to a doctor?"

"Doctors!" George said with a scowl. "What do they know? Just a bunch of high paid con artists if you ask me. I tol' that damn Doc Williams over to the medical center I have a couple a ruptured disks and need to be on disability, but he says the X-rays don't show it. 'Course they don't! You take a hard muscled man like me or you, those X-rays don't pentrate' deep enough to show anything. You know that!"

"Did you get a second opinion?" Weber asked.

"Ackk! Forget that," George said with a disgusted wave of his hand. "We ain't got no medical insurance, so I can't afford a second 'pinion. And you know what it is, it's all a big conspiracy with those there insurance companies to deny a man compensation for his injuries, that's what it is!"

Weber would have listened to more of George's problems, but he had a murder investigation to get back to, and said, "Mrs. Holman, is there someplace we can talk?"

"Sure, let me pour you a cup of coffee. Kids, you sit here and watch TV, okay?"

"I wanna watch Batman!"

"No, Georgie, I'm watching Pokeyhanes!"

"Here, let me give you some cookies and milk, and you both sit down and finish your movie, Becky, and then we'll put on Batman, okay Georgie?"

"I'm not Becky, I'm Pokeyhanes!"

Once Susan had her children occupied, she joined Weber and her husband in the kitchen, where George was busy explaining to the sheriff that if he could just get the backing to go forward with a solar powered, battery operated mini-car the size of a grocery store shopping cart, life as we know it would be changed forever. But of course the big oil companies would never let it happen because they had a stranglehold on the economy.

"It's just not fair, I'm tellin' ya! We're all slaves to their system. I wrote a letter to that there JP Getty Foundation, 'splaining how this could revolutionize the world and how I needed three million to get it off the ground, but I never got an answer. I'm pretty sure the post office filters all the mail to intercept stuff like that from minds like mine. They're in bed together, ya know, the government and Big Oil."

"George, the Sheriff's a busy man, he probably needs to get back to work. What is it I can do for you, Sheriff Weber?"

Weber would have preferred to speak in private, but it was obvious George wasn't going anywhere. So he asked Susan about the encounter between Roger Wilson and Emma Moyer. Before she could answer, her husband interrupted, waving his finger.

"Whoa! Sheriff, we don't need a rich man like Roger Wilson mad at us. How do we know you'll keep this in confidence so Susie don't get in trouble?"

"Hush, George!"

"No ma'am! Don't you be hushin' me, Susie. I know about these things. We need to talk this over.”

“George…”

“All I need to know is what happened between the two of them at Wilson’s office,” Weber said. “I’ll do my best to keep your name out of it.”

“Uh uh,” George said, shaking his head, “that ain’t gonna cut it, Sheriff. What with me down with this back o’ mine, that little bit that Susie earns is all we got comin’ in. She ain’t got no education and her prospects is limited, so it ain’t much, and it don’t stretch, but we don’t need him firing her and blacklisting her so she can’t get any more work. There’s enough folks got it in for the Holman’s in this town as it is. Jealous bastards!”

“Hush, George.” Susan said again, and turned to Weber. “He is right, Sheriff. If Mr. Wilson found out I was telling you about this, I’d be out of a job. And we need whatever I can bring in.”

“I’ll keep your name out of it,” Weber promised.

“You say that now. But what happens later if this leads to somethin’ big?”

“George…”

“Susie, you’re just a naive little old small town girl. You don’t know nothin’ ’bout how these things can explode. Sheriff, if you’re gonna be usin’ any information my wife has, and I’m not sayin’ she has any information, we need some guarantees.”

“I told you, I’ll keep her name out of it,” Weber said.

“Uh uh. What if this winds up on one of those true crime shows on TV? Or some writer comes along and turns it into a book? That true crime stuff sells good, ya know. I think we need to talk to an agent to protect Susie’s interests. We want to help and all, but a man’s got to look out for his family’s future!”

Weber hoped that George had run down, but apparently he had just paused to take a breath, because before the sheriff or Susan could say anything, George said, “Speakin’ of best interests. We’re both gonna need pert deem too. To cover our expenses and all.”

“Pert what?”

“Pert deem. You know, that daily payment the government gives to special agents and undercover opratives and such. If you’re wantin’ Susie to give you classified information about stuff that she may have seen or heard at work, and agin’ I’m not sayin’ she has anything, that makes her an undercover oprative.”

"I see," Weber said. "And why would you be getting any pert deem, George?"

George shook his head, obviously amazed that someone as dense as Weber could hold such an important position as sheriff. "Cause this here is a community property state, that's why! What hers is mine and likewise. I'm surprised a man like you don't know that."

"Well, there you have it," Weber said. "Community property is part of civil law and I deal with the criminal side of things. Thanks for clearing that up for me, George."

"Anytime, Sheriff. I'm what they call a scholar of things like that."

Susan rolled her eyes at Weber, than said, "You're probably right, George. I don't understand about needing to talk to an agent and all that stuff. But I'm glad you do. I've got to get some groceries before it gets too late. Why don't I go do that, and you can think this all over, okay? And once you figure out the best way to go, we'll call Sheriff Weber and make an appointment to go in and talk to him."

"Yeah, I think so," George agreed. "And Sheriff, if we do decide to go forward with all this, we'll both need that there pert deem payment to cover our expenses and time away from work."

Weber wanted to tell the slacker that one probably needed to actually work to earn any per diem, but he just nodded and said, "That's probably for the best. You folks just give me a call once you get the business end of things sorted out."

"You got it, Sheriff. I probably can't get hold of any of my contacts in New York or Hollywood to talk to an agent 'til Monday. But," he held a finger up in warning, "that there pert deem starts as of today if we decide to go on with this since that's when you first contacted us. That's the way these here things work, contrakshully and all. It's called retreactive' timing."

"You got it," Weber agreed, and stood up. "Mrs. Holman, you drive careful, the roads are still pretty slippery out there. I'd say to take Oak Street past the library, it's not as steep as Pinion Drive."

He thanked her for the coffee, told George he'd talk to the Town Council about the pert deem allowance, and stopped to rustle Batman's hair and give Pokeyhanes a pat on the shoulder on his way out the door.

***

Ten minutes later, Susan Holman pulled her battered Chevy Astro van up next to Weber's Explorer in the library parking lot and got into the passenger seat beside him.

"I'm sorry about George, Sheriff. He just gets off on those tangents of his, always thinking he's going to get rich quick."

"No problem," Weber told her. "I appreciate you talking to me."

"For all his faults, George was right about one thing, though," Susan said, "If Mr. Wilson found out I told anybody about what happened at his office, he'd can me. And I need the work, Sheriff. I'm not a smart woman. I don't have any skills except raising kids and cleaning up after them, but I do what I can to make ends meet. George sure isn't much help."

She was probably not much over 32 or 33 years old, but hard work, worry, and disappointment had added a decade to the woman's face. The last thing Weber wanted to do was add to her load.

"I'll do my very best to keep it between us," Weber told her. "But I won't lie to you, if Roger was involved in Emma Moyer's death, it may come up in court, and you may have to testify."

Susan thought for a minute, then said, "Just do your best, okay Sheriff?"

Her account of the altercation at Roger Wilson's office was basically the same as Ralph Tigthe had told him. On the previous Monday evening, Wilson had been working late and Susan was cleaning his office when Emma Moyer showed up. They had a screaming match that culminated with Wilson grabbing Emma by the shoulders and slamming her into a wall so hard that it knocked a couple of plaques and a framed picture of Wilson with some Hollywood personality onto the floor. Wilson had warned Emma to stay out of his business and she had left without another word. Then Wilson seemed to realize that Susan was there and had seen the entire thing. He handed her a $100 bill, apologized for losing his temper like that, and left shortly afterward without another word. Susan vacuumed up the mud Emma had tracked in, picked up the broken glass from the picture frame, and finished cleaning the office.

"Have you seen him since?" Weber asked.

"No. I clean Monday, Wednesday and Friday nights. With the storm, I couldn't get into town to clean Wednesday. My tires are pretty bald and George said his back was hurting too much to put chains on. When I cleaned Friday, the office was already closed when I got there."

"Susan, you said Roger Wilson got violent with Emma Moyer. Have you ever seen him that way before?"

She shook her head, then stopped and said, "But I'm pretty sure he beats his wife."

"What do you mean?"

"She tried to hide them, but I saw some bruises on her lower back and on her stomach when she was in the office hanging some pictures and her shirt rode up. I've seen them more than once."

Weber knew that Laura Wilson was as twisted as she was beautiful, and was aware of her sexual proclivities, having been the target of her advances himself. He also remembered Laura telling him that her husband had "punished" her by beating her when he caught her with another man. She indicated that it had not been the first time for either to happen, and seemed to accept it as part of life with Roger Wilson.

"Do you know anything about Wilson being in financial trouble, or Emma holding up one of his projects with one of her lawsuits or something?"

"I'm sorry, Sheriff, that stuff's all way over my head. All I do is clean offices and toilets. The only lawsuits I know anything about are all of the ones George is talking about filing against some big company or another in one of his schemes."

"Mrs. Holman, I appreciate your help," Weber told her. He held a $50 bill out and said, "Buy your kids a treat, okay?"

Susan looked at the money he offered and shook her head. "It's bad enough that I have to depend on my sister and Ralph. I can't take your charity."

"It's not charity. Let's call it an advance on your pert deem."

Susan laughed wryly but shook her head again.

"No, Sheriff. You're kind to offer, but I can't. I've got this mirror I have to look in every time I brush my teeth. And I have to tell you, it gets harder and harder to do it all the time."

Weber watched the Astro's taillights as she drove away, wondering why two woman, one a spoiled trophy wife and one a beleaguered mother trying her best to hold onto her last shrcd of dignity as she struggled to keep her family together, tolerated the types of abuses that came with their marriages.

Chapter 15

"Saturday night in Big Lake," Weber said, looking around the room. Mario's Pizzeria was busy, as was every restaurant and bar in town. Cash registers were ringing like sleigh bells and the business owners were reaping in the twin windfall caused by good snow and hunting season. "There was a time when we'd be surprised if more than two tables were filled in here on a Saturday in the winter. Things sure have changed."

"I miss those days, Jimmy, don't you?" Marsha Perry said.

"Sometimes I do," Weber admitted.

"Yeah, but you didn't have me back then," Parks said, and Marsha giggled and snuggled into his shoulder.

"I haven't had you in weeks," Marsha said. "You've been too busy hanging out with those Marines over in Yuma. What were you doing over there for so long, anyway? And what's with the haircut?"

"Can't tell you," Parks said, shaking his head. "Highly classified and all that. National security. If I told you, I'd have to kill you, and then Jimmy'd send me to prison. I'm too pretty for prison!"

"Awww, come on, tell us!" Marcia tickled his ribs and Parks wiggled away and caught her hand.

"Easy woman, we're in a room full of people! You can run your lecherous hands all over my firm, young body once we get back to your place, but here in public you need to behave. I know you don't care about your reputation, but folks around here hold me in high esteem."

Marsha had been Weber's sister's best friend since grade school, though they were complete opposites. Debbie, the beautiful blond, was always the center of attention, while Marsha stood to the side, always ready with a joke or some wild action to lighten any situation. She and Parks had found an immediate connection, based partly upon their shared sense of humor, and over time, Weber had watched their relationship grow stronger.

"Here you go, my friends!" Salvatore Gattuccio said as he brought a huge round metal pan to the table and sat it down on a wire rack.

"Made especially for you." The pizza was so hot the cheese still bubbled on top of it.

"Looks delicious, Sal," Weber told him and the big man beamed.

"Sheriff Jimmy, it's so good to see you relaxing for once. I think this Miss Robyn is good for you. And pretty, too!"

"Why, thank you, kind sir," Robyn said and smiled at the compliment.

"And you," Sal said, hugging Marsha, "How come you don't bring your mama in to see Sal anymore?"

"I'm afraid it's getting harder and harder to get Mom out," Marsha told him. "Ever since her stroke she seems to want to shut herself off from the world. I try, but…"

Sal frowned in sympathy and told her, "Before you go, I give you some fresh cannoli I just made. She always loved Salvatore's cannoli. Maybe it's just the thing to boost her spirits, you think?"

"That would be nice, thank you Sal."

"I give it to you before you go." Sal turned his head as the door opened and a young couple came in wearing down ski jackets. "Ciao, compagno! Welcome! Here, I have a table I saved especially for you."

"Sal never met a stranger," Marsha said. "He's a sweet man."

"And he makes a damn good pizza too," Parks said, sliding a wide slice onto his plate with a spatula.

"Eat up, big boy," Marsha told him, "Mom's going to be sound asleep by the time we get back to my place and we've got a lot of lost time to make up for. And since those damned Marines shaved all your hair off, I'll have to find something else to run my fingers through!"

"Have you no shame?" Weber asked her with a laugh.

"Hey, it's been a long time," Marsha said. "I'm going to bang him so hard we should probably exchange insurance information."

Under the table, Robyn pressed her leg against Weber's. There had been a time when Marsha's ribald sense of humor had embarrassed the more demure Robyn, but over time she seemed to grow more accustomed to the jokes and teasing that were such an ingrained part of Marsha's personality.

"So what did you find out today?" Parks asked.

"Uh uh!" Marsha said, waving her finger. "No shop talk tonight. I need you focused."

"Now, y'all just stop that!" Christine Ridgeway said. "I'm sitting here all by my lonesome and horny as a three-peckered Billy goat and you're talking about all this fornication. It's just not fair!"

Robyn's face flushed, and Weber thought that while she may have gotten used to Marsha, she was being tag teamed and was out of her league.

"What, you didn't bring any of those California surfers back with you?" Marsha asked.

"No dear, when they say hang ten, it's not at all what you think," Christine told her. "Besides the problem with those boys is, sooner or later you've got to talk to them. And while they may be pretty, they're really, really dumb!"

"Kind of like Parks here?' Weber asked.

"Aww, shucks, Jimmy. He ain't dumb. That's just an act. He's deep."

"Speaking of deep, eat up," Marsha told Parks. "Mom should be falling asleep any minute now."

They were all laughing about Marsha's latest outlandish statement when the door opened and a short, heavyset man entered and walked up to the counter.

"Who is that guy?" Weber asked. "Brian or something like that? Sells real estate?"

"Brian Oakes," Christine said with a scowl.

"Well that didn't sound all warm and fuzzy," Marsha said. "What'd he do to you? Or not do to you?"

"Oh, he tried to screw me, all right," Christine, said. "But not in a good way."

"Is there a bad way to get screwed?" Marsha asked, fluttering her eyelashes at Parks.

"He's a snake! Right after I came back to set up SafeHaven, he showed up trying to buy my parents' house and property. When I told him it wasn't for sale, he tried to tell me that the boom was going to go bust one of these days and I'd really regret it. Then he started telling me all the reasons why the place wasn't worth what he was so generously offering me."

"Nothing wrong with making somebody a business proposal, is there?" Parks asked.

"No, not if they treat you like an intelligent human being. But he talked to me like I was some damn imbecile! He kept saying that he was my friend and that was why he was making me an offer nobody else would, and I better take it while I could. I'd never met the man before, and suddenly we're friends? And even if I had wanted to sell, he was offering at least thirty percent under the market! I may have been born at night, but it wasn't last night!"

"She might be a hillbilly, but she's a smart hillbilly," Weber said. Though it was said in jest, he knew his lifelong friend had not one, but two masters degrees and was nobody's fool.

A few moments later, Oakes started for the door and Weber rose to intercept him, sticking out his hand. "Excuse me, Mr. Oakes?"

"Yes?" His smile was practiced.

"I was wondering if we could get together and talk one of these days?"

"Of course, I'm always happy to make a new friend, Mister?"

"Weber. Jim Weber."

"Why does that name sound familiar to me?"

"I'm the Sheriff. Once in a while I get a day off and they let me out of the house without my uniform."

"Yes, of course! Sheriff Weber," Oakes said, shaking his hand. "Are you a buyer or a seller?"

"Excuse me?"

"Are you looking to sell some property, or to make a purchase? I'm always looking to buy, and right now I have some prime building lots available on Flintlock Ridge."

"I'm having dinner with friends right now," Weber said. "And you don't want your pizza to get cold. What's your schedule look like?"

"I'm available 24/7, Sheriff. Here's my card, just give me a call. In the meantime, if you could tell me what kind of transaction you're looking for…"

"Let me touch base with you tomorrow or Monday," Weber said. "My dinner's getting cold, too."

"You do that," Oakes said, the smile never leaving his face. "I guarantee you, nobody can make you a better deal than I can, whether you're buying or selling."

Back at the table, Christine shivered melodramatically and said, "Bleech! That man turns my stomach, he's so sleazy."

"Seemed like a nice guy to me," Weber said. "Maybe you're missing the boat there, Hillbilly. I bet I could fix you right up."

"Oh, give me a break! Even if he wasn't such a slug, can you imagine two people built like us doing it? It'd look obscene, like a big old naked teeter-totter!"

"That's it, finish that slice so we can get out of here," Marsha ordered Parks. "If I have to wait much longer I might chase that guy down and go for a teeter-totter ride myself!"

***

"I thought Marsha was Big Lake's wild child, Robyn said on the ride home, "but I almost wet my pants over a couple of things Christine said. I like her."

"She's good people," Weber said. "She's had a run of hard luck, but she's bounced back ."

"Why do you call her Hillbilly?"

"I don't know, it's just a nickname I stuck on her back when we were kids. She was raised on a small spread up in the hills west of town and her last name was Ridgeway. It just seemed to fit."

"What's her story? I know she grew up here and then moved to California. Somebody said her husband left her and her son died?"

"Mark Wagner was one of those guys you knew was going to come to a bad end, even back in high school," Weber said. "He was a charmer and all the girls loved him, until they got to know him better."

"What do you mean?"

"Oh, some say it was all just rumors, but there were two or three girls who went out with him who said Mark didn't believe in the word "no" and tried to push things way past where they wanted it to end."

"Christine seems way too sharp to fall for a guy like that," Robyn said, and Weber looked over at her in the dashboard lights.

"None of us are the same person at 35 or 40 that we were at seventeen. Hopefully we do some learning along the way. And life's given Christine some very hard lessons."

"How bad was it?"

"Pretty bad," Weber said. "She's never gone into detail, but I know he was physically and mentally abusive, and chased anything in a skirt. One day he told her he was leaving her for some little twit he met someplace, and that was it. He walked out and left her with a nine year old kid and a lot of bills to pay."

"Bastard."

"You got that right. But she picked up the pieces and went on. Worked her way through college, got a job as some kind of social worker with the state, working with runaways and foster kids."

"What happened to the son?"

"Did you ever hear the story of the shoemaker's kids who went barefoot? The shoemaker is so busy making shoes for everybody else that he doesn't have the time to take care of his own kids. Barry believed that as he was growing up. He never understood that his mother was working hard to give him a good life, he felt like she was abandoning him just like his father did. He got into trouble, drugs and drinking, and put her through hell. Two years ago he stole a car and went joyriding. There was a police chase and he ended up crashing into another car at an intersection. Killed the woman driving it and her little girl, and left Barry brain dead. Christine had to tell them to pull the plug and let them harvest his organs."

Robyn shuddered. "I just can't imagine…"

"Me either," Weber said, as he pulled into Robyn's driveway.

"What happened to the husband?"

"Karma happened. That little twit he left Christine for? He beat her a couple of times, and one day she got tired of it and shot him dead."

Chapter 16

The ringing of his cell phone woke Weber Sunday morning, and Robyn moaned and covered her head with a pillow.

"Whoever it is, tell them it's Sunday and we're closed."

"Sheriff, I'm sorry to bother you on a Sunday morning. But I thought you'd want to know that Deputies Frost and Wright are responding to a call about a break-in at Emma Moyer's house," Kate Copley said.

Weber sat up in bed.

"A break-in?"

"A neighbor called and said somebody was breaking in. They're over there now."

"I'm on my way," Weber said.

He started getting dressed as Robyn sat up.

"I could have gone to nursing school and found myself a doctor to fall in love with. Or been a schoolteacher and hooked up with a principal. But no, I had to become a cop and end up in the sheriff's bed!"

"Doctors work longer hours than I do," Weber told her, "And you'd get bored with a school principal real quick. They don't have lights and sirens on their cars."

"True, but doctors make a lot of money, so at least I'd sit home alone in comfortable surroundings. And principals may not have lights and sirens on their cars, but they get summers off. You don't even get Sunday off!"

"Do you want to come along?"

"Oh, why the hell not?" Robyn said, pushing the covers away from her. "But you're buying me breakfast!"

***

Two Big Lake Sheriff's vehicles were parked on the street in front of Emma's house, and a red and white rental truck was backed into the driveway. Dolan Reed and Tommy Frost were talking to a man and woman who stood in the driveway in front of the truck, and when Weber got out of his unit, Dolan broke away and approached him.

"What's going on, Dolan?"

"We got a call from the neighbor lady, reporting suspicious activity. She said somebody was plowing out the driveway, and then the rental truck showed up and it looked like somebody was trying to break in. The lady there says everything in the house belongs to her."

They walked down the driveway and Weber introduced himself to the couple talking to Tommy. The man was short and round, and wore a world-weary expression on his face. The woman's resemblance to Emma Moyer left no doubt in the sheriff's mind who she was. The same slim build, the same nose and chin, though her hair was brown and she wore it longer. Leslie Ungren, Emma's half-sister. She confirmed it when Weber asked, and identified the man as her husband, Pete.

"Folks, this is a crime scene. I'm going to have to ask you to leave."

"What crime scene? I thought you found Emma out in the middle of the woods someplace. What does the house have to do with it?"

"She was murdered," Weber told her. "Until we can figure out who did it, and why, we need to keep everybody out of the house in case it holds any clues."

"If she wasn't killed here, how can there be any clues in the house?"

"Emma may have received threats, or left a journal, or something telling about anybody who was giving her problems."

"Emma didn't get problems, Emma was the problem," Leslie said. "She probably had a million enemies, with all the crap she was involved in."

"Well, be that as it may, I can't let you inside the house. And besides, we haven't found any will or paperwork that indicates what Emma wanted done with her assets."

"I'm her sole surviving relative. That makes me the heir to this house and anything in it," Leslie said. "I've been researching things on the internet. That's the law."

"When I talked to you the other day, you didn't seem to want anything to do with Emma's estate," Weber observed.

"Well, I changed my mind. After how that bitch and her mother made my parents' lives so miserable, I deserve something!"

Weber wasn't surprised, he knew how greedy people from even the best families could become when money or property was involved.

"I'm no lawyer, Mrs. Ungren, but I think a court is going to have to make that determination. But like I said, in the meantime this is a crime scene."

"So you're keeping me out of my own sister's home? Which is now my home?"

"Yes ma'am, for the time being, at least."

"You can't do that! This is my property. How can you keep me out of my own property?"

"It's not yours until a court or a will says it is. And even then, until I determine it's no longer part of my investigation, nobody goes inside."

"What about him?" Leslie asked as Richard MacEwen pulled up. "I don't want him inside there stealing everything!"

MacEwen walked up the driveway and Leslie said, "This is private property and you're not welcome here! Get out."

"What can I do for you, Mr. MacEwen?"

"I came by to feed and take care of the pets, like I did yesterday."

"You were inside the house? I want him arrested for trespassing, Sheriff!"

MacEwen looked confused, and Weber realized that he had blown it by not at least having the house taped off as a potential crime scene.

"Did I do something wrong? I was just taking care of Emma's pets. I had a key."

"No, it's okay," Weber said.

"It's not okay!" Leslie shouted. "I can't get into my own sister's house, but this... this hippy can come and go as he pleases?"

"Calm down, Mrs. Ungren," Weber said, then turned back to MacEwen."Listen, can you take the animals to your house for now? And I'll need your key. I can't let anybody inside the house until we get this all wrapped up."

"Sure, whatever you need," MacEwen said, pulling a key ring out of his pocket and taking off the brass key, which he handed to the sheriff. "I'm sorry, I was just trying to take care of them. Emma loved her animals like they were her kids."

"Emma was a crazy bitch," Leslie said. "I'm warning you, if there is even one thing missing inside that house, I'll see you in court!"

MacEwen was too consumed by grief to care, or to bother responding, but Weber stepped in.

"Mrs. Ungren, like I said, you'll have to leave now. I'll be in touch."

"No, my lawyer will be in touch with both of you!" Leslie shouted as she walked to the passenger side of the truck. "And who's going to make it right for the $60 rental this thing cost me?"

Weber and MacEwen didn't respond, but as she slammed her door, Pete Ungren took MacEwen's hand and said, "I'm sorry for your loss."

Leslie leaned across the truck's cab and blew the horn, shouting, "Come on! Maybe if we get this thing back before noon they'll only charge us for half a day!"

After the Ungrens had left, and MacEwen had retrieved Emma's pets and their food, Weber had Tommy and Dolan string crime scene tape across the driveway and around the house.

"Now what?" Robyn asked.

"Now we play snoop."

✳✳✳

Emma had not been much of a housekeeper. The small house wasn't filthy by any means, cluttered would be a better description. There were stacks of books and magazines piled on end tables, chairs, and the floor, all with an environmental theme. Edward Abbey's Desert Solitaire and Fire on the Mountain, Elinor G. K. Melville's A Plague of Sheep, William K. Jaeger's Environmental Economics for Tree Huggers and Other Skeptics, and Warren George's Call Me a Tree Hugger.

Piles of protest posters and signs were everywhere, as well as 8x10 photos of denuded mountainsides, strip-mined hillsides, and waterways clogged by garbage and industrial pollutants. More pictures showed gutted deer and elk carcasses, and others shot and left to die.

"Wow, what a cheerful place," Robyn said, holding up a color photo of a dead elephant with its tusks sawed off.

"It looks like Emma didn't know the difference between legal hunting and poaching," Weber said. "Then again, with her, everything was black and white."

"Yuck, I'd much prefer black and white," Robyn said, dropping a graphic color photo of a pile of entrails back on the coffee table.

The second bedroom of Emma's house served as an office, and there were boxes of file folders crammed with legal briefs and copies of court papers showing the many requests for injunctions Emma had filed against developers, logging outfits, construction companies, and private parties.

"For somebody who wanted to save the trees, she sure went through a lot of paper with all this stuff," Robyn said.

"It looks like anybody who even wanted to change a light bulb on their porch or paint their shutters had a good chance of getting served a subpoena from Emma. And do you know what's weird?"

"It's Sunday morning, we both have the day off, and instead of being in bed making love, we're standing in a dead woman's house looking at pictures of animal guts in living color," Robyn said. "You tell me, what's weird?"

Weber looked up from the folder he was reading. "That was an option?"

"Don't change the subject, what's weird?"

"You can't just throw that out there, and then just pretend like you never said it," Weber told her.

"I just did. What's weird?"

"I'm looking at this stuff," Weber said, thumbing through several legal folders, "And it looks like in the last eight months or so, Emma's filing of all this court stuff really increased. I found maybe a dozen filed the last two years before that. And so far, in the last few months there's maybe thirty or forty. Why?"

Robyn shrugged. "Who knows? Maybe she took a legal class? Maybe she found out it was an effective way to do things? Emma wasn't exactly predictable, from what I knew of her."

"Richard MacEwen said something about how she had been, how did he say it, extreme? That's it. Extreme. He said lately she seemed way out there. Several people who used to be involved in her protests said she went off on them over all kinds of small stuff."

"She was always extreme, wasn't she?"

"Yeah, but this was even more so. Enough that a lot of people noticed it."

They searched the house for another hour, and while they did not find any diaries, notes, or other evidence that Emma had received any threats, by the time Weber locked the door and pocketed the key, he had an even larger list of people who had reason to have a grudge against Emma Moyer.

"I hate to sound like Parks," Robyn said. "But what about that breakfast we talked about?"

Weber looked across the yard to Zehnacker's house and asked, "Would you settle for a cookie?"

***

"I knew something was going on when I saw Vic Kinney plowing Emma's driveway," Celinda said as she poured coffee. "I've lived next door to her for over ten years and I've never seen that. When we were still together, Emma used to criticize Jay for using his snow blower instead of digging it out by hand like she always did. She said it was a waste of gasoline and caused pollution. So when I saw that big truck backing in, I called your office."

"You did the right thing," Weber told her as he spooned sugar into his coffee.

"So you're the girlfriend," Celinda said, appraising Robyn with a friendly smile from across the table. "I won't lie to you, I'm a little bit jealous. And I'm not the only woman in town who is."

"Do I need to be on the alert for trespassers?" Robyn asked, smiling back.

"Not from me. I love him, but like he told me a while back, that would be almost incestuous."

Weber felt his face flush, "C'mon Celinda."

"Oh, we're embarrassing him," Robyn teased. "So tell me, what was Jimmy like when you all were growing up? Did all the girls love him back then, too?"

"Love? Oh yes, and lust too, except that we didn't know what lust was."

"Stop it, will you…."

"Look at him blush," Robyn said, laughing.

"Jimmy was the strong, silent type. And since he was older, he always tried to play it cool and not notice us girls. But we sure noticed him!"

"You're really going to do this, aren't you?" Weber asked.

"You bet we are," Robyn said with a wide grin, then turned back to Celinda and leaned her folded elbows on the table. "So tell me everything, sister. I want all the dirt. Who did he chase around after?"

"Well, there was this one girl, Kathy Pickney. Oh, they were an item! Everybody thought they'd end up married and having a houseful of kids."

"Pickney, as in the insurance guy?"

Celinda nodded and said, "Wayne's sister."

"What happened to her?"

"She went off to California and made it big in the computer business, I think. And there was this other girl, Clarissa Jackson, well let me tell you….."

***

As they drove into town an hour later, Weber said, "Well, that was uncomfortable."

Robyn laughed and said, "It wasn't for me! So tell me about you and this Kathy Pickney. Did you carve your names into a tree with a heart?"

Weber was silent, but Robyn wasn't letting him off the hook. "No comment, huh? Did you write poetry for her?'

"No comment."

"What about Clarissa Jackson? Celinda said she had a reputation for being easy. Was she your first?"

Weber's face turned red. "Can we change the subject?" he asked.

"She was!" Robyn chortled delightedly, pointing at him and laughing harder. "So tell me all about it. Where did it happen? At the drive-in over in Show Low? Out by the lake? On somebody's couch while she was babysitting?"

"We're not going to have this conversation," Weber told her.

"We're already having it," Robyn said.

"Let's change the subject."

"Forget it, you're not getting off that easy! It was on a couch, wasn't it? Oh my God!"

"Hey, I don't ask about your past," Weber told her. "Care to share?"

"No."

"No? Why not?"

"Because," Robyn said, sitting up primly in her seat and folding her hands in her lap, "I was a good girl. I'd never do anything like that!" She flashed Weber an evil grin and added, "At least not on a couch!"

Chapter 17

The daytime temperatures had warmed up enough to melt off a lot of the snow and make the road up Tomahawk Mountain passable in Weber's Explorer. The crime scene tape he and Chad had strung across the entrance to the parking lot where Emma's car had been found had been pulled down, and Coop and Dan Wright were searching the ground with metal detectors.

"What are you guys up to?" Weber asked.

"It's probably a waste of time, but I thought we'd do some looking around before the tow truck shows up to get the car. I was hoping we might possibly find something. Maybe even the spent cartridge from the shot that killed her."

"Any luck?"

"We haven't found that, but we did find these." He dug in his jacket pocket and pulled out a plastic evidence bag that held a key ring with four keys on it. "They were on the ground next to the back of the car."

One key had a black plastic end with a Toyota logo on it, and another looked like the key to Emma's house that Richard MacEwen had given Weber.

"It looks like whatever happened started here. Emma either threw or dropped the keys," Weber said, "And then she must have run in this direction." He walked toward the tree line and to the spot where they had found Emma's body and encountered the bear.

Under the trees, shaded by the sun, the snow was still deep and trampled by the footsteps from Friday's crime scene investigation. Beside him, Robyn shivered.

"Cold?"

"No, just thinking about what went on here, what you and Chad saw when you found her."

"I wish I could forget," Weber told her, and then his mind went back to the image of Steve Rafferty impaled by the steering column of a van in the crash that followed after Weber shot him three times as he tried to escape. Though the young man was a sadistic murderer who had tortured and lynched a man from the nearby White Mountain Apache Reservation simply because he was gay and an Indian, Rafferty's death still haunted the sheriff. For a moment, the sight of the bodies of his brother-in-law, Mike Perkins, and another guard in the back of their armored car flashed through his mind. There were a lot of things he wished he could forget.

He walked into the trees and spent most of the next hour looking around for any clue that they might have missed before. Weber didn't know exactly what he was looking for, maybe a hat or glove that the shooter had dropped, a discarded cigarette, anything. But whatever he hoped to find, it eluded him.

All the while, Weber was aware of the bear he and Chad had encountered, even though he knew his concerns were silly. The bear was dead, and any others in the area would have been long gone as soon as they heard Coop and Dan in the parking area.

Coop and Dan spent the hour searching the area with their metal detectors with no further success. The sound of an engine and transmission working hard began faintly, then increased, and a few minutes later Randy Laird's tow truck pulled into the clearing. The brawny mechanic surveyed the Prius and said, "I'm glad you told me about the tires, Jimmy. I don't have a flatbed. Is it okay to move it?"

"Have at it," Weber told him.

The burly mechanic backed his truck up to the Prius, hooked it up and pulled it out into the middle of the small parking area to have more room to work. Then he lifted the rear end, retrieved two tires and wheels from the back of his truck and put them on the car.

"Save those tires and wheels just like they are," Weber told him. "They're evidence."

"Gotcha," Laird said.

Once he had the car ready to go, he looked around the area and said, "Terrible thing to happen in such a pretty place, Jimmy. Old Emma could get pretty cantankerous, and we butted heads pretty bad last summer, but I still hate to see this kind of thing happen to her."

"You two butted heads? What about?"

"She showed up at my garage complaining about how the wrecked cars I was storing that got towed in were dripping fluids and polluting the groundwater table. And she wanted to know how I disposed of the waste oil from the cars I worked on. Hell, Jimmy, it's a wrecker yard and those cars have been in accidents. 'Course they're gonna leak! As for my waste oil, it gets recycled under EPA guidelines. The State boys see to that. But Emma filed one of her damn injunctions against me, tryin' to get me to cease and desist. I asked her if I should just leave all those wrecked cars the flatlanders tear up alongside the highway instead. Wouldn't that be good for the environment?"

He paused and then said, "I hope you don't think I had anything to do with this, Jimmy. I mean, yeah, there was a while there where I wanted to wring Emma's neck, but I'd never…"

"I know that," Weber told the mechanic. Laird had dropped out of high school in the tenth grade, but while he didn't have a head for schooling, he was a natural-born mechanic who could fix anything that came his way. He was well respected in town for his skill with machines and his honesty. Folks knew that when they took their cars and trucks to Randy, he never tried to pad the bill or perform unnecessary repairs to make an extra buck.

"Besides," he assured the brawny mechanic, "You'd have been standing at the back of a pretty long line. Emma seemed to have pissed off a lot of people."

"Yeah, but still, Jimmy, nobody deserves what happened to her. It just ain't right!"

"No, it's not," Weber agreed. "It's damn sure not."

"I never was much of a churchgoer, Jimmy, but I know one thing. There's a special place in hell for whoever did this." With that, he got in his wrecker and headed back down the mountain, Emma's Prius bouncing along behind him.

Chapter 18

Driving back to town, Robyn was silent. Weber wasn't sure if it was because she was angry with him for spending most of their day off doing investigative work, or because the scene of Emma's murder had upset her.

"You okay?"

"Yes."

"You're pretty quiet. What's wrong?"

She didn't reply, and Weber turned his attention back to the primitive road to navigate a particularly deep series of ruts. Weber knew Robyn well enough to know that whatever was troubling her, she'd get around to telling him in her own good time.

It wasn't until they were in the parking lot of the Roundup Steakhouse that, still looking forward through the windshield, Robyn said, "I'm mad at you."

"Okay."

"I really needed us to have this day off together, Jimmy. You didn't have to go chasing off to Emma's house. That's what you've got deputies for. Dolan and Tommy had things under control. And whatever was in that house, including those disgusting pictures, wasn't going anywhere. We didn't have to search it today. And we damned sure didn't need to spend three hours up on that mountain looking for evidence. You hired Coop because of all his experience. Dolan's been on the job longer than you. But you don't trust them to do a good job, you still want to micromanage everything yourself. That's not fair to your deputies, and it's not fair to us."

Weber knew she was right. He did have a tendency to take being a hands-on supervisor too far. But the department had been short handed for so long that it was just the way things had always been.

"I needed this day, Jimmy. And I needed to spend it alone with you, not running around playing detective."

"I'm sorry, Robyn. You're right. How can I make it up to you?"

"Damn it, Jimmy, I don't want it made up to me! I just want you to understand that we don't have to be on the job 24/7. I mean, I know there are times when we do, when something big is going down. But there's always going to be something going on."

Weber nodded, but she still wasn't looking at him.

"You have to understand something, Jimmy. This thing, this affair, or relationship, or whatever it is we're having; I can compartmentalize, okay? On the job, I can be a deputy and you can be the sheriff. That's fine. I'm good with that. I can sleep with you and make love with you half the night, and I can jump right out of your bed and put on my uniform and be your deputy when it's time to go to work. I don't ask for any special favors, and I don't expect them. But off the job, it has to be just you and me. Jimmy and Robyn. Okay?"

"Okay."

"Sitting there with Celinda this morning, hearing all those stories about you when you were a kid, I loved that, Jimmy! But it didn't last. It never lasts. Duty always calls. And even if it doesn't call, you go off searching for it."

"I'm sorry," Weber said again. "I guess I've been alone so long that I don't know how to act in a serious relationship. Hell, Robyn, this is the first serious relationship I've ever had, when it comes right down to it."

"I'm not dumb, Jimmy. I know you haven't spent every night of your life sleeping alone. And that's okay. I have my own history."

"Robyn, look at me."

She turned her head and held his eyes.

"I won't lie to you. There were a few women. Maybe more than a few. But I never felt anything close to what I feel with you when I was with any of them. I never told a woman I loved her before you."

"Not even Kathy Pickney?" Weber saw just a hint of a smile at the corners of Robyn's lips. "Or your sofa slut? What was her name… Clarissa?"

"That was kid stuff. I've never told a woman I loved her before you, Robyn."

She smiled, and said, "Tell me now."

"Robyn, I love you. I love you today, tomorrow, and forever. I love you more than anything, and I promise you that I will work really hard at trying to keep our time and work separate. Okay?"

Robyn nodded and said, "Jimmy, I know the kind of man you are. The kind of sheriff you are. It's a big part of what I love about you. I know this isn't a 9 to 5 job for either of us. Just make an effort, that's all

I'm asking."

"You got it."

"I guess being there in Emma's house and then standing right there where she died, it made me realize that none of us has any guarantees in life. Even more so in our line of work. I just don't want something to happen to one of us someday, and regret any time we could have had that we missed."

A lifetime in police work had taught Weber just how fragile life could be, and he understood where Robyn was coming from.

"I'll work harder at making sure our time is just that, our time. Okay?"

"Okay." She leaned across the console and kissed him, than drew back and smiled. "Now feed me! And I don't want any salad either, I want the biggest steak this place has!"

***

Three hours later, lying curled up with her head on his chest in her bedroom, Robyn asked, "What about kids, Jimmy?"

"Kids?"

"Yes, kids. Like real people, only smaller, and usually with runny noses."

"What are you asking me, Robyn? Is this one of those biological time clock things?"

"We've never talked about it. Do you want kids?"

"I've never given it a lot of thought, to be honest with you. Do you?"

"Would it be a deal breaker if I said I did. Or didn't?"

"Where are we going with this, honey?"

"Just answer me, Jimmy. Would it make a difference?"

Weber sighed, "Robyn, nothing would make a difference in the way I feel about you. Have I ever thought about being a father? Yeah, in kind of an abstract way. I guess most guys think about it. Do I feel a burning desire to be a father? No, not at this time."

"But will you? Or does the idea of having kids scare the hell out of you?"

"It doesn't scare me. I don't know. I guess if it happens, it happens."

She rolled over and put her chin on his chest and looked at him, concern in her eyes.

"What if it never happens? What if I can never give you a baby, Jimmy?"

A single tear rolled down her cheek and dropped onto his chest.

"Honey, what's this all about?"

"I wasn't a slut like your high school sofa sweetie, but I wasn't a nun either. There was this guy, David, and we were head over heels in love our senior year. Or at least I was in love. I thought he was too, until I got pregnant."

"What happened?"

"I told him as soon as I found out. It was the week before graduation. We were at the drive-in, and he said it didn't matter, we'd graduate and get married. It was still early, nobody would even know. We'd tell them I must have gotten pregnant on our honeymoon. Then we made tender, sweet love in the back seat of his Chevy Blazer. He drove me home and dropped me off, and the next day he left town and joined the Air Force. I never saw him again."

"Damn. What happened to the baby?"

"Jimmy, you have to understand, I was seventeen years old. I was a good girl. Those kinds of things didn't happen to good girls. I could never have told my parents. They had such high expectations of me."

Her tears were falling freely now, he could feel them make a track through the hair on his chest and down his side, but he didn't move to wipe them away. He just held her.

"I had this friend, Andrea Sheppherd. She was my best friend since fifth grade. She was the only one I could trust enough to tell. A few days after graduation, we drove down to Nogales, parked the car on the American side, and walked across the border. Andrea's brother had given her the name of a clinic. He thought it was for her, and she never told him otherwise."

"Robyn..."

"Wait, I'm not done, Jimmy."

"Honey, it..."

"Please, let me say this, Jimmy! I have to get it all out in the open, and then if you want to get dressed and go home, I'll understand completely."

He nodded, and Robyn continued. "Driving back to Glendale, I started to hemorrhage. I was losing blood really fast and Andrea drove me right to the first hospital we could find, in Tucson. I was pretty much out of it by then, but they told me later she saved my life. When I woke up, my parents were there. I had never seen those looks on their faces before. I know they were really hurt, but I guess that they were so glad that I was alive that they didn't say anything. Then the doctor came in and told me that there had been a lot of damage done, and my chances of ever conceiving again were impossible. So you have to know, Jimmy, if you ever want kids...."

He raised his hand and tenderly wiped the tears from her cheeks, then pulled her on top of him and held her close as she sobbed.

"It's okay, baby. It's okay," he whispered, kissing the top of her head. "I don't care if we ever have kids or not, Robyn. All I care about is that you're right here in my arms forever."

He held her like that for a long time, letting her cry herself out. Finally Robyn fell asleep, and he eased her off him and onto her side, then held her close, listening to her breathing in the darkness of the bedroom.

Chapter 19

Monday morning Weber called Brian Oakes and asked if he had time to get together.

"Of course," the real estate man said enthusiastically. "I've always got time for a friend! Come on over."

Premier Real Estate was housed in a new A-frame office on the business route on the south side of town, across from a new convenience store that had opened in the last week. Judging by the vehicles with ski racks lined up at the pumps, they were doing a booming business. Weber could recall the days when if you needed gas in Big Lake, you had to make it to Howard Brubaker's Texaco or old man Morgan's Gulf station on the other end of Main Street by 6 p.m., when they both closed and went home for dinner. And if you forgot to fill your tank on Saturday, you walked to church on Sunday.

"Welcome friend," Oakes said, wearing a maroon and white ski sweater. He crossed the room to greet Weber as he walked in. The man's handshake was firm and he made eye contact with the sheriff, working hard to demonstrate his sincerity in wanting to establish a good relationship with his new friend.

"Sit down, sit down," Oakes said, leading him to a padded armchair in front of the gas fireplace and taking the one next to it, which was turned at a strategic angle to allow them to converse easily. Friends didn't do business across a desk. "Coffee?"

"No thanks," Weber said, looking around the office, which was one big open great room with a glass front and knotty pine walls and ceiling. The walls were decorated with prints with a western theme, lots of mountain meadows, snowcapped peaks, elk, and wild horses.

"So, Sheriff Weber, I've been checking up on you."

"You have?"

"Yes sir, and I think I know why you're here."

"You do?"

"Yes," said Oakes. "It's about your ranch out on the west side of town."

Weber and his sister Debbie had grown up on the ranch, but ranching and livestock had never appealed to the young man, and after their parents' deaths he soon remembered why he had joined the Army.

Before two years had passed, Weber had sold off the cattle, leased out the acreage with the exception of the family home and surrounding ten acres, and been hired by Pete Caitlin as a deputy. After Debbie's murder convictions, Weber had developed a phobia about the old home place and had not been able to do more than pull into the driveway and sit in his vehicle, haunted by the ghosts of his past. Molly Bateson, a psychiatrist Weber had been seeing after he suffered a meltdown in the wake of his shooting of a young murder suspect months earlier, had suggested that the empty house symbolized all that Weber had lost in the last year.

"What about the ranch?" Weber asked.

"Jimmy… may I call you Jimmy? I won't try to gloss it over. That's a very valuable piece of property. But its value is diminishing every day. Nobody wants big, old fashioned two story houses these days. No sir, they want small, cozy little chalets, like this," Oakes said, waving his hand around the room.

"Like this?"

"Yes! Lots of glass, lots of logs, cozy! I'm afraid that old house is an albatross around your neck, Jimmy. Best thing you could do is knock it down."

"Knock it down?"

"I'm afraid so, my friend," Oakes said with a frown as he nodded his head. "But the good news is, that ten acres is prime development land! Yes sir, prime land. But there's a problem?"

"A problem?"

Oakes frowned and nodded again as he commiserated with his new friend.

"What's the problem?"

"Money," Oakes said, looking him in the eye. "Times are getting tough and nobody has the money to develop land any more. Why, a year ago? That land would go for twice, maybe three times as much as it's worth now. You came to me too late, Jimmy."

"I guess that's the story of my life," Weber said. "I'm always a day late and a dollar short."

"You're a good man, Jimmy. That's what I hear all over this town. Jim Weber? He's a good man."

"I guess it's good to know that I have friends," Weber said, "since my land isn't worth much of anything."

"I'll tell you what I'm going to do," Oakes said, reaching out to put his hand on Weber's arm. "I know I'll probably lose money on the deal, but a good man like you shouldn't be saddled with a place that's only going to drag him down. I do have some resources available that a lot of folks don't have. Jimmy, I'm going to offer you $120,000 for the place."

"You don't say?"

"That's right, Jimmy. Cash money."

Weber scratched his head and frowned. "I seem to remember that when Wayne and Sally Lambert sold their place next to mine, it went for over $40,000 an acre."

"Could be," Oates said. "But like I told you, times have changed. Why, when it was booming last year you might have found somebody to pay that. But not now, Jimmy! And think of the liability that place exposes you to every day. If a couple of kids break into that old house, then get themselves cut on a piece of window glass or something, you could get sued and lose everything. You don't want that, do you?"

"No, I guess not."

"Jimmy? Let's cut to the chase. You're my friend, and I don't want to see you getting stuck with some lawsuit over that darned old house. I'll go $125,000 dollars. You could have the money in your bank account tonight. That's life changing money, my friend!"

"Well, I kind of like my life just like it is," Weber said. "So let's talk about something else. Why were you fighting with Emma Moyer in front of Matt Well's sporting goods store a while back?"

Oakes seemed taken aback by the question, and sat back in his chair with his brow furrowed. "That's why you're here? Emma Moyer?"

"I heard you and her went at it out in the parking lot. Now she's dead."

"And you think I had something to do with it?"

"I didn't say that," Weber said. "I just asked why you two were arguing."

"Sheriff, I didn't have anything to do with her death. I mean, yes, we argued, but I didn't have anything to do with what happened to her!"

"What did you argue about?"

"She showed up here a while back when I was having my open house, right after I opened. She was waving some kind of protest sign, yelling that I was just another carpetbagger who came here to rape and pillage the mountains. Claimed that all I was out for is the almighty dollar. She created an ugly scene."

"When was this?"

"Last summer. Spring actually, May 15th to be exact."

"And you waited until last week to confront her about it?"

"No, we crossed paths a few times after that. Every time I went before the Town Council about subdividing land I had purchased, she was there trying to make them keep me from going forward. And when they approved a project anyway, she filed injunctions to stop it."

"That's what the argument was about last week?"

"Yes! I filed papers to develop twenty acres I bought out by the ski lodge. The Town Council approved everything over Emma's objections, and then on Monday I got served with an injunction saying it was the habitat for the purple goldfinch or the Albanian sparrow or some such nonsense! So everything comes to a halt while I have to prove no such habitat exists on the property. I have three projects going on, and she did the same thing with every damn one of them! It's cost me a fortune. When I saw her protesting in front of that gun store I stopped and told her exactly what I thought of her, and that I'd fight her tooth and nail before I'd back down. I told her I was going to file a countersuit against her for malicious use of the judicial system."

"What did she say about that?"

"She told me to go for it."

The real estate developer stopped for a minute, and a strange look came over his face.

"What is it?" Weber asked him.

"She said something else. I never gave it any thought, and to be honest, I forgot all about it until just now."

"What did she say, Brian?"

"She said to go right ahead and sue her, that she wouldn't live long enough to have to deal with it anyway. But in the meantime, if she stopped me for even a day or a week, it was worth it."

***

"So do you think Emma had some kind of premonition about her own death?" Coop asked when Weber reported on his meeting with Brian Oakes.

"I don't know," Weber said.

"Or maybe she got a death threat that she was taking seriously?"

"If she did, she never reported it," Weber said.

"Sounds like this real estate guy might be sleazy, but he may have hit on something to fight back against all of her lawsuits. Give her a dose of her own medicine."

"He's not sleazy," Weber said. "After all, he wanted to take the ranch off my hands."

"Hey, at that price, I'd buy it," Coop told him. "If you're going to get screwed, it might as well be by a friend, right?"

"Oh, we're friends, Oakes and me," Weber assured him. "I know, because he told me so several times."

"So is Oakes a suspect?"

"As much as anyone is," Weber said. "He certainly had a motive. Emma was tying him up in court, like she was every developer, it seems. He said he had appointments all day and evening Tuesday. I've got Tommy checking on his alibis."

Mary knocked on his office door and poked her head inside. "Jimmy, Emma's sister is on the phone threatening all sorts of things. Do you want to talk to her?"

"Not really."

"Well, do it anyway. I'm tired of listening to her."

Leslie Ungren not only resembled her late sister in many ways, she obviously shared her temper too, and wasted no time holding anything back when Weber picked up the telephone.

"When can I get into my house?"

"It's not your house at this point," Weber told her. "Like I told you yesterday, I don't know what Emma's will calls for, or if she even had a will. That's a civil issue and out of my area of responsibility."

"If it's not your responsibility, how can you keep me out?" Leslie demanded. "I want inside that house to see what that boyfriend of hers has stolen."

Weber rubbed his forehead and wondered why every Monday had to start out this way.

"Mrs. Ungren, I'm sure Richard MacEwen has not stolen anything. He and Emma seemed to have had a committed relationship."

"Committed? The only thing that psycho was committed to was making trouble for people! She was the one that needed to be committed!"

Weber let her rant for another minute or two and then ended the call, telling her once again that no, she could not enter Emma's house until a will was found, if Emma had one, and until Weber had decided that the house was no longer part of his homicide investigation. Leslie was just as angry when she hung up as she had been when their conversation began, but she had succeeded in making Weber's own mood turn sour.

His mood hadn't improved when Mary stuck her head back inside the door again a few minutes later and said, "You'd better get out to SafeHaven, Jimmy. Christine Ridgeway's got a problem."

Chapter 20

When Weber pulled to a stop in front of the old farmhouse, a heated conversation was going on between Christine, who stood blocking the door, and Mayor Wingate, who stood on the wide front porch with another man.

I don't care what you say, this is wrong! I won't have it here inBig Lake."

Christine stared back at the little man with her arms crossed over her formidable chest, her jaw set and fire in her eyes.

"Now what?" Weber asked.

"I was just telling this… this woman that she is way over the line and can expect no support from the Town of Big Lake for her facility. And I am going to help this gentleman speak to his wife, whether she wants him to or not."

Weber tried to place the other man, who was in his early twenties and dressed in a red plaid shirt and worn jeans. Ben something… Ben Houser, that was it. One of Bill Houser's sons. They ran a small logging operation, with beat up equipment held together with bailing wire and hope.

"She doesn't want to talk to him right now," Christine said. "And I'm not gonna make her! And Chet Wingate, you are way out of line even bringing him here!"

"Now you listen here, missy, I'm the mayor of this town and my word is the law!" Chet shouted, shaking his finger at her.

Arms still folded, Christine took a step forward and peered down at the obnoxious little man, whose head barely reached her shoulder.

"Do I look like a Missy to you, you little pissant? Back off before I step on you and grind you under my foot! Your word don't mean spit around here, and if Jimmy doesn't lock you up for trespassing, I'll kick your fat butt clear off this property!"

"Alright, that's enough," Weber said, putting his hand on the mayor's shoulder and pulling him back. Chet started to shrug it off, but when Christine took another step forward, almost touching him, he stepped backward.

"Okay, what's going on?"

Christine and Chet both started to speak at once, but Weber held his hand up. "One at a time. Go on, Christine."

The mayor started to protest, but Weber shot him a withering look and he held his tongue.

"I've got a young woman who came here last night because she needed to get away from a situation at home. The mayor and her husband showed up and Chet was trying to make me let him in and wouldn't take no for an answer."

"A man's got a right to talk to his own wife, don't he?" Ben Houser asked. "I just want to talk to her, that's all!"

"Yes, you do have a right, son," Chet told him, "and I'm going to make sure you do."

"Over my dead body!" Christine said.

"Okay, enough! Deputy Cooper, please take Mayor Wingate and this young man down off the porch."

"You can't do that!" Chet insisted. "I'm the mayor!"

"And if Mayor Wingate resists, put him in handcuffs and in the back of your unit. In fact, if he says one more word, do it. Ben, you go on with this deputy and wait by the cars until I get this sorted out, okay?"

"I just want to see her," the anguished young man pleaded. "I won't hurt her or nothing. I'd never hurt my Traci. I just want to tell her I'm sorry."

"I'll see what I can do, okay? But go on down there and wait for now."

After they were off the porch and out of hearing range, Weber followed Christine inside.

"Jimmy that man had no right coming out here like that. I don't care if he is the mayor! He just put this place, and everybody in it, in jeopardy."

Weber couldn't disagree, but instead said, "Tell me what's happening."

"About three o'clock this morning I got a call from Traci Houser, saying she needed to get away. She was calling from the Fast Stop, and I went out and picked her up."

"Wait, you went out at 3 a.m., alone, to meet somebody? Christine, that's dangerous."

"Well, what could I do, Jimmy? She didn't have a car and the poor thing had hitchhiked a ride into town with the D-Licious Bread truck.”

“You could get yourself killed doing that,” Weber admonished her. “You don’t know who might be on the other end of the phone line.”

“Oh push, Jimmy! Nobody’s gonna hurt me, and there’s no way I can just roll over and go back to sleep when I get a call like that. You know me better than that.”

“If that happens again, please call the office,” Weber told her. “Have a deputy go with you, just in case, okay?”

“Whatever, Jimmy, you old worrywart. Anyway, she was waiting inside the store when I got there, so I brought her out here and got her warmed up. First thing this morning, her husband was calling and I told him I could not tell him if his wife was here or not, due to confidentiality. He called back a couple of times, and he was polite and all, just about begging me to let him talk to her. Then here comes old Chet Wingate pulling in with the husband right behind him, and Chet just started barging right in here, telling me I couldn’t keep him out. I couldn’t decide whether to wring his neck or call you. And I’m still not sure I made the right choice.”

“Back to the woman,” Weber said. “Has she been abused?”

“Well, yes and no, depending on how you look at it. He didn’t beat on her or anything, he just… well hold on a minute.”

She left him alone for a moment and returned with the most pregnant young woman Weber had ever seen. Traci Houser was a slender, dark haired woman whose huge distended belly seemed to proceed her into the room like a pilot car before a wide load going down the highway. She waddled into the room, and seeing Weber, asked in alarm, “Is Ben in trouble? Please tell me that he’s not.”

“Nobody’s in trouble,” Christine assured her. “Here honey, you sit down.”

She brought Traci a straight backed kitchen chair and the woman eased herself down into it, holding her belly with her hands. Christine squatted down next to her and said “Traci, I need you to tell Sheriff Weber why you’re here.”

“I can’t,” Traci said. “I’ll just go on home with Ben. I’m sorry to get you all involved in our silly little problems.”

“No,” Christine said, shaking her head. “That’s not going to solve anything.”

“I can’t,” Traci said again, shaking her head. “I don’t want to get Ben in trouble. He’s never raised a hand to me or nothing like that, he’s a good man and a good husband. He just don't understand."

"What doesn't he understand?" Weber asked her.

Traci's face was red and Christine squeezed her arm. "It's okay, honey, you can tell him."

Traci looked down at the floor and said, "He just won't stop poking that thing of his at me. He says it's my duty. And I liked it when I wasn't this way. But now… well it hurts, and I'm afraid for the babies."

"Babies?"

"Traci here is gonna have triplets," Christine told him. "But it seems like Ben has an overactive libido and won't give her any peace. Finally she just couldn't take it any more, and after they had sex last night she waited until he was asleep and left."

"I love my husband," Traci sobbed. "But I can't take it any more. I can't! Once these babies are out of me, I want to make him happy. But he just don't understand. I thought maybe if I left for a while, at least I could get some rest and maybe he'd come to realize what I've been telling him."

"Traci, I don't want to embarrass you, but I have to ask just so we're all on the same page here. Did your husband force himself on you? Did he hit you, or hold you down, or threaten you in any way?"

"Oh, no sir," Traci said, shaking her had empathically. "He just keeps asking and rubbing himself against me when I say no, and I finally give in just to get some rest."

"Okay, what do you want to happen, Traci?"

"I don't want him to get in trouble, or nothing. I just want him to understand that I can't do it right now. At least not every morning and again every night. I want to be with him, I do. I miss him. But he just don't understand!"

"Honey, if we can help make Ben understand what you need, and that you can't do those things right now, would that help?" Christine asked.

The young woman turned to her and nodded, crying. "I want to go back home! But it just hurts right now."

Christine held her while she cried, and when Traci had regained her composure, she nodded to Weber and said, "Jimmy, why don't you go talk to Ben a little bit, and then bring him inside? Would that be okay, Traci?"

The girl nodded into Christine's chest. "I love him, Miz. Ridgeway. I just…"

"It's okay, honey, we'll get this all worked out," Christine assured her.

As Weber turned toward the door, she added, "But don't you let that damn Chet Wingate in here, or I might be sleeping in one of your jail cells tonight!"

Apparently the mayor had managed to keep himself out of trouble, since Coop had not locked him inside his patrol car, but seeing Weber come down off the porch, he started forward.

"I've wasted enough time out here this morning, Sheriff. Now, I want you to let this young man talk to his wife right now! That's an order."

Weber stepped in front of him, wanting desperately to throttle the stubborn little dictator. "Chet, I'm going to have a little chat with Ben, and then he's going to get to talk to his wife. If everything works out okay, she'll be going home with him in just a little bit. But I want you to understand something right now. You're a complete idiot. Ben's a pretty good guy who just wants his wife to come home, but he could have been a damned ax murderer for all you know. And you bringing him out here could have led to a dangerous situation."

"How dare you talk to me that way!" the mayor said shrilly, "I was just looking after the best interests of one of my constituents."

"I'll talk to you any way I want to, you blockhead. Did you ever stop to think that his wife is one of your constituents, too? What about her best interests? What if he would have pulled out a gun and started shooting the minute you got here?"

"If this place wasn't here, that woman would be back at home where she belongs," Chet said. "That's the problem! This shelter! It's only been open a few weeks and it's already breaking up families."

Weber could feel the anger building inside of him. Chet Wingate had pulled some pretty dumb stunts over the years, but this was inexcusable. Recognizing the signs of an impending explosion, Coop stepped forward and took the mayor's arm.

"I think you'd better leave now," he said, pulling Chet away and walking him to his car.

Chet started to resist, but seeing a look on the sheriff's face he had never seen before, he backed down.

Once he left, Weber turned toward Ben Houser, who was sitting on the open tailgate of his rusty Chevrolet pickup. The sheriff sat down beside him and asked, "Do you love your wife, son?"

"Yes sir, I do," Ben said.

"Then why would you rape her?"

Ben turned to Weber incredulously. "Rape… No, I didn't rape her. It's not rape if a man and woman are married. I just made love to her, that's all."

"You're wrong," Weber told him. "It's called spousal rape, and you can go to prison for it. Is that what you want to do, go to prison and never see your wife or those babies she's carrying?"

"Oh God no, Sheriff! I love my wife. I never raped her. I'd never do that to any woman, especially my Traci!"

"What you don't understand is that if a woman tells you no, and you still have sex with her, it's rape. You don't have to beat on her or hold a gun to her head. Even if it's your wife."

Ben looked at him, his jaw hanging open.

"When you two were dating, did you ever want to do it, and have her tell you no?"

"Yeah, she wouldn't do it until we got married. That was important to her, to wear white at our wedding."

"And what did you do when she said no, Ben?"

"Nothing."

"Nothing?"

"I stopped whatever I was doing. Or trying to do."

"So why is anything different now? That marriage license isn't like a bill of sale for a horse, or a title to a car. Traci still has a right to say no, and you still have to honor that."

"But I thought she liked it. She always said she did!"

Weber could tell that the young man wasn't trying to argue with him, he was honestly confused.

"I'm sure she does, when she's not all swollen up and pregnant like that."

For a moment, the image of a pregnant Robyn came into his mind, and Weber realized that he still had not fully processed her revelation from the night before. He had told Robyn that he didn't care whether they had children or not, but was that true? He really had not given the matter a lot of thought before. But he knew one thing, that he would rather be with her than with any woman he had ever known, children or no children.

"Sheriff, I love Traci. I never knew…"

"You got a couple of brothers, don't you, Ben?"

"Yes sir, Alan and Donald. I'm the youngest."

"I remember Donald. He was quite a football player in high school a few years back."

Ben nodded and Weber asked, "How do you get along with your brothers?"

"Alan and Donald? We get along fine. Always have."

"You being the baby of the family, I bet they tease you to all get out."

"Oh, maybe when I was younger, but not so much any more," Ben said. "They're good guys."

"Do they give you a lot of advice on things?"

"Yeah, I guess so."

"How about on being married and all that? They ever give you advice or talk to you about women?"

Ben nodded.

"How many times those two brothers of yours been married, between them?"

The young man shrugged his shoulders. "Let's see, Alan's been married three times. And Donald's on his second."

"Uh huh. Let me ask you something, Ben. I bet those boys can run any kind of machine there is, right? A skidder, bulldozer, backhoe? And if you need to know how to operate that stuff, you'd ask them, right?"

Ben nodded, and said, "They and my Dad taught me how to when I was still a kid."

Weber continued, "I don't think either of your brothers were ever in the military. But you see Deputy Cooper over there? He retired after twenty years in the Army. Served all over the world. Iraq, Afghanistan, Germany, Korea. So if you were thinking about joining the Army, who would you take advice from, one of your brothers, or Deputy Cooper?"

Ben shrugged, "Deputy Cooper, I guess. It just makes sense."

"Why's that, Ben?"

"Because he knows what he's talking about. He's done it."

"Okay, so do you think you should be taking advice from somebody who knows what he's talking about? Or somebody who keeps trying to get it right but hasn't yet? Do you see where I'm going with this, Ben?"

Ben nodded, and wiped tears from his eyes.

"I guess I messed up pretty bad, didn't I, Sheriff?"

"You messed up. But it isn't the end of the world. That little girl in there loves you, son. And she wants to be a good wife to you. But you have to understand that making love and having sex are two different things. You can make love to her by holding her and telling her how beautiful she is, even when she's all big in the belly like she is now and may not believe it herself. You can make love to her with just a look, or holding a car door for her, or maybe giving her a foot rub when she's all sore and tired. But when you have sex with her this pregnant, it's painful for her. It hurts her physically and it hurts her emotionally. When she tells you no and you do that anyway, you're telling her that she don't matter to you, that's it just all about you and what you want. That could leave her not liking you very much. Resenting you even. Do you want that?"

"No sir, I don't," Ben was openly crying now. "I'm sorry, Sheriff. My brothers are always saying stuff like women want it even when they say they don't, and it's a man's job to show them that they do."

"Yeah, and you can see how successful their love lives have been."

"I never knew it was hurting her. I just remember that she used to like it. She liked it a lot."

"And she will again, once those babies come out of her. But she may not if she sees it as just something you're going to take from her whether she likes it or not. It's supposed to be something you two share. And you need to understand something else too; Traci is going to need a lot of help from you with those babies. That's a lot of diapers that are going to need changed. Are you up for that?"

"Yes sir. I just want to make this all better. I love that girl so much. I'll never do that to her again." Ben stopped, then said, "Well, I want to do it to her again, I just mean…"

Weber smiled at him and slapped the young man on the back, then put his hands on the tailgate and shoved himself off. "Come on, let's go talk to your wife."

***

An hour later, after a lot of tearful recriminations on Ben Houser's part, and promises from his wife that once she had given birth to their babies and had a chance to recover from their delivery, she was looking forward to getting their love life back on track as much as he was, they stood on the porch watching as the couple rattled down the driveway in Ben's old truck.

"You think they're going to be okay?" Weber asked.

"I think so," Christine said. "They're kids and they've got some growing up to do. They've only been married a year and she's seven months pregnant. Right now he's like a kid with a new toy. But once he learns that nookie is a renewable resource and doesn't have an expiration date, he might slack off. Besides, they'll both be so darned worn out chasing after those babies that I don't think either of them will have any energy for it until those kids grow up and go off to college."

Weber laughed and started down off the porch, then turned back. "I was serious earlier, Hillbilly. I don't want you to go traipsing off at night to meet somebody like you did. There could be a crazy husband waiting out there with a gun."

"I've had a crazy husband," she said. "Don't you worry your little self about me. Besides, I've still got my Daddy's old Detective Special and I know how to use it. And I'll tell you something else, if that danged Chet Wingate ever shows up here again, I may use it on him!"

Weber laughed as he put his Stetson on. "And there's not a jury in the land that would convict you."

Chapter 21

"Sounds like you had a busy weekend, for having a day off," Kirby Templeton said as they gathered around a large table at the back of the ButterCup Café for lunch.

"Too busy. I had to jump down Chet's throat this morning, so he'll probably try to suspend me again this afternoon. I may just take him up on it. I could use a vacation."

"Do you think he'll ever get the message that he isn't the entire Town Council and doesn't have the power to suspend or fire you?" Paul asked.

"No use trying to confuse the man with facts when his mind's already made up," Weber said.

"Anything new you can tell me about the investigation into Emma Moyer's killing?"

"We're interviewing people, we've got some leads, but nothing solid at this time."

"What, you went to lunch without me?" Larry Parks demanded, sliding into the last empty chair. "I swear I'm never leaving town again! How quickly you forget."

Before Parks could continue his pity party, a beanpole of a man came in wearing boots, jeans, and a Carhartt jacket. He paused at their table to say, "Why, hello, Kirby, fellows." He tipped his cowboy hat to Robyn and said, "Miss" and nodded toward Parks.

"Long time, no see," Templeton said. "How are you doing Josh? How's Sarah?"

"Oh, fine as a couple of old farts can be, I guess. Every day we can get out of bed's a good one. Did you get your deer yet, Kirby?"

"Didn't get drawn for a tag this year. Second year in a row."

"It's those damn bureaucrats down in Phoenix," Josh lamented. "Was a time a man just bought his hunting license and went out and got himself a deer. Not any more. We've got to have a drawing. What's this country coming to, anyway? You remember those days, don't you Paul?"

"Not Paul," Weber said. "It may be a small town, but he's still a city boy at heart. He's out of his element if he gets ten yards off pavement."

"City boy? I was born and raised right here in Big Lake, just like you!"

"That's right, I said city boy," Weber said. "Tell us about the one and only time you went deer hunting, Paul."

Paul's chubby cheeks turned red at the memory. "I don't want to talk about it."

"Tell them," Weber chided. "Don't make me do it. Because I will."

"Yeah, and you'll make it even worse than it was," Paul said with resignation. He looked around the table, and every eye was on him. "You're really going to make me do this, aren't you?"

Seeing no way out, he sighed and told his tale. "We were sixteen and Jimmy here decided we needed to go deer hunting. But could we buy a six pack and cruise the back roads in a pickup truck like normal country boys? Oh no! He says we're going to take a couple of his dad's horses and do it up right. Says we can see a lot more from the back of a horse, and cover a lot more territory."

Robyn couldn't help giggling at the vision of the portly man, even as a teenager, trying to get up into a saddle on a horse's back. Paul gave her a hurt look and went on with his story.

"So what happens? The day we're supposed to go hunting, Jimmy gets in trouble with his old man for something and can't go. But he says there's no reason I can't. He takes me out to the corral and introduces me to this old swayback roan that must have been a hundred years old."

"She wasn't swayback until you got on her," Weber said, and Paul ignored him.

"They called her Sunflower. He gives me a quick lesson on how to drive the nag, and away me and Sunflower go. I ride way back into the mountains…"

"He wasn't more than a mile back behind the barn," Weber interrupted, "up by that stock tank on the back side of Strawberry Gully."

Paul shot him a look. "Who's telling this story, you or me?"

Weber raised his hands in surrender and Paul continued, "Anyway, I get back there seventeen miles from nowhere and it's going okay. Jimmy and Mr. Joe, his daddy, had both assured me that the horse was nice and well trained, and that she'd come right back home at the end of the day. So once I get halfway used to riding that old mare, it wasn't too bad."

Paul was a good storyteller and his audience was hooked, so he continued.

"So anyway, things are going pretty good, and lo and behold I see this big old buck. Not a spike or a yearling, this was a Boone and Crockett trophy, I tell you. So I pull this old lever-action Winchester that Jimmy loaned me out of the saddle scabbard, and I rack a round into the chamber, and get me a good sight picture, right behind the shoulder, like Jimmy told me to do, and I squeeze the trigger." Paul held up an imaginary rifle, closed one eye as he sighted down the barrel, pulled the trigger and said, "Pow!"

Nobody said a word and every eye was on him as he relived the event. "And then all hell broke loose! Did you know that no matter how they do it in those old cowboy movies, a horse gets really mad when you shoot a rifle off right over its head?"

Robyn was raising her glass to her mouth and had to set it quickly down at the mental picture Paul was painting.

"That damned old hayburner went wild! She farted and reared up and threw me into a bunch of rocks and pissed a stream as big as the Mississippi River, stomping all over me in the process. Then she ran off a few steps, and I swear to God, she thought it over and came back and stomped on me again!"

The table broke up in laughter, and even Josh McCabe, normally a stoic man, had to lean on a chair to hold himself up.

"Well, old Sunflower, she lights out and leaves me out there a thousand miles from nowhere, all bruised and scratched to pieces, and covered in horse piss and shit."

"She came right back to the barn, just like we told him she'd do," Weber cut in. "My old man says we better go find him. So we jump in the pickup and head out, and eventually we find Paul limping down the road, looking like a refugee from a tornado or something, dragging his rifle behind him. He smelled so bad my dad made him ride in the back of the truck!"

Fists pounded the tabletop and diners at other tables turned to see what the commotion was about. When they finally got themselves under control, Robyn asked, "What about the deer? Did you ever find it?"

"Sure did," Weber told her. "Dead as a doornail, not 50 feet from the trail. And it was just as big as Paul said it was. A rack as wide as Texas, and it must have weighed 325 pounds."

"You actually hit it?" Robyn asked Paul, impressed.

"Oh, he didn't hit it," Weber said. "There wasn't a scratch on it anywhere. Best we could figure out, that old buck busted a gut laughing at Paul and died right there on the spot!"

They were all still busy wiping tears from their eyes when Weber's cell phone rang. He answered, listened for a minute and said, "We'll be right there."

"What was that?" Bob Bennett asked.

"Do you remember after Lenny Dewitt's arraignment, when you said his kind never learns how to stay out of trouble? I want a peek at your crystal ball now and then. He's dead. His son-in-law shot him."

Chapter 22

Lenny Dewitt had never been a handsome man, and death hadn't done him any favors. He was sitting half slumped against the outside wall of the Mountain Mist Motel in a large pool of blood, with a slack jawed expression in his face. A Buck folding knife, with its four inch blade open, lay near his feet.

When Weber exited his vehicle, he saw Sam Gibbons standing in front of the dead man's sons with his arms spread wide, as if to hold them back, while his brother Jake was talking to Brad Gleason, who was sitting on the open tailgate of the guide's pickup truck. A bolt action Remington .308 rifle with a scope lay in the parking lot.

Dolan Reed had arrived seconds before Weber, and Buz Carelton was right behind him. Dolan immediately started stretching yellow crime scene tape across the parking lot, while Buz moved to stand near the rifle to secure it until photos were taken to record everything's location.

Weber put his fingers alongside the man's neck, feeling for a pulse that wasn't there.

"Jesus Christ, Sheriff, I never saw this coming!" Jake said. "If I would have…"

"What happened?" Weber asked, but before Jake could reply, Brad said, "I shot him."

"Don't say another word," Weber ordered him. "Robyn, read him his rights and handcuff him. Jake, come with me."

He led the guide out of earshot and said, "What happened here, Jake?"

"I'm sorry, Sheriff, I'm responsible for letting it happen."

"It's okay, Jake, just tell me what happened. Start at the beginning."

"Everybody got their deer, except the kid. I had him out with me, because I didn't want to deal with Lenny. I don't like to talk bad about the dead, but I can't say he didn't get what he had coming."

Jake was shaking and Weber asked, "Do you need to sit down?"

"No. I've never seen anything like that. I'm rattled, is all."

"I understand. It's okay, just take your time."

Jake took a couple of deep breaths, then said, "You saw how Lenny could be, he was always ridin' the kid's ass, putting him down. And those two aren't any better." He nodded toward Chuck and Richey.

"We extended their hunt because of the time we lost with the storm and that woman's death, and this morning was their last chance because they were due to fly out tomorrow. I took Brad out and Richey rode along. Sam had Lenny and Chuck out riding the back roads, just kind of givin' them a tour and keeping them busy and out of my hair. Before we left, Lenny told the kid that if he didn't get a buck, he'd be walking back to Pennsylvania."

As he told the story, Jake seemed to be calming down just a bit, and his shaking had stopped. "Anyway, we were back off the fire road that runs along Fetterman's Ridge and spotted a nice six point, an easy shot. The kid tried, but he couldn't do it, Sheriff. He had a good rest, a clear shot, but he just couldn't pull the trigger. He started shaking, but it wasn't buck fever. I've seen that before. No, he just didn't have it in him to kill something. I don't fault him for that. Some people can't. He just handed me the rifle and said he wanted to go home."

"Then what?"

"I told him not to worry about it, that it didn't make him any less of a man or anything. Some of us just aren't cut out to be hunters, I guess. But right away Richey starts calling him a pussy and telling him how the old man's going to kick his ass when we got back here. I told him to shut up, but he's as bad as Lenny was."

Weber looked up as an ambulance pulled into the parking lot and Robyn, having put Brad in the back seat of her patrol car, started talking to the paramedics.

"Sam was back with the other two when we got here, and right away Richey starts telling his dad and brother how Brad had this easy shot and wouldn't take it. That set Lenny off like I had never seen him before. He started calling the kid every name in the book, telling him how worthless he was, and how much money he wasted on this hunt trying to make a man out of him. Sam and me both told him to shut up, but he wouldn't listen. Then he pulls out his knife and says since the kid ain't got any balls anyway, he might as well turn him into a real pussy so at least he'd be useful for something."

As his story neared the end, Jake started to shake again, and Weber put a steadying hand on his arm. "Take your time, Jake."

"He kind of jabbed at Brad with the knife. I don't think he really was going to cut the kid, Sheriff, but who knows what goes on in the head of a man like that? Anyway, Brad had his rifle in his hands, and when Lenny did that, the kid just jerked it up about halfway and pulled the trigger. I think it surprised him as much as me. They were by the door of the room there, and Lenny just sort of fell down right there. Brad didn't say a word, just backed up and dropped the rifle, and stood there."

"Why was the rifle loaded?" Weber asked, knowing that standard safety procedure called for unloading all firearms before getting into a vehicle after a hunt.

"The damn thing was," Jake said. "I unloaded it myself. But as we were getting ready to drive out, Richey was sitting in the back and he put a round in the chamber. Said if we saw a deer he was going to shoot it to fill out Brad's tag. I told him to unload the damn thing, and he worked the bolt. I thought he did, but apparently not. I couldn't see from in front. And to be honest, I was busy tryin' to keep him from bullying Brad and wasn't paying enough attention. If I had been, maybe Lenny would still be alive."

Weber could see the anguish in the other man's face, and put both hands on his shoulders. "Jake, listen to me. This isn't your fault."

"Yes it is! If I would have…"

"We can play woulda, shoulda, coulda till the end of time, and it doesn't change a thing," Weber said. "You're right. If you would have stopped your truck and taken that gun away from Richey, this might not have happened. If Judge Ryman would have ordered him to jail Friday, Lenny might still be in there and alive. If I would have broken his arm when he poked his finger in my face the other day, maybe he couldn't have gotten that knife out. But none of those things happened. Lenny is the one who decided to push the issue. Brad is the one who pulled the trigger, whether it was an accident or if he had just been pushed too far, one time too many. It's that simple. Don't you wear this, my friend. I know a lot about guilt, and trust me, it's not a burden you want to carry around with you."

Weber hoped his words were getting through to Jake, but he suspected that they were falling on deaf ears. And he knew from his own experiences that words alone could not ease the man's conscience, whether he was right or wrong.

Chapter 23

"Sounds like self-defense to me," Bob Bennett said late that afternoon, after he had read the reports from everybody involved in Lenny Dewitt's death. "That's what happens when you take a knife to a gunfight."

"Part of me wants to buy the kid a drink and say "Well done" and part of me thinks he overreacted and a man would still be alive if he hadn't."

"What's that old saying, the son of a bitch just needed killing? Lenny Dewitt is dead because he poked at that young man with a knife and threatened him. A young man that he had a long history of verbally abusing. Now, whether he would have actually cut him or not is irrelevant. He did it, and even his own sons said they saw him. Any defense attorney six months out of law school would get an acquittal."

"The kid's screwed either way," Weber said. "Life as he knew it is over."

"Could be. But from everything I've heard so far, maybe he'll be better off. Look, Jimmy, if you want to file a murder charge, I'll give it consideration. But I have to tell you, I just don't think we have much of a case."

"You're right," Weber said, standing up and stretching, "Let's go talk to him."

***

Brad Gleason seemed to have aged ten years since Weber had seen him at the motel right after the shooting. His face was haggard with grief and his eyes showed the pain that was ripping his heart in two when he looked up as Weber unlocked his cell.

"How are you doing, Brad?"

He looked at Weber dully and shrugged, but didn't reply.

"Come with me," Weber said, and led him out the door from the small cellblock and into the Sheriff's Office's one interview room.

Weber motioned him to a seat across the table from himself and Bennett. "You've been read your rights, and those still stand. But I'm going to do it again, okay?"

The other man didn't say anything, so Weber read him his rights again. "Do you understand your rights as I've explained them to you, Brad?"

He nodded.

"We need you to say yes or no, for the camera," Bennett told him.

"Umm, yes, I understand."

"I know we've been all over this a couple of times before," Weber said. "But we need to be sure you've told us everything you can remember. Do you want an attorney here to represent you?"

Brad shook his head, and Bennett reminded him to speak.

"No, I don't want an attorney. I did it, I shot Lenny."

"Brad, I want you to go over the whole thing again, from when you were on the mountain and saw that deer but couldn't shoot it, to what happened at the motel this afternoon."

The young man's story remained the same, and matched everybody else's statements. Jake Gibbons had taken him out one last time to try to get a deer, and Richey Dewitt had gone along for the ride. After three hours of hunting, they had spotted a nice buck and Jake got him into a position for a good shot, but Brad couldn't pull the trigger, even with Jake encouraging him and Richey scoffing at his "weakness." He had handed the rifle to Jake and said he couldn't do it, and they had left. Back at the trailhead, Jake had unloaded the rifle and put it in a rack across the back window of the crew cab pickup. Richey had continued to mock him, telling him how mad Lenny would be when he heard that Brad had "pussied out" again and how he was going to go ballistic. He said that as they started back to town, Richey, sitting alone in the back of the truck, had removed the rifle from the gun rack and loaded it, saying that if they saw a deer on the ride back to the motel he would kill it and they could put Brad's tag on it. Jake had ordered him to unload the gun and they heard the rifle's bolt being opened and closed and assumed he had complied. Back at the Mountain Mist Motel, Richey had been the first out of the truck, and had quickly told his father and brother about Brad's latest failure, and as predicted, Lenny had gone into a rage. He had cursed Brad, then started jabbing him with his knife, threating to emasculate him. At that time, Brad had shot him.

"Why were you carrying the rifle, Brad?" Weber asked.

"It was one of the ones we brought from back home. Lenny bought us all matching rifles and scopes. He said that way, if one got broke or something, we'd be able to use one of the others. I was just taking it back inside the room to put in the case."

"Did you know it was loaded?"

"No! Mr. Gibbons unloaded it before we got in the truck, and when Richey put a bullet in it again, he told him to unload it. It sounded like he did, and he never said he had only opened and closed the bolt, but left the bullet inside."

"Why did you point the gun at your father-in-law?"

"I don't know… he kept jabbing that knife at me and saying he was going cut off my… you know. It just happened!"

"Did you think you were defending yourself? Do you think Lenny would have cut you?"

"I don't know," Brad said. "It all happened so fast, it was like a blur."

"Had he threatened you before?"

Brad shrugged and nodded, and Bennett reminded him to speak.

"He was always saying stuff like that."

"Like what, Brad? Tell me specifically anything you can remember from the past. Times he threatened to hurt you."

"The day me and Sherry told her parents we were going to get married, he said he'd kill me and dump me in a ditch before that happened. Her mom and Sherry got him calmed down, but he was always saying stuff like that. Always saying he was going to kick my ass or cut my nuts off or cut my throat, something."

"Had he ever assaulted you before?"

"He got mad and punched me a few times, or pushed me against the wall and choked me."

"Did you ever report any of that to the police?"

"No."

"Why not, Brad?"

Brad had been looking down at the table during most of the interview, but he looked up and said, "I was married to his daughter and worked for him. I knew if I ever did report him to the cops, it would only get worse. Sherry was Daddy's little girl, and I knew if it ever came down to it and she had to choose him over me, I'd lose."

"Did Lenny ever assault Sherry, or her brothers, or mother?"

"Never Sherry. Like I said, she was his little princess. But I guess growing up, he beat on the boys a lot. Said it was for their own good, to toughen them up and turn them into men."

"How about his wife? Did you ever see him abuse her?"

"Stella's probably as crazy as he was and they fought a lot, but I think if he ever raised a hand to her she'd have killed him in his sleep."

"Brad, did you ever think Lenny would make good on his threats to hurt you, to cut you?"

"At first it scared me, but then I guess I got used to it." He paused, then said, "There was one time… two Christmases ago. I got Sherry a little French poodle for Christmas because she always said she wanted one. When we went over to their house for Christmas dinner Sherry brought it along and Lenny was making fun of it, saying only a little faggot like me would buy his wife a little faggot dog like that. Sherry just kind of laughed about it. But later in the day, we were all in the living room and Lenny went into the kitchen for something and the dog had pooped on the floor. He was kicking it and screaming at it, and I picked it up to try to get it away. He grabbed a big butcher knife that was in the sink and said he was gonna cut its head off. I tried to keep the dog away from him and he slashed my arm instead."

"He cut your arm? Where?"

Brad rolled up his shirt sleeve to show them the six inch scar along the side of his right forearm. From the look of it, it had been a deep wound.

"What happened then, Brad?"

"Sherry wrapped it up and tried to stop it from bleeding, but it wouldn't. Sherry and Chuck took me to the emergency room, and all the way there they kept telling me to say it was an accident, I had reached inside the dishwasher to unload it and got cut on a knife in there. I don't think the doctor or nurse believed it, but they didn't push it and I didn't want to make matters worse."

Weber wondered just how much worse things could have been.

"What happened then?"

Brad shrugged. "Nothing happened. Nothing was ever said about it again. And when we got back to the house, the dog was gone and I never saw it again."

Weber and Bennett looked at each other, not needing words to communicate.

"Back to today," Bennett said. "Brad, did you willfully kill Lenny DeWitt? Did you act in self-defense? Were you mad and wanted to show him he couldn't push you around anymore? What was going through your head when you raised that rifle and pulled the trigger?"

"I honestly don't know," Brad said, crying. "I wish I had just gone ahead and let him cut me! Maybe then he'd be sitting here and I'd be dead and not have to deal with it any more!"

They allowed him to cry for a few moments and then Weber said, "Brad, you and the witnesses have all said you brought the rifle up about waist high and pulled the trigger, all in one motion. Is that right?"

He nodded then remembered the camera and said, "Yes."

"You didn't shoulder the rifle like you did when you were practicing for the hunt?"

"No sir."

"Brad, I have to ask again, when you raised that rifle and pulled the trigger, had you reached a decision to shoot Lenny? Yes or no?"

"No sir. It just happened. I didn't even know it was loaded!"

"Did you want to shoot Lenny?"

"No! I don't know why I did it, I just raised the gun up and the next thing I knew, he was dead! I wish it was me, instead."

He broke down in sobs again, and they sat in silence for a few minutes, then Weber and Bennett stepped out into the hall and closed the door behind them.

"This kid's not a murderer," Bennett said, and Weber nodded.

"No use in dragging this out any longer."

They went back into the interview room, and Bennett said, "Brad, we're not going to charge you with Lenny's death. Sheriff Weber and I are both convinced it was accidental, and was a result of Lenny's own actions. You're free to go."

"Go? Go where? I killed my father-in-law. I don't have anywhere to go. Sherry won't want me around after I killed her dad. My parents are both dead and I don't have any other family I'm close to. And if I go back to the motel, Chuck and Richey are going to kill me. They're as bad as Lenny was!"

Weber thought for a moment, then said, "You're not a prisoner and you're not charged with any crime. You're free to go, but I want you to stay here in your cell for a little while longer while I try to work something out. The door won't be locked. Is that okay?"

Brad shrugged again and said for the third time during the interview, "I'd have been better off if Lenny would have killed me instead."

***

"What do you think?" Weber asked when the video of the interview with Brad ended, and Christine shook her head sadly.

"That poor boy has been abused physically and psychologically as much as any woman or child I've ever worked with. It happens, you know. The latest figures I've seen say over 800,000 men become victims of domestic violence every year."

"That's amazing," Weber told her. "I don't think we've ever had a reported case that I can remember."

"Don't mean it don't happen," Christine told him. "A lot of men are embarrassed, or think they'll be ridiculed for not standing up for themselves. And even though this young man may not have lived in the same house with his father-in-law or his wife's brothers, it's the same thing."

"He can't go back to that motel," Weber said. "I've no doubt that his two brothers-in-law will hurt him. Maybe even kill him. And I can't keep him in jail forever."

"Well, I can't take him back with me," Christine said. "It just wouldn't work having a man inside a shelter for women."

"Miss Ridgeway, somebody has to do something for this young man. You said yourself, he's as abused as any woman victim. He needs a safe place to stay, and I believe he needs the same kind of counseling you talked about providing for women at the Town Council meeting last week," Bob Bennett said.

Christine put her elbows on the table and massaged her temples for a moment, then opened her eyes, resting her chin in her hands and said, "You're right, darn it. Just because he's got outside plumbing, instead of inside, don't make him any different emotionally. I've got two women in the house right now, but there are three cabins sitting there empty."

"You'll do it?" Weber asked, smiling.

"Aww heck, you little twerp, you know I can't say no to you. We'll give it a try and see what happens. But," and with that she turned to Bennett, "I want something in return."

"Name it."

"I want to file a restraining order against that little troll you call a mayor. I don't want him coming anywhere near SafeHaven again. He could have put everybody out there in danger with that stunt he pulled today. And we all know it wasn't about helping that boy get his wife back. It was because his daddy buys a lot of supplies at Chet's hardware store. That, and Chet Wingate wanting to show how powerful he is."

"You're kidding me, right?" the Town's attorney asked.

"I'm as serious as a bad case of diarrhea in a Los Angeles traffic jam," Christine replied.

Bennett buried his face in his hands, and for a minute Weber didn't know what to expect.

"Bob?"

When he looked up, he had an evil grin on is face. "I'll talk to Judge Ryman and have it ready to serve on him first thing in the morning."

Chapter 24

"So you're really going to do it?" Parks asked the next morning, as he snatched a buttermilk cruller from a stack of pastries before Archer Wingate could finish the one he was busy stuffing into his mouth and reach for another.

"Right now, and I'm taking Paul along to report it for the newspaper."

"Oh, you are a devious man, Jim Weber," Mary Caitlin said. "I'd give a week's pay to be a fly on the wall!"

"What are you gonna do?" Archer asked, spitting bits of dough out as he talked around a full mouth. Parks moved the rest of the goodies out of spitting range, but not out of arms reach, as Archer snagged a blueberry donut.

"You probably don't want to know," Weber told him, and Archer shrugged and went to work on the donut while giving Parks a baleful look as the FBI agent helped himself to a chocolate long john. Weber turned away from the two eating machines and grinned at the newspaperman.

"Shall we?" Weber asked, and Paul nodded. His own grin was wide as his belly as he followed Weber out the door.

***

Main Street is the center of activity in Big Lake, housing a dozen or so small shops catering to both the tourist trade and full time residents, several restaurants, and most recently, an art gallery or two. The Sheriff's Office is located in the middle of town, with the Big Lake Town Offices located next door, across a small parking lot. On the far side of the Town Offices, Judge Ryman's courtroom occupied a large block building that also held two small meeting rooms used for various purposes. In the rear was a depository for records dating back to the earliest days of the community. The newspaper office is directly across the street from the Sheriff's Office.

At the north end of town, Main Street continues on past a convenience store, Arby's and McDonald's, and eventually out to the ski lodge at Cat Mountain. Looking south, Main Street appears to end at the foot of Apache Mountain, an imposing monolith that towers over the town, but in reality the street turns left sharply at the last minute and connects with the state highway a mile away, completing a loop begun on the north end of town. Wingate's Hardware & Lumber was located six blocks from the Sheriff's Office at the left turn, where they found Chet Wingate busy barking orders at Darrel Meecham, as the clerk tried to assemble a pyramid-shaped cardboard display of batteries.

"No, no, Darrel! The D cells go on the bottom, then the C's and double A's above them, and the triple A's on top! Can't you get anything right? Hurry up and get that darned thing together so you can restock the rock salt. Chop, chop, time is money!"

Darrel was a short, balding man who always seemed nervous, no doubt due to his employer's non-stop verbal barrage of orders and criticism that began the moment he walked in every morning and followed him out the door at the end of the day. Darrel fumbled and dropped a box of batteries that spilled out and went rolling across the floor, earning more abuse from Chet.

"Now look what you've done! Do you suppose my customers want to buy merchandise that's been dropped and dinged up? If even one of those batteries has a scratch on it, it's coming out of your paycheck."

Weber always wondered when the call would come in to his office that Darrel had finally snapped and bashed in Chet's head with one of the sledgehammers or mauls the store sold, and also wondered why it hadn't happened already.

Seeing Weber and Paul Lewis, Chet left Darrell to clean up the mess and said, "I hope you're here to tell me that with the death of that unfortunate man yesterday, you've closed the case on Emma Moyer's death. This negative publicity is going to kill our tourist traffic."

Weber wanted to tell him that, judging by how busy the town's restaurants, motels, and shops were, the murder investigation had not had much impact on business. Instead, he replied, "No, I'm here on another matter."

But Chet didn't want to discuss other matters, he wanted the case closed, and demanded, "Why not? Everybody knows that fellow from back east killed that poor woman. Now get this whole ugly mess wrapped up. Today!"

"Well, I don't know where everybody is getting their information, but apparently I'm not privy to it," Weber said. "I don't know who shot

Emma, but I'm working on it."

"Oh, come on, Sheriff! The man shot at her before and threatened her, he disappeared from his guide and later showed up in town with no alibi for where he was in the meantime, and Emma was found dead just up the road from where he was last seen. Who else could it be?"

Weber wanted to tell him that who else was a long list, but he didn't care to share the details of an open investigation with the mayor in public, or in private, for that matter. Besides, he had other business to attend to, and the fact that several customers were lurking nearby, hoping to pick up some tidbit of information about the homicide case, only added to his secret pleasure when he said, "Actually, Chet, I plan to get back to work on figuring out who killed Emma as soon as I'm done here."

With that, he handed the mayor a document as Paul raised his camera and took a photograph of the exchange.

"What's this?"

"Chester Wingate, you have been served. That's a restraining order preventing you from going anywhere closer than a thousand feet from SafeHaven or Christine Ridgeway, and from contacting or harassing Ms. Ridgeway or anyone working or staying at SafeHaven by telephone or any other means. Per Arizona Revised Statute 13-3602, if you violate this order, you are subject to immediate arrest on a Class One misdemeanor, and can be sentenced to up to six months in jail and a fine of up to $2,500 plus court costs."

Paul Lewis may have only been the editor and publisher of a small town community newspaper with a limited circulation, but he had grown up in the business, starting out cleaning lead type in the old letterpress days under his father's tutelage, and he knew a good story when it came his way. And one of the benefits of being a small town editor was that he knew his community and the people in it. So after getting the picture of Weber serving the mayor the restraining order, he kept his camera focused on Chet Wingate, anticipating the explosion that would follow. The little martinet did not disappoint him.

"What? You can't do this! I'm the mayor!" he bellowed.

"Don't shoot the messenger," Weber told him. "I didn't do anything. I'm just a humble public servant doing my job. Christine Ridgeway requested the order, and after hearing what you pulled out at SafeHaven yesterday, Judge Ryman issued it. All I got to do was serve it on you. That's part of my job, you know."

"I won't have it! I don't accept it," Chet said, ripping the document in half and throwing it on the floor and stomping on it, then kicking the pieces away from him.

"You can throw any kind of tantrum you want," Weber told him, "it's your store and I'm sure your customers appreciate the show. But you've been served. You have the right to contest the order with the judge in the next ten days. In the meantime, I've got a murder to solve."

Paul followed the sheriff out the door, but not before pausing to get one last picture of an enraged Chet Wingate shaking his fist, his mouth open, and his eyes bulging in rage as he roared threats of a ruined career in Weber's wake.

***

"Well, that was fun," Paul said, as they drove back toward the Sheriff's Office.

"Did you get some good pictures?"

"Oh yeah! This week's front page is going to be a keeper!"

"Not afraid of losing Chet's advertising business?"

Paul shook his head. "All he ever did was run a little business card sized ad, and he cancelled that and hasn't advertised with me in over a year. He got mad because I wouldn't give him his own weekly column on the front page to talk about his vision of the town's future. Most of which praised Chet Wingate. I guess he figured not getting his $50 a week would starve me into submission. When I wouldn't cave in, he tried to get the Town Council to bully me into it."

"Oh, payback time!"

"Yeah, Jimmy, but you remember what my old man used to say, never fight with a man who buys his ink by the barrel."

Weber laughed, but the laughter died off as they pulled into the parking lot of the Sheriff's Office just in time to see a man in a green Army field jacket going in the door.

"Looks like you've got company," Paul observed.

"Oh joy," Weber said. "If there's anybody I can't stand more than Chet, it's that jerk. Come on in, you might get to watch me choke the life out of him. Now, that'd be a front page picture for you!"

"I'll pass," Paul said as he got out of the Explorer. "Between Emma Moyer's murder, the snowstorm, and our good mayor blowing his cork for the camera, it's going to be a full issue already. Besides, then I'd be a witness, and I'd feel bad having to testify for the prosecution and helping to send you up the river. I'd do it, mind you. I'd just feel really, really bad about it."

"It's nice to know you've got my back," Weber said.

"I'll tell you what. This thing with Chet will blow over soon enough and you'll catch whoever murdered Emma. Once that's all done, I'll be back to running pictures of kittens and puppies on the front page. If you could hold off on strangling him until things slow down a little bit, I'll sure be happy to come back and cover the whole story."

"I'll try to control myself," Weber told him as Paul headed across the street to the newspaper office, "But I'm not making any promises."

***

Gordon Hahn, the Bureau of Indian Affairs investigator assigned to the nearby White Mountain Apache Reservation, was a thoroughly unlikeable man; big, florid-faced, and lacking any kind of social graces. A web of tiny broken veins around his bulbous red nose identified him as a heavy drinker, and Hahn preferred to bull his way through life, counting on his bulk and loud voice to cover his lack of professional skill.

When Weber entered the office, Hahn was busy telling Dan Wright about how much he disliked working with the Apaches, whom he considered to be unwashed savages. The man's own body odor made his criticisms not only offensive, but ironic. Seeing the sheriff, the young deputy found an excuse to break off the conversation and walk away from Hahn.

"I went to the Mountain Mist with Tommy and we collected all of Brad Gleason's clothes and stuff and took them out to SafeHaven. They wanted to know what was going on with the case, but we didn't tell them anything about no charges being filed or anything. As far as they know, he's still in jail."

"Good work. I appreciate that."

"Jimmy! What's going on, son?" Hahn interrupted, pumping Weber's hand like a politician on the campaign trail. "I hear they're dropping like flies around here these days. That's the way to do it, let them all kill each other and save your ammo. Wish those damn war whoops on the Rez would do the same thing. It'd sure make my job easier."

"What are you doing here, Hahn?"

If he recognized Weber's animosity, Gordon Hahn didn't acknowledge it. "I'm getting together with my man Parks to update him on this case with the credit cards. I've been carrying the load while he was off on some hush-hush secret assignment."

While he had a good working relationship with the White Mountain Apache Police, Weber didn't have any jurisdiction on the Reservation, and there were enough problems to deal with in Big Lake that he didn't have time to pay much attention to what was happening anywhere else. He remembered Parks saying something about a credit card scam based down in Whiteriver, the capital of the Reservation, and his friend lamenting about having to work with Hahn on the case.

"Yeah, sons-a-bitches are two weeks out of the freakin' Stone Age and they've already jumped from raiding wagon trains to hustling stolen credit cards. I'm telling you, it's a new world, Jimmy."

Weber was familiar with Hahn's crude ways and racist attitude and wondered, not for the first time, how the man had avoided ending up facedown on some back road on the vast Indian reservation with a bullet in the back of his head some dark night.

Proving that he was as much a misogynist as he was a racist, Hahn changed the topic to Christine Ridgeway and SafeHaven. "So what's this I hear about this women's shelter that big ol' blond gal opened up? Johnny Yazzie's wife works at the hospital down in Whiteriver and your pal that runs the place was down there meeting with her last week. Far as I'm concerned, all that abused woman bullshit is just that, bullshit. I've known more than a few damn broads that need a little abusing now and then to keep 'em in line."

"You're a real asshole, do you know that?" Mary said. "I guess a guy like you thinks abusing a woman is okay because you'd have to beat a woman into submission just to touch her."

"Oh Mary, don't get your knickers in a twist. You know I'm just having fun. All I'm saying is a woman can run faster with her dress up than a man can with his pants down!" Hahn laughed at his own sense of humor and Weber felt his jaw tighten. "But I did tell your buddy there that she was way outta her league coming down on the Rez talking all that nonsense and she'd better watch it before some buck made her his squaw."

Hahn was saved from Weber's growing fury when Parks came through the door.

"Larry! How you doing? Glad to see you. The redskins are about to go on the warpath and I need all the backup I can get."

Parks was no more a fan of the BIA man than anyone else, and every time he had worked with Hahn on the Reservation he had been appalled at the man's lowbrow attempts at humor and blatant contempt for the Apache people, not to mention his disgusting personal habits.

"What do you need, Hahn?"

"I left a message yesterday that I was coming to town to meet with you on the credit card case. Did you forget all about me?"

Hahn wasn't easy to forget, but Parks obviously had. Weber knew his friend would rather do anything than spend time in a meeting with his counterpart from the BIA, but he took advantage of Parks' arrival to escape to his office, with Mary close on his heels.

"God, what a disgusting excuse for a human being," she said as she plopped herself down in the chair next to Weber's desk, still fuming over Hahn's comments.

"Well, if it's any consolation to you, Paul got some great pictures of Chet going ballistic when I served him his restraining order."

Mary laughed and asked, "Is he really going to put them in the paper?"

"Front page," Weber assured her. "You know Paul, he's got a nose for news."

"He's going to have to print extra copies," Mary predicted. "Everybody's going to want a copy. This issue will sell out."

"I'm ordering a dozen myself," Weber said, and they were laughing over Paul's impending financial success when Judy Troutman knocked on the door, then stuck her head inside.

"Sheriff, the medical examiner down in Tucson's on the phone. He has the preliminary autopsy report on Emma Moyer."

***

"Sheriff, Cliff Hurlburt here. I'm an Assistant Medical Examiner and I was told you needed any info on Emma Moyer ASAP," said the voice on the other end of the telephone. He sounded young, and Weber pictured somebody fresh out of college and full of enthusiasm, working his first job. He wondered how long it would be before the caseload and bureaucracy wore him down.

"I appreciate the fast service," Weber told him. "What can you tell me?"

"Well, as you know, there was significant damage done to the body postmortem by the bear. I don't think I've ever heard of a case here where somebody was actually eaten by a bear before. Or partially eaten."

Weber had to suppress a shudder at the vision of the bear savaging Emma's body.

"You said postmortem. So she was definitely dead before the bear got to her?"

"No question about it. She was shot with what looks like a large caliber weapon, probably a high powered rifle, based upon what I read in your report. The bullet shattered her spine at the fifth thoracic vertebrae, T-5, passed through her heart, and exited through her chest. Death would have been instantaneous. Whatever the animal did to her, she was gone before it happened."

Weber was grateful for that news at least.

"There was no indication of gunshot residue on the body, which given the weather up there, is not surprising. I'm assuming she wore several layers of clothing. A jacket, a shirt, and undershirt, which would have prevented GSR from reaching the body. I did find traces of fabric in the wound canal that are consistent with the clothing that was sent down with the body. Those would have been forced into the wound as the bullet passed through."

"Thank you," Weber told him. "So can I confirm that you are calling this a homicide?"

"These are only preliminary observations, as you know. It will be at least two weeks before I can send you the full report, but this death can definitely be classified as a homicide."

"Thanks," Weber said, although the determination only confirmed what he already knew.

"However, there's more," Hurlburt told him.

"More?"

"Yes. Even if she had not been shot, the deceased probably only had a short time to live. I'd estimate six months at best."

"What are you talking about?" Weber asked.

"She had cancer. I haven't determined where it originated yet, but I found tumors in the chest cavity and what remained of her abdominal organs. To be honest, I'm amazed that somebody in her condition was even able to be out in the mountains like you described in your report. She must have had an extremely strong will."

As Weber thanked Hurlburt and hung up, he recalled his conversation with Brian Oakes and the real estate developer's threat of a countersuit against Emma. She said to go right ahead, that she wouldn't live long enough to have to deal with it anyway.

Chapter 25

A tall, thin woman with the palest skin Weber had ever seen on a living person, greeted him at Roger Wilson's office and offered him a seat while she excused herself to see if her boss was available. Except for her carefully coiffed blonde hair and blue eyes, he would have thought the woman was an albino. Her bright red lipstick and matching nail polish seemed even more vibrant against her nearly translucent skin and the white pantsuit she wore.

She returned a moment later and said Wilson was on a long distance call, but would be free shortly. Weber studied her as she sat back down at her desk and began typing on a keyboard, her long fingers flying over the keys. A nameplate on her desk identified her as Tamara Radcliffe. There was nobody else in the office and she didn't seem inclined to small talk so Weber picked up a copy of People magazine and leafed through it. He was pretty well convinced that nobody in Hollywood was capable of living a normal life or maintaining a healthy relationship by the time the telephone on Tamara's desk buzzed, fifteen minutes later. She picked up the receiver, listened for a moment and hung it back up as she pushed her chair back from her desk.

"Mr. Wilson will see you now," she said, and led Weber through the office past several empty desks to Wilson's private office.

Roger Wilson was Big Lake's golden boy, born with a silver spoon in his mouth that he had worked hard to turn into gold. The son of a successful investment banker who had retired early to trade corporate boardrooms for the good life in the mountains, Wilson's first car was a Porsche when he turned sixteen. He had been a high school and college football star who went on to become a real estate speculator, land developer and all around success story. There were rumors that he planned to run for State Senator in the next election.

"Sheriff Weber, it's good to see you! I apologize for keeping you waiting. I was on a conference call with some foreign investors. The Japanese are great businessmen, as I'm sure you know, but their insistence on formality does take a lot of time."

Wilson was a handsome, well built, tanned man in his late 30s, and he shook Weber's hand and smiled like they were old friends. Though Wilson had been a year behind him in school, they moved in very different circles and had been no more than nodding acquaintances. Still, Wilson acted like having the sheriff dropping in for a visit was an everyday occurrence. He waved Weber to a chair across from his desk and dropped back into his own.

"Why is it we never seem to get together, Jimmy? I mean, it's a small town, but sometimes it seems like we live in two different worlds."

Weber wanted to tell him that they did indeed live in two very different worlds, but didn't bother, since no one knew that better than Wilson himself.

"We'll have to get together and go squirrel hunting someday."

"Squirrel… oh, a joke! You were always a kidder, weren't you?" Wilson pointed his finger at Weber with the thumb up like a pistol and showed off his perfect white teeth as he laughed, but when he saw that Weber wasn't sharing in the humor, his face turned serious and he leaned forward, putting his arms on his desk.

"Anyway, what can I do for you today, Sheriff? I'm assuming this isn't a social visit."

"I'm afraid not. I need to talk to you about Emma Moyer."

If the dead woman's name alerted him to anything, Wilson covered it well. He shook his head with a sad look on his face and made a tsk-tsk sound. "I was shocked to hear about that. Things like that never happened around here in the old days. This just isn't the same town we grew up in, is it Jimmy?"

"I understand you had problems with Emma a while back?"

"Problems?" Wilson wrinkled his brow in thought, but didn't offer anything else.

"Yes, problems. I understand she had stonewalled some of your development projects?"

Wilson's face screwed up in a grimace and he shook his head. "I won't lie to you, Sheriff, Emma Moyer was a real nightmare at times, with her protests and injunctions. She cost me and every other developer, construction company, and real estate agent in the area a lot of time and money. I just happened to be one of her targets."

"I imagine that could be pretty frustrating."

Wilson nodded and said, "Where are we going with all this?"

"I understand you and Emma had a run-in a while back."

"Is that a question or a statement, Sheriff?"

"What was it about?"

Wilson shook his head but the wide smile never left his face.

"What was what about?"

"Don't play games with me, Roger. I know that Emma came in here a while back and you two got into an argument about something, and I know that you got physical with her."

"Physical?"

"You slammed her against the wall and warned her to stay out of your business."

Wilson laughed. "That's absurd, Sheriff. Where do you get your information? Do I look like a man who would do something like that to a woman?"

"I've met your wife," Weber told him, and watched as Wilson's eyes narrowed and the smile left his face. He sat back in his chair and said, "If you have anything else to say to me, you can contact my attorney, Sheriff."

"Is that really the way you want to play it?" Weber asked him.

Wilson opened a drawer and pulled out a business card, which he dropped onto his desktop. "My attorney is Conrad Gilbert, in Phoenix. You give him a call and relay any further questions you have for me through him." He stood up and said, "Have a good day, Sheriff."

Weber remained seated and said, "I'll tell you what, Roger, how about if you call your man and tell him to come up here and we'll have us a little chat in the interview room at my office."

"I don't have time for this…"

"You'll have to make time," Weber told him. "Because it looks like the only way we're going to get anywhere is if I arrest you."

"Are you mad, Sheriff? Arrest me for what?"

"Well, you told me that Emma was costing you a lot of time and money. I know you physically assaulted her right here in this office and threatened her. And now she's dead. So unless you have a really good alibi for where you were last Tuesday afternoon, that makes you my prime suspect."

Wilson dropped back into his chair heavily and the color drained from his face. Probably not so much that he resembled his receptionist, but close. He held his hands palms up and said, "Stop."

Weber regarded him in silence. He had never seen Wilson lose his composure like this. The man was usually calm and in control no matter what was happening around him. Weber wondered if Roger Wilson really had killed Emma.

"Look, Sheriff, you may have heard a rumor that the Republican party is backing me for State Senator next November. It's true. I'll be kicking off my campaign right after the first of the year. I can't have any hint of scandal like this associated with my good name. It could ruin my chances for election. Do you understand what I'm telling you?"

"Seems to me it might be in your best interest if we settle this here and now, between us," Weber said.

Wilson regarded him for a long moment and then asked, "How much?"

"How much?"

"Yes, Sheriff. How much do you want?"

"Are you trying to bribe me, Roger? Because if you are, you're gonna have one hell of a scandal attached to your good name."

"I just meant.... what is it you want, Sheriff?"

"Did you kill Emma Moyer?"

"No! No, I never… no. I didn't kill her."

"But you did bounce her off the wall right here in this office, didn't you? And you threatened her. What was that all about?"

"I don't know what she told you, but it wasn't like that."

"Like what, Roger?"

"Damn her," Wilson said, rubbing his hands across his forehead, "Emma had me so tied up with her damn injunctions that work was at a standstill on my newest project. I have a lot of money riding on it, both my own and my investors', and I couldn't afford to lose any more time. These Japanese, they're sharp businessmen, but they don't like getting involved in things like that. They were threatening to take their money and walk. These days they have too many opportunities to choose from. If a project looks like it's going sour, they're done."

"What project are we talking about?" Weber asked.

Wilson met his eye and said, "Sheriff, I need to ask for your discretion on this. Until we get all of the land purchases finished and the Town Council approval and building permits we need in place, this whole thing could blow up in our faces. What I'm telling you can't leave this office."

"I don't care what your latest scheme is, Roger, except as to how it relates to Emma's murder."

"It's going to be called Cimarron Ridge. A master planned community out at the T intersection."

"At the T? Isn't that Forest Service land?"

"Part of it is, and part is private property. But we're doing a swap for 250 acres of land our group owns along the north end of the lake that the state wants to preserve for public use as a park. So everybody wins. The Forest Service gets a prime piece of lakefront access that they will in turn lease to the state. The folks who own land adjacent to the T are going to make a killing, and Big Lake gets a wonderful new development that includes both upscale residential and commercial parcels."

"Sounds like a big project," Weber said.

"It is! We're talking about a shopping center, townhomes, condominiums. It's going to change the face of Big Lake forever. But if any word of it gets out, it could ruin us. There are a lot of people who don't want any changes around here. They'd still be happy to be stuck back in 1963, when a dog could sleep in the middle of Main Street all day long and never have to worry about getting run over. And Emma Moyer was the worst of them."

"Maybe those folks are right," Weber suggested.

"Those days are over! This town is growing every day and fortunes are being made. And it's not just the developers, Jimmy. A lot of people have made a lot of money around here."

"By selling off their land?"

"Yes! Land that was costing them more in taxes than they could afford. The days of the small ranches are gone. There were fools who worked their whole lives trying to make a go of it with a hundred head of cattle, holding on by the skin of their teeth and getting nowhere. And then passing that same dead end dream on to their kids to follow."

"My father was one of those fools," Weber said.

"Yes, he was," Wilson said. "And what did it get him? I remember how it was when we were growing up, Jimmy. You drove that rusty old pickup truck and worked whatever jobs you could find after school to earn a buck or two, and helped your old man brand cows and mend fences while other kids were playing sports and chasing girls. The only difference between you and some of these guys is you got out! You left Big Lake, and let's be honest, if your parents had not died and you had to come back here to take care of your sister, you'd still be gone."

Weber couldn't deny what Wilson was saying. He had chosen a

different life than that of a small rancher scrabbling for every dollar just to pay the taxes and feed bill, always hanging on by a thread. But he had never felt cheated when he had to go off to work while Roger Wilson and his crowd hung out and enjoyed the good life. He decided to change the subject.

"And Emma was standing in your way?"

"Emma was standing in everybody's way! I don't care if you were building a shopping center or a birdhouse, she was right there trying to stop you."

"What happened last week, Roger?"

"I don't know how she found out about it, but Emma came in here and told me that she knew about the plans for Cimarron Ridge and she was threatening to put a stop to it. She even had the names of my principal investors at Kanagawa Limited and said she was going to call them and let them know she was filing an injunction to stop the land swap."

"What happened then?"

"I admit it, I lost it. But you have to understand my position. Everything I have in the world is tied up in this project. Everything. If it fails, I'm done."

"And if it succeeds?"

"Then, I'm rich."

"You're already rich, Roger. How much is enough?"

He shook his head. "You don't get it, Sheriff. For a true visionary like myself, there is never enough. Yes, I'm well off, I won't deny that. But it takes hard work to maintain our lifestyle. I'm always involved in some new project, flying off to build a shopping mall or a high rise someplace, and as soon as it's done there's another one. But this project, I'm talking millions! I can stop all that and concentrate on the next phase of my life."

"Politics."

"Yes, politics! State Senator is just a steppingstone to the Governor's office, and from there…. I can do great things for this town, Jimmy. For this state. Hell, for the whole country! But I need to be able to focus all my energies in that direction. Cimarron Ridge gives me the freedom to do that."

"So when Emma came in threatening to expose your project, you lost it."

"I'm not proud of it," Wilson said. "But yes, I did. I was just so tired of her interfering in everything I tried to do that I shoved her up against the wall and told her I'd see her dead before I'd let her stop this project." He met Weber's eyes and said, "But that was it. I heard a gasp and looked over and saw my cleaning woman staring at me in horror and I came to my senses. I stepped back and Emma flew out the door. I never saw her again, and I didn't kill her. I swear."

"Where were you Tuesday night?" Weber asked.

He wouldn't meet Weber's eyes when he said, "I was… busy."

"Busy?"

"Yes, but I can't tell you what I was doing."

"Can't or won't?"

"It has no bearing on any of this."

"Look Roger, you're still my best bet for this murder, and I don't have time for any bullshit. In fact, given what you just told me, I have even more reason to think you're guilty. I'm about to put the handcuffs on you right now unless you can tell me where you were Tuesday night."

Weber could tell that Roger Wilson was desperate and at the end of his rope. He may have had dreams of political glory, and maybe even saw himself in the White House someday, but right then all he could see was his life going down the drain.

"Sheriff, again, I have to appeal to your discretion. If word gets out that I…"

"Roger, I don't care if you were dressing up in your wife's underwear and getting spanked by a big, hairy truck driver, or standing in front of the mirror practicing your inauguration speech, as long as you weren't up on the mountain shooting Emma Moyer. So out with it."

"I was… Tamara and I were together."

"When you say together you mean…?"

"You're going to make me say it, aren't you?"

"Yes I am, and then I'm going to confirm it with her, so think very carefully about what you say."

"You're enjoying this, aren't you?"

"I'm just doing my job, Roger. And yes, to be honest, some parts of my job are more enjoyable than others. Now, out with it."

"We were at her condo on Porcupine Lane from a little after 2 p.m. until about 7."

"And what were you doing there, Roger?"

"What do you think?"

"I'm thinking you were doing to her what you've done to a lot of your small investors over the years and are now looking forward to doing to the people you think are going to elect you to office."

Wilson's eyes hardened. "You think you're funny right now, but I'm not a good man to have as an enemy. You might want to remember that, Sheriff."

"You're not a good man, period," Weber told him. "But don't think you can threaten me, Roger. I don't care if they elect you Emperor someday, you and I both know I'll smash you like a bug if you get out of line in my town. I may only be a fool rancher's son, and I may not have had all of your advantages growing up or your bright future, but I'll do it. You can take that to the bank."

Wilson's last attempt to preserve any dignity evaporated and he said, "Tamara and I were in bed."

"For five hours? Maybe you're a better man than I gave you credit for."

"Don't be crude, Sheriff. We made love, then we fell asleep for a couple of hours, and when we woke up it was snowing hard. We made love again and then I showered and drove home."

"Get her in here."

"Do we really have to do this?" There was just a hint of a whine in Wilson's voice. He looked at Weber's stony face and picked up the telephone on his desk. When Tamara came on the line he said, "Could you come back here, please?"

Chapter 26

"I don't get it. The man's got more money than God, a beautiful wife who was a movie star, and a house that's almost a mansion up on that mountain. Why does a guy like that cheat on his wife?"

"I don't know. I think part of it's about power and a sense of entitlement as much as anything else, Tommy," Weber told the young deputy. "Just like movie stars and politicians and professional athletes who do things like that. I think they get to thinking that they're so important that the rules that the rest of us live by don't apply to them any more."

The young deputy shook his head. "I still don't get it. If I had a nice lady I loved, I'd treat her right and never do something like that."

Weber wanted to tell him that he knew Roger Wilson's wife, and while she was beautiful, she was far from innocent and had her own twisted sins. But Parks spoke up, saying, "From what I saw, you had a good woman, son, but you threw her away for your life of sin and debauchery with that guy from the bookstore!"

At the memory of Tami Gaylord's pursuit of him, Tommy blushed again and shook his head, saying, "That lady… that's just not right."

"So where are we now?" Coop asked. "Between us, Tommy and I have talked to everybody on the suspect list, and while we've eliminated quite a few, there are still plenty of people who had a grudge against Emma Moyer. And we still can't rule out Lenny Dewitt a hundred percent. Robyn had a lot of good reasons why he was unlikely, but we still know he had a hot temper, he was up there on that mountain unaccounted for and carrying a rifle during the approximate time she was killed, and we know that he shot at her earlier the same day. There are as many reasons to believe he did it as there are to believe that he didn't."

"I know," Weber agreed. "There are a lot of people here in town who think he did it, and it would sure be easy to just say he did and close the case. But Emma deserves better than that. We have to be sure."

"How can we be sure? The man's dead," Tommy said. "It's not like he can tell us anything. Or make a confession.”

“Did you get anything when you talked to his sons again?”

“No. To hear them talk, their old man was a saint,” Coop said. “They’re more interested in getting him shipped back home for burial and wanting to know when Brad Gleason goes on trial. They said they were headed home tomorrow unless you still need them here as part of their dad’s murder investigation.”

“I’ll feel better when they’re gone,” Weber replied. “If they find out we’ve released Brad, they’re going to be looking for him.”

“They’re going to find out no charges are being filed against Gleason sooner or later,” Coop said.

“Yeah, but I’d prefer they do it in Pennsylvania. I think I’ll drive over to the motel and talk to them one last time.”

***

The Dewitt brothers were all packed and ready to go, a stack of suitcases, duffel bags and cased rifles piled along the wall of their motel room. Both were unshaven and disheveled looking, and Weber wasn’t sure if that was due to their shock and grief over their father’s death, or if they routinely neglected their personal appearance.

“What’s happening with that little prick that killed my Dad?” Chuck, the older of the two, demanded when he opened the door to Weber’s knock. “I told those two deputies that came to get his shit that we want to see him before we leave.”

“I can’t let you do that,” Weber said. “In a felony investigation, witnesses and suspects have to be kept apart. Otherwise it can taint testimony, and you know how juries can be these days.”

“Yeah, well you can tell that little bastard that our sister Sherry has already filed for divorce. She never should have married him in the first place! If she hadn’t our Dad would still be alive.”

“How’s your mother holding up?” Weber asked, trying to move the subject away from Brad Gleason.

“How do you think she’s holding up?” asked Richey. “Her husband was murdered, we’re stuck here, and we don’t even know when we can go home and plan a funeral.”

“I just need to talk to you one last time,” Weber said, “and than you can go ahead and head back home. I just called the medical examiner’s office in Tucson and they will be releasing your father’s remains to be shipped home tomorrow. He was going to call your mother to make arrangements for transporting him home."

"Why's he in Tucson anyway?" Richey asked. "That's 200 miles from here."

"We're a small town," Weber told him. "We don't have the facilities for an autopsy here. We have to farm things like that out to Tucson and Phoenix."

"I don't know why they had to cut him up anyway," Richey complained. "They know what killed him, he was shot!"

"It's the law," Weber said. "Any unattended, unnatural death requires an autopsy if there is any question of a crime being committed."

"Any question?" Chuck exploded. "We all know a crime was committed! Brad murdered him in cold blood! All you need to do is sit his ass in the electric chair and fry him! Or let us handle it for you."

Weber didn't bother telling them that Arizona used lethal injection for administering the death sentence, let alone that he and Bob Bennett had decided that the case did not merit filing charges against Brad. As he had told Coop, he would feel better if Chuck and Richey found out about that decision once they were back in Pennsylvania.

"Anyway, I know we've been over all of this before, but I need to ask you some things."

"What things?" Richey demanded. "We've told you. Brad shot our Dad. We saw it, Jake and Sam Gibbons saw it, and Brad even admitted it! What more do you need?"

"Actually, I need to talk about last week, when your father went missing."

"What's that got to do with any of this?" Chuck asked, then stopped and pulled his head back. "Wait a minute, you're gonna try to pin that woman's death on our Dad, aren't you? That's it, isn't it? He's dead and can't defend himself and that makes it easy for you to wrap up that case. You dirty, rotten son-of-a bitch!"

"Calm down, son," Weber told him. "Nobody's trying to…"

"Don't call me son!" Chuck interrupted hotly. "I'm not your son. And if you think we're going to let you smear our Dad's name to make it easy for you to close that woman's case, you'd better think again! Dad was a good man and he never hurt anybody!"

Weber wanted to tell them that their father was a bully at best, and maybe even a psychopath, based upon what Brad Gleason had told him about the man. But he knew that wouldn't accomplish anything except to further antagonize them. Good or bad, Lenny Dewitt was still their father, and they were loyal to him in life and in death.

"I'm not trying to pin anything on anybody," Weber said. "I'm just trying to find the truth. There are a lot of people who think your father did kill Emma Moyer, and the easiest thing in the world for me to do is to just say "Okay" and close the case. But that's not the way I do things. Now, you tell me your dad didn't do it, okay, then help me prove it so I can clear his name."

Richey seemed to be the more reasonable of the two, and before his older brother could reply, he said, "Fine, ask your questions. But I don't know what more we can tell you. We've been over this again and again."

"You never know," Weber said. "Sometimes some little thing you forgot all about, because it didn't seem to matter, can be the key. Your dad said two hunters picked him up after he left Brad and Jake Gibbons, and they stopped and had a couple of drinks. Were you guys here when he got back?"

"Yeah, we were both here," Richey said.

"Do you remember what you were doing? It was snowing. Were you looking out the window for him? Were you watching TV? What?"

The brothers thought for a moment, then Richey said, "I was in the shower in the room next door that I was sharing with Brad. When I got out and was drying off, Chuck came in and said Dad was back."

"So you never saw the guys who dropped him off?"

"No."

"How about you, Chuck? Where were you?"

"In our room laying on the bed, watching TV."

"Did you see the two guys your dad was with, or their truck?"

"No. The door just opened and the old man came in. I told him they had a search party out for him, and he said that was stupid. He said he'd gotten a ride with a couple of guys and they stopped at some bar and he bought them a couple of beers and they shot the shit for a while."

"Did you hear the truck? Did it have loud pipes, maybe a loud stereo playing?"

"No, man, nothing. The TV was on and I didn't hear anything."

Weber tried to rock their memories for anything else they might have forgotten, to no avail. Whoever had picked up Lenny Dewitt, if anybody actually had, seemed to be as big a mystery as everything else associated with Emma's murder. He expressed his sympathies for their loss, wished the brothers a safe trip home, and promised to be in touch if there were any new developments.

"The only new development I want to know is when they execute that bastard that killed our Dad," Chuck told him. "Because I plan to be right there watching and laughing at him as he goes to Hell."

Chapter 27

"Emma had cancer? I had no idea. She never said a word about it to me."

The last few days had taken a toll on Richard MacEwen. He seemed to have aged and shrunk since Weber had seen him at Emma's house on Sunday. His eyes were lifeless and his shoulders slumped as he sat in his mail truck outside the post office.

"Had she been seeing a doctor, that you know of?"

MacEwen shook his head. "I think Emma hated doctors almost as much as she did developers and hunters. She thought most of the medicines they dispense do more harm than good, and that the body could heal itself with natural remedies."

Weber remembered seeing an assortment of supplements and herbs from the health food store in Springerville in Emma's medicine cabinet.

"I wonder…," MacEwen said, and then his voice trailed off.

"What, Richard?"

The mailman shrugged his shoulders, then said, "I don't know. Like I told you before, the last few months Emma had changed. It was like she was mad at the world and she kept pushing and pushing, kind of like she had to stop everything she could and there was no letup. Maybe she knew time was running out?"

"It makes sense," Weber told him. "The medical examiner I spoke with said it was pretty advanced, and he was amazed that she was even able to be out in the woods like that, chasing down the hunters, in her condition."

"It doesn't surprise me. You knew Emma, Sheriff. She was committed to her work and lived and breathed it. I just wish…," his voice broke and he couldn't hold back his anguish. Weber put a hand on his shoulder as he lay his head down on the steering wheel and sobbed. After a moment or two, MacEwen raised his head and wiped away his tears. "I just wish I had known. Maybe I could have made her get some kind of treatment."

"You're right. I knew Emma, too," Weber told him. "And you and I both know that nobody could make her do anything she didn't want to."

"At least I could have been here with her last week, so she wouldn't have died alone up there on the damn mountain!"

"Listen, Richard, you have to stop beating yourself up like this. You had no way of knowing that Emma was sick, or that some psycho was going to be waiting for her up on that mountain. Your daughter needed you to be there for her birthday. That's where you belonged. None of us can predict the future. All we can do is make the best decisions we can at the time, with the information we have available."

Even as he spoke the words his mind flashed back to recent events in his own life, and Weber knew that they offered little comfort. But they were all he had to offer.

"I'll tell you this," MacEwen said, sitting up in his seat and looking through the windshield, "I'm a pacifist. I've never had a fight in my life, Sheriff. But if whoever the bastard is that hurt my Emma was standing here in front of me right now, I'd rip his head off and stomp it flat!" He turned his face to Weber and met his eyes with determination, then started his truck and drove away.

As Weber watched the mail truck make the turn at the end of the block, he thought of Richard MacEwen and Ralph Tigthe, two men that have loved the same woman a lifetime apart. Men who were as different as night and day, but who were united in their love for Emma Moyer, their grief over her death, and their loathing for whoever had pulled the trigger and taken her away.

***

Brad Gleason sat with Christine at the scarred wooden kitchen table in the small three room cabin at SafeHaven, staring listlessly off into space.

"How are you doing?" Weber asked him.

Brad shrugged, but didn't reply.

Weber pulled a business card out of his pocket and put it on the table. "This is a friend of mine named Molly Bateson. She's going to be stopping by this afternoon to talk to you, Brad. She's a psychologist, and she's on call for SafeHaven."

Brad shook his head. "A shrink isn't going to make what happened go away."

"No, it's not," Weber agreed. "But she can help you deal with all of this."

The young man didn't react, just shrugged his shoulders again.

"Listen, Brad, I know what you're going through," Weber told him. "A while back I had to shoot a young man who had killed and mutilated somebody, and then shot one of my deputies. And even though I didn't have a choice, just like you didn't with Lenny, the guilt eats you alive. I know that. Talking to Molly has really helped me learn how to handle it. Just talk to her, okay?"

Finally Brad looked across the table at Weber.

"Why are you doing this, Sheriff? All of this? You, Mr. Bennett, Miss Ridgeway and everybody? I don't deserve any of this. You people don't even know me. Why do you care?"

"Hon, we care because you're a good person who's been stuck in a bad situation for a long time," Christine said, reaching her arm across the table to put a hand on Brad's. "None of this is your fault. Not what happened yesterday, and not any of what's been happening all along. You deserve to be happy, Brad, and you deserve to be treated with respect, not spending your life being abused and called names."

A tear rolled down Brad's cheek and he looked at them with the haunted eyes of a dog that has been beaten too many times, but he couldn't speak. Weber wondered if the sad young man had been pushed too far and would ever be happy again. But he knew that if anybody could help him regain his self-respect and sense of self-worth, it would be Christine.

In the meantime, he still had Emma Moyer's death to investigate. Unfortunately, Brad could offer him no more than Chuck and Richey had. He had been reading a book in the motel room he shared with Richey when Chuck came in and told them that Lenny had returned. He had not been aware of the sound of a vehicle coming or going, and had heard nothing that might identify the men Lenny said had given him a ride.

Driving away from SafeHaven, Weber wondered if the men were real or just an alibi Lenny had made up to cover for him shooting Emma, and if there was any way he could prove it, one way or the other. He wished he could simply take the easy route and blame the crime on the dead man and get on with his life, but that wasn't Weber's way. He believed in justice, even though he knew it wasn't always found in a law book, and Emma deserved justice. It was Weber's job to see that she got it, no matter how long it took him to find the truth.

***

Jake Gibbons was splitting firewood with a hydraulic splitter when Weber pulled into the ranch yard. He shut the motor down and walked over to the Explorer.

"Howdy, Sheriff. What can I do for you?"

"Sorry to interrupt your work there, Jake."

"Hell, you grew up on a ranch," Jake said, breathing hard. "Never a shortage of work. It ain't going anywhere."

"Jake, I have to ask you about the thing with Emma at the gun shop. Matt Wells said Emma was really creating a scene."

"Yeah, she was about as out of control as I'd ever seen her. And believe me, I've seen her go off more than once!"

"Matt said you picked Emma up and carried her out of the shop and you two went at it pretty hot and heavy."

"If you're asking me if I killed that woman, Sheriff, no I didn't. Yeah, I'd have liked to have wrung her neck a time or two, but that's not my way. Tell you the truth, as much as she pissed me off from time to time, I admired Emma in a way, too. I'd rather have somebody look me in the eye and tell me that they hate me than mess with some of these new people coming into town slapping you on the back with one hand and sticking a knife in you with the other. And I sympathized with a lot of what Emma was trying to do. There was a time when I knew everybody on this mountain at least enough to wave to. Now we've got some fancy new place going up every week and I'm a stranger in my own hometown. Couple months ago I was on Old Dan, riding along the road out there one evening, and some gal in a little car that cost more than I'll make in a year came roaring up and screeched to a stop beside me, complaining about having to drive over horse shit in the road. Hell Sheriff, horse shit in the road! For all her craziness, maybe Emma was right."

Weber chuckled and said, "You and me, we've shoveled some horse shit in our time."

"Tell you the truth, Sheriff, it ain't the horse shit that bothers me as much as the chicken shit. That seems to be piling up deeper and deeper around here these days."

Chapter 28

The sheriff knew that evening's Town Council meeting was going to be a hot one, and he wasn't disappointed. Councilwoman Gretchen Smith-Abbot, Chet Wingate's staunchest ally, fired the opening salvo.

"Sheriff Weber, how dare you humiliate our mayor with this restraining order of yours? It's simply unconscionable!"

"It wasn't my restraining order," Weber told her. "All I did was serve it, which is part of my job."

"Nonsense! This is just one more attempt on your part to besmirch the good name of Mayor Wingate."

"Sheriff Weber is right," Bob Bennett said. "The restraining order was filed by Christine Ridgeway, on behalf of SafeHaven. Part of the Sheriff's duties include serving legal documents like this."

"Do you have any idea how this made me look to the voters of this town?" Chet demanded. "My reputation has been ruined!"

"Voters, Chet? They're not citizens to you, they're just voters, right?"

"Enough," Kirby Templeton said, rapping his gavel and sending Weber a stern look. "We're not going to turn this into another episode of the personal soap opera you two are always embroiled in." He turned to Bennett and asked, "What's this restraining order all about, Bob?"

"Yesterday Mayor Wingate took a young man out to SafeHaven whose wife was staying there, demanding that he be allowed to talk to her. Sheriff Weber and Deputy Cooper responded to keep the peace."

Kirby looked at the mayor is surprise. "You really did that, Chet?"

"A man's got a right to speak to his wife," the mayor said. "This is a perfect example of how that place is already destroying the very fabric of this community and tearing families apart!"

"Chet, do you realize the danger you put Ms. Ridgeway and her clients in? Not to mention the position you put this town in? What if that man had pulled a gun and started shooting? Not only could we have had a tragedy out there, but the liabilities are terrifying."

"All I was trying to do was help put a family back together. After all, the woman wound up going home with her husband when it was all over. Right back where she should have been in the first place!"

"Are you crazy, Chet?" Councilman Frank Gauger asked. "Of all the dumb stunts you've pulled, this tops the cake!"

"I was just doing my job," the mayor said stubbornly. "And that's not the point of all this anyway."

"Then what is the point?" Gauger demanded.

"The point is, Sheriff Weber publicly humiliated me by serving that paper on me in public, in my own store. And he brought the newspaperman along to photograph it!"

"If anybody humiliated you, it was yourself," Weber said. "Throwing a tantrum and ripping the restraining order up, right on camera."

Before Chet could respond, Templeton rapped his gavel again. "Enough! Sheriff, you and I both know you could have handled serving those papers in a more discreet way. I usually support you, but this was pushing the envelope way past what's acceptable, and I'm not impressed."

Weber expected the reprimand, but it was worth it to him to get a jab back at the mayor after all of his attacks over the years. Still, he did his best to look chagrined as he nodded in acknowledgement of the senior councilman's comments.

"Now, as for you," Templeton said, turning to the mayor, "I'm a heartbeat away from asking for a vote of No Confidence in you, Chet. You stay away from SafeHaven and mind your own business from now on."

"Anything that happens in this town is my business," Chet said, "And you don't have the authority to order me to do anything. You're just one member of the Council." He sat back with his arm folded stubbornly.

"That's simple enough," Frank Gauger said. "Enough of this nonsense. I make a motion that the Town Council order Mayor Wingate to stay away from SafeHaven in his official capacity."

"Seconded," said Templeton. "All in favor, raise your hand and say aye."

Every member of the Council, except Chet Wingate and Councilwoman Smith-Abbot, voted in favor of the motion and Templeton rapped his gavel once again, putting the matter to rest. "There you have it, Chet. You pushed the issue and now it's official. Let's move on to the next order of business."

The mayor had lost battles with the Town Council before, and with a couple of exceptions, most of the members supported Weber more often than not, but this overwhelming defeat seemed to rock his world and he was subdued during the rest of the meeting.

After dealing with a few other issues, such as approving overtime pay for the town employees who had worked to clear the roads after the blizzard, Councilman Mel Walker asked, "Sheriff, can you give us a update on these two shootings?"

"We made an arrest in the shooting of Lenny Dewitt, and after examining all of the evidence, Bob Bennett and I determined that no crime was committed and that the shooting was accidental. Mr. Dewitt was shot by his son-in-law, Bradley Gleason, after threatening the young man with a knife, in front of several witnesses."

"Accidental and not self-defense?" Councilman Walker asked. "Why is that?"

"If I may," said Bob Bennett, before Weber could reply, and Kirby Templeton nodded, "We'll share information on the shooting, but we ask that what we are going to tell you be kept confidential for a while yet."

"Why is that?" Walker asked.

Bennett explained the situation and the fear that if Lenny Dewitt's sons knew that the man who had shot their father had been released, his safety would be in danger. As expected, Councilwoman Smith-Abbot mumbled something about the public's right to know, but when the mayor remained silent, she let it drop.

"Okay, that's one down. What can you tell us about Emma Moyer's murder?" Councilman Walker asked.

"I'm afraid I can't tell you much, since that's still an open investigation," Weber replied.

"I've heard a lot of talk around town that this Dewitt fellow that got himself killed did it."

"Mel, I'd tell you more if I could," Weber said. "Mr. Dewitt was a suspect, but I can't prove he did it, at this point. He's still a viable suspect, but I'm looking at other avenues too, which I'm not at liberty to discuss."

Walker nodded and let the subject drop, and Weber expected the mayor to push the issue as he had in past criminal investigations, but he remained quiet. Whether Chet Wingate was truly contrite in the face of his official censure or was just pouting, Weber found the silence from his direction refreshing, and the meeting soon ended.

Kirby Templeton caught up with Weber and Paul Lewis outside on the sidewalk. "I don't suppose I could convince you not to run those pictures on the front page tomorrow could I, Paul?"

"Kirby, you know better than to ask me that. The mayor losing it and making even more of an ass out of himself in public than usual? There's not a newspaper in the world that could pass that up."

Templeton shook his head. "I understand where you're coming from, but this town has taken one hit after another lately. I had to ask."

"Hey, look at it this way," Paul said. "Between the Council's vote just now and tomorrow's paper, maybe the good citizens of Big Lake will finally get enough and boot Chet out of office come next election. That would make you a shoo-in for his job."

"No thank you," Templeton said, shaking his head again. "I don't want it. I've got enough to do already between running the pharmacy and moderating the Council meetings."

"You know I'd support you with the paper," Paul said.

"I appreciate that, Paul, I really do. But I really don't want the job."

"Well, we need somebody new," Paul said. "It's time, Kirby. Chet gets worse every day. This stuff with SafeHaven, it really could have turned out bad."

"I'm not disagreeing with you," the councilman said. "But not me. Who knows? Chet was pretty quiet after the vote tonight. Maybe he learned a lesson. Anyway, I promised Angela I'd be home as soon as the meeting was over. She's feeling poorly."

"Nothing serious I hope," Weber said.

"Naa, she took a fall stocking a top shelf yesterday and is down with her back. I keep telling her to stay off ladders. That's what we've got hired help for, but she's a stubborn old woman. But don't worry, I'm going go home and rub some liniment on her and she'll be back to work tomorrow, ordering me around like a drill sergeant."

As they watched the councilman's car disappear down the street, Paul said, "He's a good man. I'd sure like to see him challenge Chet for mayor."

Weber nodded, then the newspaperman asked, "Do you want a look at the layout for tomorrow's front page?"

"Does a bear go caca behind a cranberry bush?"

Laughing, Paul led him across the street to his office.

Chapter 29

The weekly edition of the Big Lake Herald hit the street Wednesday morning and was sold out by noon. Just as Mary had predicted, everybody in town wanted a copy of the paper, where four photos spread across the top of the front page under the bold headline Mayor Explodes, showed Weber serving Mayor Wingate with the restraining order, him ripping the papers in half, then kicking them across the floor of his hardware store in a rage, and finally shaking his fist at the sheriff. The bottom half of the page was split in half, one reporting on Emma Moyer's murder, and the other, the shooting death of Lenny Dewitt. Paul had agreed to withhold information on the decision not to charge Brad Gleason until after Chuck and Richey had left town, writing only that a suspect was being questioned and the investigation was still ongoing at press time.

"Look at you gloat," Parks said to Paul over lunch at the ButterCup Café, "You must be very happy with yourself. Three big stories on page one. How often does that happen? I can see a Pulitzer in your future."

"It's a good day to be a newspaperman," Paul agreed.

"Well, here's a head start on next week's issue for you," Parks told him. "My new office is getting delivered next Monday."

"Really? I hadn't heard that," Weber said.

"Just got the call this morning," Parks told him.

"Does this mean I get the extra desk in my office back?"

"Yes it does, Bubba, but that don't mean you can rent your spare bedroom out. I plan to keep freeloading off you until we're both old and gray. And when you get old enough to turn senile, I'm going to start charging you rent!"

"Hell Parks, you're at Marsha's more nights than you're at my place. You should just make it official and move in with her and her momma."

"Uh uh," Parks said, "I do that and the next thing you know she'll be making me kick in for half the groceries and carry out the trash!"

"He really has perfected the art of mooching, hasn't he?" Paul said.

"Oh, yes sir!" Parks assured him. "This ain't my first rodeo, just a different arena."

"So tell me about your new digs," Paul said as Dan Wright and Coop joined them, taking the empty seats across from Weber.

"It's one of those park model trailers like the old farts live in down in those retirement communities in Phoenix and Apache Junction. Except when we got the Town Council to approve it, one of the requirements was that it come with fake log cabin siding to blend in with the town's ambience. We're gonna put it in the back corner of the Sheriff's Office parking lot so I can be close at hand, in case Jimmy needs me. Or if Archer brings in fresh donuts."

While they were laughing, the waitress came by to take their orders, and after she left Coop said, "I talked to Jake Gibbons this morning. He said he was taking Chuck and Richey Dewitt to Sky Harbor in Phoenix this afternoon to fly back home. They wanted to know when they could get the rifle back that we seized after their father's shooting. I wasn't sure how you wanted to handle that, since technically it isn't evidence if the case is closed, but we don't want them to know it yet."

"We'll wait until they're home and ship it to a gun shop back in Pennsylvania, and they can pick it up there," Weber said.

"Personally, that seems pretty ghoulish to me," Dan said. "Would you want to have a gun back that killed somebody, let alone somebody you knew?"

"To each their own," Weber said, thinking about the fine Colt .45 semiautomatic pistol he had killed Steve Rafferty with, now cut into pieces and resting on the bottom of the lake.

***

"Looks like somebody wants to talk to you," Coop said, nodding at a couple standing in the parking lot of the Sheriff's Office when they returned from lunch.

Weber recognized the woman as Sharleen Collins, who worked in the high school cafeteria. She wore a strained expression and was wringing her hands nervously. He thought that the man with her was her husband, Rocky or Ricky, something like that, but he wasn't sure.

"I'll see you inside," Weber told his deputies and approached them. "How are you folks doing today?"

"We're sorry to bother you but we need to talk to you, Sheriff," Sharleen said, obviously apprehensive. The man didn't say anything, but looked worried. Weber wasn't sure what their concern was, he had only met the woman a couple of times and didn't know her husband except by sight.

"How about we go inside where it's warm," he suggested, and they exchanged panicked looks.

"Look, Sheriff, we're trying to do the right thing. But we can't afford any trouble."

"Okay."

"Rocky did something stupid last week, and we're trying to make it right. But we can't afford any trouble," the woman said again.

"Rocky, unless you robbed a bank or killed somebody, we can work it out one way or the other," Weber said. "You didn't do something like that, did you?"

"No sir," Rocky said, shifting from one foot to the other, either from the cold, nerves, or a combination of the two. "It's about that fellow that got himself shot. The one that's picture was in the newspaper."

"Let's talk inside," Weber said.

***

"We can't afford any trouble," Sharleen Collins told Weber a third time as they took the chairs indicated next to his desk. "We really can't."

"Like I said, unless you committed a major felony, we can work something out," Weber assured them. "What do you know about the man in the newspaper?"

Rocky cleared his throat and looked toward his wife, who said, "Go on, Rocky, tell the Sheriff."

"I'll just lay it out and hope for your understanding. Everybody says you're a good man, Sherriff. I try to be, too."

Weber tried to hide his impatience and waited for Rocky to go on. Finally, he did.

"Well sir, I knew it was wrong. My license is suspended because of a DUI, but with hunting season, well, we depend on that meat to get us through the winter. So yeah, we went hunting, my brother Mitchell and me. And I was driving. Please, Sheriff, I can't afford to go to jail! I just got hired at the new carpet store and I can't lose my job."

"That's your big crime, you were driving a car with a suspended license?"

"Yes sir. My truck, actually. I'd have made Mitch drive, but he can't drive a stick shift. Never was able to learn how. Stalls it out every time."

"Okay, what about the man in the newspaper?"

"We come up on him when he was walking down the road up there on Tomahawk Mountain and gave him a ride. He seemed like a nice guy, kind of pissed off at the world at first, but we got to talking and then he warmed right up. Even bought us a couple of beers when we got back to town."

"I don't know what you were thinking, Rocky," Sharleen snapped. "One DUI and a suspended license already, less than a month to go before you get your license back, and you not only go driving, you stop at a bar! Every time you get together with that brother of yours it leads to trouble."

"Baby, I know. I just..."

"Okay, you two can discuss this later," Weber told them. "Tell me about the man you picked up. You're sure it was the same one whose picture is in today's paper?"

"Yes sir," Rocky said. "I even remembered his name. Lenny. I've got a cousin back in Michigan named Lenny."

"Yeah, and he's just as big a loser as that brother of yours," Sharleen said sharply.

"Now Baby, that's just not true. Lenny can't help it if he's had a run of bad luck."

"Four wives in eight years isn't bad luck, Rocky, it's ridiculous! How many times has he called us and..."

"Let's get back to the man you and your brother picked up," Weber interrupted. "Did he tell you what he was doing up there all alone, on foot?"

"He said he got in a fight with his guide and was walking back to town. It was snowing pretty hard and we gave him a ride. He was complaining about his kid or somebody not shooting a deer and some crazy lady shooting a gun off in the air."

"What time did you pick him up?" Weber asked.

Rocky shrugged. "Not sure. It was late afternoon and it was snowing hard."

"Where along the road did you pick him up?"

"We were at the third parking area, just getting back to the truck, when he came walking past. We thought he was lost at first."

"Hang on," Weber said, and left the office to return in a moment with Chad and the topographic map they had used to plan the search for

Lenny Dewitt the week before. Chad listened to Rocky's story, studied the map, and asked, "You're sure it was the third parking area?"

"Yes sir. That's where we always park and hunt from."

"That's right here," Chad said, showing Weber the spot on the map. "Maybe a quarter mile down the mountain from where Jake Gibbons said he was parked. Maybe a little more."

"Did you see any other vehicles up there on the mountain?" Weber asked. "Either parked or going up or down the road?"

Rocky shook his head.

"And where did you go for these beers he bought you?"

"The Antler Inn," Rocky said. "It's the first place we came to. It was packed, but we managed to get a booth in the back by the pool table."

Fifteen minutes later they had learned everything Rocky could tell them, and Weber thanked them and sent them on their way with a strong warning to Rocky to stay out from behind the wheel until it was legal for him to drive again. Though, given the story and the stop at the Antler Inn, he suspected it was only a matter of time before the man found his license suspended again.

"Well, that pretty much rules Lenny Dewitt out as Emma's killer," Chad said once the couple had left. "He met up with Rocky and his brother before Jake and Brad came down the mountain looking for him, and they were parked downhill from where Jake had left his truck. Emma was uphill from there. There's no way he hiked up to where she was and came upon her at just the right time, cut her tires, shot her, then hiked back down past where Jake was still parked and got picked up by those two. It just doesn't add up."

"I agree," Weber said. "Which means we still have a killer on our hands."

He stood up and said, "You run down Rocky's brother and see if he has anything to add. I'm going to see if I can catch up with Jake before he takes those two guys back to Phoenix. Their father may have been a jerk in a lot of ways, but they deserve to know he wasn't a murderer."

***

Jake Gibbons was just pulling out of the parking lot of the Mountain Mist Motel when Weber got there. He bleeped his siren to get Jake's attention, and the guide pulled over.

"I hope you came to tell us that Brad hung himself in his cell," Chuck said when Weber walked up to the truck.

"No, but I do have some news for you."

When he finished telling them what he had learned about their father and where he had been after he left Jake and Brad on the mountain the day of Emma Moyer's murder, Chuck was just as hostile as he had been all along.

"We told you our Dad wasn't a murderer! But you wouldn't listen to us, would you?"

"I'm sorry," Weber told him. "But I had a job to do. I still do."

"I could give a damn about that silly assed woman who got herself shot up there on that mountain," Chuck said. "How about you just do your job and make sure Brad fries for killing our Dad?"

Weber stepped back and watched Jake's truck pull away, thinking that the old saying about the acorn not falling far from the tree was certainly true of Lenny Dewitt and his sons.

Chapter 30

"All I can say is, if I had known this was such a busy little town, I'd have asked for more pay before I signed on," Coop said. "Folks around here sure weave some tangled webs."

"So we've eliminated Lenny Dewitt as a suspect," Chad said. "Now where are we?"

"I have a question," Coop said. "Do we know Roger Wilson's alibi is good?"

"He called the receptionist back to his office and she gave basically the same story, without any coaching. They left the office in early afternoon and drove to her condo in separate cars but got there within a couple of minutes of each other. They had sex, slept for a while, woke up and did the deed a second time, then Roger took a shower and drove home about 7. She knew the time because she flipped on the TV while he was in the shower and the six o'clock news was just wrapping up."

"I know it's a long shot," Coop ventured, "But could they have rehearsed all of that in advance, just in case somebody came around asking questions?"

Chad shrugged. "If I were a married man getting ready to announce a run for Senate, I think I'd find a better excuse than that I was shacked up with my secretary all afternoon. A scorned wife isn't too good for a man's political aspirations. My MaryAnn's a sweet lady, but if she ever caught me fooling around on her, my head would be hanging over the fireplace beside a couple of deer I've taken over the years."

Something nibbled at Weber's mind as they continued to talk, running down and eliminating other suspects on their list, or shifting their priorities around, and as the meeting went on, a thought was beginning to form.

"In spite of his alibi, out of everybody we've talked about, Roger Wilson is still the one person who had the most to lose by Emma's interference. He was seen assaulting Emma and was heard warning her to stay out of his business. He even admitted to me that he told her he'd see her dead before he'd let her stop this latest project of his. Parks, you've got more resources than we do in the technical area. Is there any way you can take a deeper look at his financial situation? In the past he's used mostly investor money for his projects, but he told me everything he has is wrapped up in this new Cimarron Ridge development. Given enough money, and with his political future on the line, who knows what lengths a guy like that would go to?"

"I'll see what I can dig up," Parks said.

"Anybody have anything else to add?" Weber asked.

"I went by the garage and talked to Randy Laird," Dolan said. "All four of Emma's tires had been slashed with what had to be a heavy-bladed knife. The cuts were each four to six inches long. You don't do that with a kitchen knife."

"No chances of getting any fingerprints off the tires or wheels?"

Dolan shook his head. "With the snow and getting moved around and all, nothing."

"I think those condos where Tamara Radcliffe lives on Porcupine Lane have security cameras," Tommy Frost said. "Do you want me to go by and see if they maybe caught Roger Wilson coming and going last week?

"Good idea. Check it out." Weber said. Anything else?"

Nobody had any more to offer and the meeting broke up.

***

Chad's comment about a scorned wife and Weber's own remark to Roger Wilson that he had met the developer's wife, nagged at the sheriff. As Chad had said, MaryAnn Summers was a sweet woman who was proud of her small town background and morals, but Laura Wilson was a different creature altogether.

A stunning redhead with big green eyes, an amazing body, and perfect skin that had taken her all the way to Hollywood, Laura was proof that beauty was only skin deep, no matter how enticing that skin may be. Weber knew that what lurked beneath the surface was a twisted woman with a taste for rough sex and a devious mind. Laura was an accomplished actress who could play the role of an airhead or a scheming seductress just as easily, and he had seen her jump from character to character instantly, right in front of his eyes.

Among Laura's many extramarital dalliances had been a man

named Phil Johnson, who had ended up dead in the back of an armored car, murdered by the sheriff's own sister in a crime that had rocked the little town of Big Lake to its very foundations. The investigation into that crime had revealed Laura's sexual appetite, and the fact that when caught cheating, her wealthy husband would beat her as punishment. But even when cuckolded, Roger Wilson was always aware of the importance of keeping up appearances. "Roger is always very careful when he bruises me. He always hits me on the body, never on the face or arms, so nothing ever shows. Can't cause a scandal, you know," Laura had told the sheriff, matter-of-factly.

To add yet another facet to Laura, during the investigation into the armored car hijacking that had left Phil Wilson and Mike Perkins, Weber's brother-in-law, dead, he learned that she had once shot a movie producer to death, claiming he attempted to rape her. While most people in the know in Hollywood said it was actually a case of a newer actress who used the casting couch to get a starring role in a film that had been promised to Laura, she still managed to walk free on a self-defense plea.

"I'm going up to talk to Laura Wilson," Weber said, "do you want to ride along?"

Well aware of the other woman's background and that fact that she had offered herself to Weber in the past, Robyn wasted no time following him out to the Explorer.

"So what's up with Laura?"

"Well, I know Roger and her seem to have this weird relationship where he almost seems to accept her hopping from bed to bed, but I'm wondering if she is aware that he's doing some fooling around, too."

"You're going to tell her about him and the receptionist?"

"I thought I'd just kind of feel her out and see if she says anything about it."

"Oh, bad choice of words!" Robyn said. "Talk about scorned women, don't make me go seven kinds of crazy on you, Jimmy. This girl don't share her toys!"

"Jealous?" Weber teased.

"No, possessive," Robyn told him, taking his hand.

"Well, you've got nothing to worry about there," he assured her, squeezing her hand.

"Yeah, you're faithful as an old dog, right?"

"Well, that, and I've seen how good you can shoot!"

Chapter 31

Weber had not seen or spoken to Laura Wilson in months, but she acted like they had just had lunch together at the country club the day before, when she opened the door.

"Sheriff! What a pleasant surprise. Please, come in."

They stepped inside, wiping snow off their shoes, and Laura turned a dazzling smile on Robyn. "You must be Deputy Fuchette? I've heard so much about you. My, you are pretty!" She touched Robyn's cheek with three fingers, almost a caress, then looked at Weber with what bordered on a leer, "You're a lucky man, Sheriff!"

Weber didn't reply, but he saw Robyn color slightly, though he wasn't sure if it was embarrassment that their personal relationship was so well known, Laura's unexpected touch, or anger over the other woman's veiled compliment on her looks. In Laura's world, pretty could never compete against beautiful.

Laura showed her visitors to seats on a leather sofa with an awesome panoramic view of the town and lake below them through the floor to ceiling windows. Dressed in a red silk pantsuit with enough buttons open at the top to show plenty of cleavage and the fact that she wasn't wearing a bra, she sat across from them on a loveseat.

"So, to what do I owe the pleasure of your visit?"

"Laura, have you ever heard of a woman named Emma Moyer?"

"Oh, so this isn't a social visit?" she replied with an exaggerated pout. "You really need to let him off the leash more, Robyn, dear. All work and no play and all that. Although, who knows, maybe Jimmy likes being on a leash?"

When a man works with a woman every day and sleeps beside her a lot of nights, he learns to read her body language and moods, and Weber knew that Robyn didn't find Laura Wilson at all charming, but she masked it well and didn't reply.

"Emma Moyer," Weber repeated. "Is that name familiar to you, Laura?"

"Yes, I know who she is. That crazy, activist lady who's always making Roger so mad. He's thrown more than one tantrum over the things she's done to interfere in his business."

"Are you aware that Ms. Moyer was murdered last week?"

"Surely you don't consider me a suspect, do you, Sheriff?"

Weber had not considered that possibility, but it was one to look into. Emma's constant interruptions were causing Roger Wilson to lose a lot of time and potentially, a lot of money. Had his wife been involved?

"Where were you last Tuesday afternoon, Laura?"

"Oh my God, I am a suspect?" she asked, laughing musically. Apparently she found the idea of being the focus of a murder investigation a novel idea. But Weber reminded himself that Laura was an actress so one could never know what was real in her world.

"Last Tuesday, Laura?"

"Oh, you're like that grouchy old Sergeant Joe Friday in that old TV cop show from when I was a tiny little girl," Laura pouted, changing roles. "Just the facts, ma'am. Don't you ever believe in having any fun?"

Before Weber could reply, Laura leaned over the heavy wood coffee table toward Robyn, giving the deputy a good view down her blouse. "How about you, pretty lady? Do you like to have fun? Or maybe you're the one who prefers being on a leash?"

Robyn kept her eyes focused on Laura's and didn't reply, and the other woman sat back down. "Why is everybody so serious in this town? To answer your question, Sheriff, I was home all day last Tuesday, watching the storm come in and waiting for Roger to get home."

"Do you know where your husband was?"

"Of course I do. He spent the morning in his office on a series of conference calls and the afternoon in bed with his receptionist."

So much for the scorned woman theory, thought Weber. If Laura Wilson was upset by her husband's infidelity, she hid it well.

Laura laughed again, and said, "Oh, you should see the look on your faces! You two seemed so shocked. Don't you at least watch television or go to a movie once in a while? You know, dear, there are more positions than just missionary with the lights off," she told Robyn.

The deputy didn't answer, and Laura smirked at them. "In the real world, outside this provincial little town with all of its hang-ups and inhibitions, people understand that sex isn't this big romantic thing with fireworks exploding and hearts throbbing. It's just physical fun and it doesn't have to be limited to the bedroom, or to whatever society thinks is the sacred institution of marriage. So yes, I know all about my husband and Tamara. Just like Roger knows that I have an occasional fling. It's no big thing. She's his current plaything, just another toy, like his fancy cars and his airplane."

"And you?" Robyn asked, speaking for the first time.

For just an instant Laura's look turned icy. "Yes, I'm a toy too. But some toys a man keeps and some he plays with for a while and throws away when he loses interest. Have you figured out which one you are, dear?"

Robyn didn't reply, though Weber felt her stiffen imperceptibly beside him. Laura switched roles again, back to the charming hostess she had been upon their arrival.

"Sheriff, neither myself nor Roger had anything to do with the death of that woman. As I said, I was here all afternoon and I made a series of telephone calls to my mother and sister in Tucson and to a friend in Los Angeles. I'm sure if you check our telephone records you can confirm that, as well as the fact that Roger was in his office during the morning and at Tamara's during the afternoon of the storm. You'll have to look elsewhere to solve your crime. Now, can I offer either of you a drink, or perhaps a cup of coffee?"

With nothing more to be gained from talking to Laura, Weber thanked her for her time and they started to leave. As she showed them to the door, Laura touched Robyn's arm and said, 'I'm sorry if I shocked you, dear."

"To each their own. If your husband wants to boink his secretary and you don't care, it's none of my business," she replied.

"Well, as I said, Roger's not the only one who has 'friends.' And he is a very generous man. In fact," she said stepping closer and leaning in as if to share a confidence, "He likes to share his toys with me. You should try it some time." And with that she kissed Robyn.

***

"She stuck her tongue in my mouth!" Robyn shouted as Weber drove down the mountain. "Ackkk! I'm gonna puke."

"Damn, you can hit hard!" Weber told her. "Remind me never to piss you off. She must have landed eight feet away."

"Yeah, and did you see the smirk she gave me when she wiped the blood off her mouth and cooed and said she likes it rough? And then she said butch women turn her on! Butch? Me?"

Weber laughed in spite of himself as Robyn took a long pull from a bottle of water, swished it around in her mouth, and then spit out the window. She wiped her mouth, not for the first time, and glared at him.

"Not one word, Jimmy! Not to Parks, not to Mary, and not to Marsha. Oh God, especially not to Marsha. And wipe that grin off your face."

"My lips are sealed," he promised. "Kind of makes you wish yours had been too, huh?"

"Jimmy, I'm warning you…"

"Okay, okay. Not a word."

He rounded a curve and tapped the brake pedal to slow down as two cow elk ambled across the road.

"Can I ask just one thing, Robyn?"

"What?"

"Was it as good for you as it was for me?"

Weber was shocked. He knew Robyn wasn't a child and that she had grown up in the big city, but he had no idea that the usually modest woman he loved knew so many filthy words.

Chapter 32

"The security video Tommy got from the condo office confirms it," Chad said, pushing the play button on the video player. "There's no way Roger Wilson was up on the mountain last Tuesday." The timestamp on the black and white video showed Tamara Ridegway's Lincoln Navigator pulling into her parking slot at 2:06 p.m. Tuesday. Three minutes later Roger Wilson's white Ford Expedition slid in next to it and he went into the condo. Chad fast forwarded, the video becoming a blur that stabilized when he released the button. It took a couple of attempts for him to reach the frames that showed Wilson leaving. By then snow was falling hard and the quality wasn't as sharp, but there was no question that it was Roger Wilson who left Laura's apartment at 7:13 and got into his SUV and drove away.

"After Tommy was done with it, I watched every minute of the video twice, at about three times faster than normal," Chad said. "The camera is pointed toward the condo door and nobody else came or went between the time they got there until he left. The only other door opens onto a tiny little patio completely enclosed with a six-foot high redwood fence. So unless he climbed over it and left on foot, then came back and climbed back in, he was there all along."

"So where does that leave us?" Weber asked, sitting back in his chair in frustration. "Lenny Dewitt didn't do it. Roger Wilson didn't do it. Brian Oakes didn't do it. Richard MacEwen was down in Tucson so he didn't do it. And Emma damned sure didn't shoot herself in the back!"

"Could Roger have hired somebody to do his dirty work?"

"It wouldn't be above him, Coop. Something to consider."

"Robyn, did you get anything out of Laura Wilson yesterday?" Chad asked.

She shot Weber a look and then said, "Nothing except that she's a twisted bitch. She knows about her hubby's girlfriend and doesn't seem to care. She was home all that day and has telephone records to prove it."

"Have we considered the sister?" Coop asked. "She sure seemed eager to get Emma's house and we know they didn't get along."

"Buz checked her out. She has an alibi," Chad said, shaking his head. "And by the way, according to her attorney, Emma left her house and a couple thousand bucks she had in a small bank account, and a money market fund with about $60,000 in it, all to several different environmental and animal rights groups."

"Damn it, Emma didn't shoot herself," Weber repeated. "We know she made a lot of enemies. Somebody has to know something! Start on our list again and look at everybody one more time, guys. We need to keep going over it all until we figure out who did this."

A loud discussion coming from the main office interrupted the meeting and Weber went out to find Archer Wingate being harangued by George Holman.

"It ain't right, I'm tellin' ya," Holman was shouting at the pudgy deputy, who regarded him as impassively as Archer did anything in life that he couldn't eat. "We tried to do the right thing and now my wife's outta work. Now how we gonna feed our young'uns?"

"What's the problem?" Weber asked.

"The problem is that you blew Susie's cover and that Roger Wilson fired her! And with me not able to work 'count of my back and all, now what're we supposed to do? A man tries to provide for his family and this is what happens!"

"Roger fired Susan? What did he say?"

"Didn't say a word. Didn't even have the spine to tell her in person. That gal that works for him called Susie and told her to come to the office and drop off her key 'cause her services were no longer needed. No explanation or nothin' and when she got there the secretary took the key and gave her a envelope with her check in it. Not even any sevrinse' pay or nothing.' I'm gonna need to collect some of that pert deem you owe Susie."

"Pert dee... never mind. Look George, I never told Wilson I had talked to your wife. Maybe this is just a coincidence."

"No sir!" George said, shaking his head emphatically. "No sir, don't you try to make out like it ain't your fault, Sheriff. We had us what's known as a implicet agreement that Susie'd be your undercover opritive, what they call a mole, and you'd pay her pert deem. Now I want what's coming' to us!"

Weber wanted to tell the fool that if he was really concerned for his family's welfare, he'd quit being such a slacker and know-it-all and get a job to support them. But an old line he'd once heard came to mind - Never try to teach a pig to sing; it wastes your time and it annoys the pig. Trying to reason with a man like George Holman would be a waste of breath. He dug into his pocket and pulled out some money.

"Here's sixty dollars. Give it to your wife so she can get some groceries. I'll talk to Roger Wilson and see what this is all about."

"Sixty dollars! I can't feed my family on that, Sheriff! We ain't rich people, but we got a standard of livin' to maintain."

"George, take the damn money and get out of here," Weber said. "I'll talk to Roger."

"This ain't right," George said, pocketing the money. "It ain't right at all! I'll be talking to my legal reprensentive' if this don't get resolved real fast. I'm usually a mild mannered man, but you push George Holman into a corner and he comes out fightin' all the way!"

Weber had to take a deep breath to keep from exploding, but he managed to avoid it as he pointed George toward the door. When he turned around, Archer stood in the same place. "Are you a statue or something, Archer? Move, flap your arms around, do something before Coop forgets he's not in the Army any more and paints you!"

***

Tamara Ridgeway looked up from her computer and regarded him coolly when Weber came in, but didn't greet him.

"I need to talk to your boss," the sheriff said.

"He's unavailable."

"His car's in the parking lot."

"I didn't say he wasn't here, I said he's unavailable."

"Well go tell him he'd better become available," Weber told her.

Tamara stared at him and said, "You don't impress me. You're nothing but a bully and I'm not the least bit intimidated by you."

"Lady, I don't give a tinker's damn what you think of me," Weber said and walked past her into the inner office.

"Stop! You can't go back there! This is private property!" Tamara shouted, hurrying after him.

"Call a cop," Weber said over his shoulder.

When he pushed the door to Roger Wilson's office open he was shocked to find the real estate developer locked in an embrace with Juliette Murdoch, the director of the Chamber of Commerce.

Chapter 33

"Sheriff Weber! What are you doing here?" Roger demanded as Juliette turned quickly away.

"I'm sorry, Mr. Wilson. I told him you weren't available, but he barged right past me!" Tamara said.

"Mr. Wilson? Gee, why all the sudden formality?" Weber asked. "I mean, it looks like I'm the only one who isn't making it with old Roger here. Shouldn't we all be on a first name basis? And as for you Juliette, I have to say I'm disappointed. Does the mayor know where you are and what you're up to?"

"This isn't what it looks like," Juliette said. "Roger… Mr. Wilson and I were just discussing the town's future and…. please, Sheriff Weber, don't put me in this position."

"It kind of looked to me like Roger was about to put you into some kind of position," Weber said.

"You have a filthy mind!" Tamara hissed.

"Me? I'm not the one sleeping with my boss. And his wife," Weber said.

"What? With her?" Juliette demanded indignantly.

"Please, Juliette, it's not like that," Wilson said, "I can explain…"

But she glared at him and said, "You go to hell, Roger," then seemed to reclaim her dignity as she straightened her shoulders and stalked out of the office.

All pretense of the refined businessman was gone as Wilson shouted, "Who in the hell do you think you are, coming in here like this? You have no right!"

"Can it," Weber said. "Jesus, Roger, aren't you afraid you're going to wear that thing out? You must live on raw oysters."

"You're a pig!" Tamara said.

"Go sit on an icicle, sister, your temperature is almost above the freeze line," Weber told her and the receptionist turned on her heel and fled back to her desk.

"Get out of here," Wilson ordered, pointing at the door. "Mayor Wingate's going to get a call from me about this, Sheriff!"

"I'm not going anywhere," Weber said. "And if you saw yesterday's paper, Chet Wingate's got problems of his own. Speaking of the paper, I bet Paul Lewis needs something for next week's front page. I bet this new, super secret project of yours, and the fact that you're romancing Juliette to get the Chamber's support when you announce it, would really get folks in town talking. So if you really want me to go….."

Wilson closed his eyes and tilted his head upward, then asked, "What do you want?"

"Why did you fire Susan Holman?"

"The cleaning woman? How did you hear about that?"

"I've got my sources."

"What's that got to do with anything?"

"Answer the question, Roger."

"I fired her because her husband's been shooting his mouth off around town about some book deal or movie deal he's working on about Emma Moyer's murder. He said his wife saw me assault Emma and threaten to kill her."

"Where did you hear this?"

"I've got my sources too, Sheriff."

"You can tell me here or you can tell me through the bars of a jail cell, it's up to you Roger. What's it going to be?"

"You listen to me," Wilson shouted, "I don't have to take this from you! You're a two bit sheriff in a one horse town, and I'm going to make it a point to laugh when you find yourself out on the street."

"No, you listen," Weber told him, "You can glad hand all the investors and politicians you want, and screw your way through the female population of the whole damn state if you want to. But you and I both know what you really are, Roger. You're a cheating, scheming, wife beating coward who has used your Daddy's money and name to scam your way to the top. You're big and tough when you're throwing a helpless woman against a wall, but I'm not a woman and if you get in my way or play any more games with me I'm going to rip off one of your arms and beat you with it. I'm trying to find a murderer, and every time I turn around your name pops up to the top of the list."

Roger Wilson glared at him with hatred in his eyes and Weber hoped the man would make a wrong move. He needed to hit somebody, and just as the real estate developer was at the top of the suspect list in

Emma's murder, right that moment he was also at the top of Weber's list of potential punching bags. Wilson seem to read that in his eyes and backed down, as Weber knew he would. "It was George Holman."

"George?"

"Yes, he called here telling me that if I wanted to look good in his wife's book deal, he needed some financial incentive from me."

"George was trying to shake you down? You're kidding me."

"I've already told you how sensitive my position is right now," Wilson said. "The last thing I need is him running around spreading rumors. So I paid him, and then told Tamara to get his wife in here and tell her she was fired. I don't need somebody with a big mouth working in here around all of the sensitive documents in this office."

Weber couldn't believe it, but at the same time he could. George Holman had spent his life working one scheme after another. Now it seemed like he was playing both ends against the middle, pleading the poor mouth to Weber and trying to blackmail Roger Wilson at the same time.

"How much did you give him?"

$2,000."

"That was it? If I were going to blackmail somebody, I'd want more money than that."

"What can I tell you, Sheriff? He wanted $2,000 to keep his mouth shut and that's what I gave him."

"And what did you plan to do if he comes back next week wanting more?"

"All I need is three more weeks to wrap this deal up. If I have to buy some more time, I will."

Weber wanted to ask Wilson why he didn't threaten George Holman like he had Emma Moyer, but he already knew the answer. Holman wasn't much of a man, but Wilson was a coward. While he was capable of getting rough with women, even a no-account man like George Holman intimidated him.

"So what's the deal with Juliet?" Weber asked instead.

"What do you think?"

"I think she doesn't hold a candle to your wife or to the Ice Princess out there in the front, so there must be a reason. I suspect that reason is to have the Chamber of Commerce behind you on this project."

Wilson shook his head, smiling at the sheriff like he was a backward child. "Like I told you the other day, Sheriff, we live and work in two very different worlds. Juliette Murdoch owns three acres of land right in the middle of where Cimarron Ridge will be built."

"Damn man, is there nothing you won't do to close a deal?"

Wilson just looked at him. They both knew the answer.

***

"Sheriff Weber? Can we talk?"

There was no love lost between the sheriff and the director of the Chamber of Commerce. Juliette Murdoch was a single mother who had never forgiven Weber for arresting her twin sons three years earlier after they were caught vandalizing vacant summer cabins. While she dismissed their crimes as no more than youthful pranks, the cabin owners who had to replace broken windows and doors, shattered bathroom fixtures, and furniture that had its stuffing ripped out and strewn across the floor would disagree.

But it was a different Juliette who approached him in the parking lot of Roger Wilson's office. She was shaking with fear and tears filled her eyes.

"What is it, Juliette?"

"Sheriff, what happened in there…. please, if word of this got out…."

"Word of what, Juliette? You rubbing bellies with Roger or the Cimarron Ridge project?"

Her cheeks colored and a small part of Weber, one that he wasn't particularly proud of, enjoyed her humiliation for a brief moment.

"I'm sorry," he apologized. "I was out of line."

"Sheriff, I know we've had our problems in the past. But if anybody found out about Roger and me, my reputation would be ruined."

"Listen, Juliette, all I'm trying to do is find out who killed Emma Moyer. Anything else is none of my business."

She regarded him for a long moment, not sure how to react.

"Juliette, I know Emma Moyer was a pain in the ass to a lot of people around here. Hell, she was a pain in the ass to me a lot of times! But nobody deserves to die like she did. Now, I know that you hate me because of that thing with your boys and I'm not going to get into all that again. But as far as this thing with you and Roger, if it doesn't involve my case, I don't care. Although personally, I think that you could do a lot better than him. But if I find out that he or the Cimarron Ridge project had anything to do with that woman's death, nothing's gonna stop me from getting to the bottom of it."

Juliette wiped tears from her eyes, careful not to smear her mascara. "Roger is an ass. He thought he needed to romance me into selling him my land up there, but I'd have done it anyway. It's a sweet deal and I'll make a nice profit. Several people stand to make out if this deal goes forward."

"So why give in to him with the other?" Weber asked, confused.

Juliette looked away and said, "Sheriff, you're not a 46 year old woman with a muffin top and stretch marks. The prospects aren't too bright around here. A man sees a couple of gray hairs and he's off looking for something younger and firmer. I knew the thing with Roger was just physical, but sometimes you reach a point where you're willing to settle."

Weber shook his head and reached out, placing a finger on her chin and turning her face back to him. "Juliette, you're a good looking, smart woman. You don't have to settle."

He wasn't sure if he saw gratitude or skepticism in her eyes before she turned away again and said, "Remind me of that some long, cold winter night when the wind's blowing hard and the only company I have is the television and a bottle."

Chapter 34

As so often happens in the White Mountains, a week can make a tremendous difference. While they had been wading through knee deep snow at the parking area where Emma Moyer had been killed seven days earlier, now there were just a few small patches left in the open area, and even along the edges where trees shaded things, the snow had melted down to just a few inches of muddy slush.

Coop had spent the afternoon searching the entire parking area with his metal detector once more, hoping to find an ejected shell casing or some other clue, with no success.

"It was worth a try anyway," Weber told him.

They stood together looking toward the break in the tree line where Emma's body had been found.

"Any luck in that area?"

Coop shook his head as he turned the metal detector off and laid it across the back seat of his patrol unit. "I had Tommy and Dan wading around up there half the day looking, but it would take a week under the best of conditions. There's still a lot of snow once you get under the trees. There's not a mark on a tree or any indication where the bullet went after it exited her body. It could be anywhere. We're talking needle in a haystack at best, Jimmy."

In the short time Coop had been with the Sheriff's Office, Weber had developed a lot of faith in the experienced lawman's abilities and judgment. If Coop believed he could find any evidence by searching the thick forest terrain with his metal detector, he'd do it. If he said it was a lost cause, Weber was willing to take him at his word.

"We've only got an hour or so of daylight left. Might as well head back to town."

Coop nodded and stretched his back, which cracked audibly, even under his coat.

"Getting old there, Deputy?"

"Naa, just stiff from all that bending over working the metal detector. I can still run with the big dogs, don't you worry about that, Sheriff."

"Yeah, well there's something to be said for just laying on the porch in the sunshine," Weber told him.

Coop laughed, then paused with his door open and turned back to Weber. "We're going to figure this out, Boss. It may take a while, but we'll do it."

Weber nodded, then stood alone in the parking area listening until the sound of Coop's vehicle faded away and the forest was silent. He didn't know what he was expecting, maybe Emma's ghost to whisper a clue to him on the wind that rustled the needles of the pine trees. But no spectral voice called a name from the darkening forest, and finally the chill of the coming night air seeped into him. Shivering, Weber walked back to his Explorer, but before he opened the door, he made a promise, repeating Coop's words. "We're going to figure this out, Emma. It may take a while, but we'll do it. I won't stop until I do."

***

Driving back into town, Weber played a hunch and drove through the parking lot of the Antler Inn. As he suspected, an old Astro van, its maroon paint dull and faded, was parked on the side of the building, nosed in between a new Dodge dually pickup and a rust bucket International Scout. George Holman was sitting at the bar, explaining his system for winning the Lotto to a grizzled old cowboy who looked at him through bleary eyes and burped in response.

"You're slackin' Margo," George said to the overweight blonde woman behind the bar. "Another round for me and my friend Jerry here. It was Jerry, wasn't it?"

"Jerry, Harry, Larry, I don't give a shit," the cowboy told him, trying to focus.

George laughed and said, "Set 'em up Margo. In fact, I'm buyin' the whole bar a drink! Let the good times roll."

"You ain't getting anything until I see the money," Margo said. "I've been stiffed by you before, George!"

"Well here you go, darlin', help yourself," George said slapping a $50 bill down on the sticky bar top. "And let me know when that's gone. There's plenty more where it came from."

Margo reached out for the money, but Weber beat her to it, slapping his hand down on the bill.

"What the hell? Get out of here, Weber!"

"Sorry, Margo, the party's over," Weber said. "Outside, George, now."

"You can't come in here and start ordering my customers around," Margo shouted, but Weber ignored her. He stuck the money in his pocket, and grabbed George by the arm and started steering him toward the door over the man's protests that he hadn't done anything.

There were only a few patrons in the bar, but one of them was a big logger with a bulging gut that hung over his belt, and a scattering of yellowed teeth when he opened his mouth to talk. He stepped in front of them, blocking their path.

"The man ain't done a damn thing, why are you hassling him?"

"It'd probably be a good idea for you to mind your own business, sir," Weber told him.

"Maybe I'm making it my business."

"See, now, that would be a bad idea," Weber said.

"All he was doing was sitting at the bar minding his own business and you come in here rousting him for nothing. That's wrong!"

"Step aside, sir," Weber ordered. "You really don't want to take this any further."

"How about you just let the man go and get back to writing tickets out on the highway and I won't break your back? How's that sound?"

"It sounds like you're threatening me," Weber said. "What's your name?"

"You can just call me Badass. Mister Badass! That's all you need to know."

"Well, Mr. Badass, you and I seem to have a problem, and that's unfortunate. Now, you came in here to have a few drinks and a good time, so how about you get back to that and I'll go on about my business? How's that sound?"

"No, how about you get your hands off my friend here and you won't be in a wheelchair tomorrow? How's that sound?"

"It sounds to me like you're letting your alligator mouth write checks that your hummingbird ass isn't going to be able to cash. Step aside."

"I'm not going anywhere. And neither is my friend there."

"You're really going to take this all the way, aren't you?"

Mr. Badass just folded his arms and stood his ground.

At a shade over 5'10" and 170 pounds, Weber wasn't a small man, but the big logger was over a head taller and had at least 100 pounds on him.

Weber held his portable radio to his mouth and said, "Dispatch, this is Sheriff Weber. Is Mary still there?"

"10-4, Sheriff, stand by."

A moment later Mary Caitlin's voice came through his speaker. "What do you need, Jimmy?"

"Can you have Buz and Dolan come out to the Antler Inn with a crime scene kit? And alert Doc Williams over at the medical center that he'll be getting a DOA in with multiple gunshot wounds."

"Will do, Buz and Dolan are on their way. Should I get the ambulance rolling too?"

"Tell them not to rush. They've got plenty of time. They'll be picking up a DOA, not a live patient."

"10-4."

"Gunshot wounds? I never said I was going to shoot anybody," the big man said, dropping his arms to the side. "What's that shit all about?"

"No, I'm the one that's going to be doing the shooting," Weber told him. "You've already threatened to do me serious bodily harm. And since you're twice my size and seem pretty intent on breaking my back, there's no way I'm going to get into a fight with you. I'm just going to pull out my pistol and shoot you. And as big as you are, I'm not going to stop shooting until it's empty. It's a Colt .45 and it's loaded with eight rounds of 200 grain jacketed hollow points, seven in the magazine and one in the chamber. I know they work, because I killed a bear with one last week."

"Hey, I don't want no part of no shooting!" George said. "I just come in here to have a couple beers and relax."

"Shut up, George," Weber said. "But you should probably step aside so that when I start shooting you don't get any blood splatter on you."

"Just hold on a damn minute," Mr. Badass said. "You can't threaten me like that. I've got rights."

"Sure I can," Weber told him. "You threatened to do me serious injury in front of all these people. Do you have a next of kin you want notified?"

"Listen, I don't even know this asshole. He's just a guy in a bar. I'm not getting killed over him!"

"Well, that's certainly up to you," Weber said. "With the cost of ammunition these days, and all the paperwork this is gonna cause me, I'd just as soon we let this whole thing drop. But I do already have the crime scene crew and the ambulance on the way…"

"Well, I ain't gonna be here when they get here!" Mr. Badass turned his back on the sheriff and made a quick exit, the hoots and jeers of the rest of the bar's patrons following him out the door.

"Damn, Sheriff, we sure showed him!" George said, slapping Weber's shoulder like they were best buddies.

"Shut up," Weber told him, grabbing him by the arm again and hustling him out the door.

Once outside, Weber keyed his radio again and said, "Dispatch, this is Weber again. Disregard previous communication. It looks like reason has prevailed."

"10-4," Mary said, and Weber could hear the chuckle in her voice.

Leading the other man to his van, Weber said, "Okay George, you and me are going to have a talk."

"You got no right to come in there and embarrass me like that," George protested. "And I want my $50 back that you stole in there!"

"No, you're going to give me my other $10 back of what I gave you today," Weber told him.

"That was pert deem!"

"The term is per diem, you ignorant ass," Weber said. "I gave you money because you said your wife lost her job, so your kids would have something to eat. Not so you could sit in a damn bar and buy drinks for a bunch of losers who wouldn't even give you the time of day if you were the one mooching drinks, which you usually are."

"You got no right…"

Weber punched him hard in the stomach and stepped back as George doubled over, then sank to his knees and retched. When he had emptied his stomach and wiped his face with his jacket sleeve, Weber jerked him upright and slapped his face hard, then slammed his back against the side of the Astro and put a forearm across his throat. "Listen to me, you lazy, worthless piece of shit. I know you shook Roger Wilson down for two grand. That's a felony and I can send your ass to prison for it. And if I did, it would be the best thing that ever happened to your wife and kids. Is that what you want?"

All bluster gone from him, George shook his head and gagged for breath.

"Now here's what's going to happen," Weber said. "As far as Wilson is concerned, that $2,000 is chump change, and if he was dumb enough to give it to you, that's his problem. You are going to get in that van of yours and drive home, and I'm going to follow you. And when we get there, you're going to give Susan that money and you are going to keep your mouth shut and your hands off of it. That money is to hold her over until you start earning a paycheck, which you are going to do, starting tomorrow. I know that Russ Havins needs a man to work at the propane company, and that's going to be you. I'll talk to him tonight and you'd better be there at 7:30 tomorrow morning. You go to work, you keep your mouth shut, and you do your job, got it? And if I hear of you slacking off, or calling in sick, or any of your other bullshit, you and me are going to have another talk. Trust me, George, you don't want us to have another talk. Is that clear?"

His eyes huge in the light of the security lights mounted alongside the building, George nodded.

"You stay away from Roger Wilson, you stay out of this bar, and you start acting like a man, beginning right this minute. You're going to be washing dishes and running the vacuum and helping your wife with those kids. I plan to drop in once in a while for a visit, George, and when I do, I'd better not find you laying on your ass on the couch. Any questions?"

George shook his head again, terrified. To reinforce his point, Weber pressed his forearm harder across his throat, cutting off all air, and felt the other man's fingers clawing ineffectually at his coat sleeve. Then he let up the pressure and stepped back.

George bent over gasping, trying to draw air into his lungs. Weber gave him a moment, then asked, "Are you ready to go home now?"

George nodded.

"Do you have any questions about what we just talked about? No? Good, now just one more thing. You still owe me $10."

Pulling a thick wad of bills from his pocket, George thrust it toward him. Weber peeled off a ten and handed it back. "Enjoy the feel of that money, George, because it's the last time you'll ever have that much in your pocket. Because you're going to give your paycheck to your wife every week and she's going to give you an allowance. That way you won't be tempted to come back in here, got it?"

Still afraid to speak, George nodded once again and stuck the rest of the money back in his pocket.

***

Susan Holman was spooning macaroni and cheese into bowls when Weber and her husband walked into the mobile home. Becky jumped up from her chair and ran to hug her father, with her brother right behind her. Weber was reminded that, whatever his shortcomings were, to his two young children, George was still Daddy.

"Sheriff Weber? George? Is everything all right?"

"Just fine," Weber assured her. "Why don't you get the kids situated and then the three of us will have a little chat."

With concern in her eyes, Susan poured milk into the kids' plastic glasses and watched while they said grace, then returned to the living room.

"What's this all about? What have you done now, George?"

"Well honey…."

"George hasn't done anything wrong, Susan," Weber interrupted. "In fact, you should be pretty proud of him. He went and had a talk with Roger Wilson, and while he couldn't get your job back, he did convince him that you deserved severance pay. Show her, George."

"Yes ma'am, sevrinse' pay," George said, digging the money out of his pocket and handing it to his wife. Susan looked at it is disbelief and Weber was sure it was more money than she had ever held in her hand at one time in her life.

"There's more good news," Weber told her. "George found a new job. He starts tomorrow. And it looks like his back is on the mend, so he won't have any trouble getting there, will you George?"

"No sir, looking forward to it."

"In fact, George is feeling so much better you won't believe the energy he has, will she George?"

"No sir, lots of energy. I'm feeling like a new man."

"Well that's good, George. Why don't you use some of that new energy of yours and go give those kids a second helping. And while you're in there, you could wash that pot for Susan, couldn't you?"

"Right on it. Kids, ya'll want some more mac n' cheese?"

When he was in the kitchen, Susan looked at Weber and asked, "What did you do?"

"Not a thing. I think George just had an epiphany today."

"An epiphany?"

"Yes ma'am. Hey, George, I'm out of here. But don't you worry, I'll be around, okay?"

"Yes sir, lookin' forward to it," George said over the excited chatter of the children.

Susan followed Weber outside to his Explorer.

"An epiphany? George?"

"Yeah, it's a miracle," Weber told her. "I think you might find yourself married to a brand new husband."

"Sheriff Weber, I..." She stood on tiptoe to wrap her arms around his neck and kissed his cheek. "Thank you."

Weber hugged her for a minute, then felt her shiver through the thin sweater she was wearing. "It's cold out here. Go back inside with your husband and kids. I'll see you around, Susan."

He watched her go back inside the little trailer and the sound of happy voices floated to him on the crisp night air. For just a moment Weber stood there watching the scene, then climbed into his vehicle and drove away.

Chapter 35

"You got George Holman a job? And he took it?" Buz asked in disbelief.

"Sure did," Weber said. "I had to do some fast talking with Russ over at Hi-Country Propane, but he owed me a favor or two and agreed to give him a chance."

"But Jimmy, you know how George is," Dolan said. "He'll be there a week and be out the door. Either Russ will get tired of listening to George tell him how to run his business, or else he'll come down with some pain or injury and say he can't work."

"You see, that's why I'm the Sheriff and you're the Deputy," Weber told his old friend. "As a supervisor, I know it's all about incentive. You give a man the proper incentive and he'll do a good job for you every time. And trust me, I'm pretty sure old George has got some real incentive to make this work."

They were interrupted when Parks hustled into Weber's office with a folder in one hand and a grin spread across his face. "You're looking happy this morning," Weber said. "Marsha make you a double omelet for breakfast?"

"As a matter of fact she did, but that's not what's got me smiling. No sir, I'm just happy for the good fortune of my fellow man. And from the look of this," he said, waving the folder, "some of my fellow men and women around here are going to be enjoying good fortune very soon."

"What is it?" Weber asked, taking the folder and opening it.

"First of all, here's the master plan for Roger Wilson's Cimarron Ridge development. For a guy that's normally pretty boastful, I think he understated things to you."

"What do you mean," Weber asked?

"Well, good ol' Roger told you about the condos and shopping mall and all that, right?"

"Yeah. So what's your point?"

"Well bubba, my point is that if a snake has as many heads as that guy does, maybe at least one is speaking with a forked tongue. Get it, forked tongue?"

"Yeah, you're hilarious," Weber said. "Get on with it."

"Ohhh, somebody didn't get their bran muffin this morning!"

Enjoying Weber's glare, Parks took the folder back and flipped through the pages, before pulling one out and saying, "This here is a list of all of the properties in private hands that will be incorporated into the project. There are seventeen different parcels ranging from a half acre to over 1,000 acres."

"Jesus, how big is this place going to be?"

"Glad you asked that, Bubba. According to this, between the land Wilson's been buying up quietly all along and what's here, almost 25,000 acres."

Dolan whistled. "That's a lot of condos and restaurants."

"That can't be," Weber said, "most of that land is Forest Service, isn't it?"

"No, only that strip right alongside the highway, which is going to be traded for the park land along the lake. Actually, a lot of it was part of the old Washburn Land and Cattle Company that Lucy Washburn's daddy acquired way back when you and me's daddies were jumping from one testicle to another trying to keep from being born bastards. And Roger Wilson now owns most of it. For the rest, if Wilson gets this thing approved, the people that own the land he has options on stand to make a lot of money."

"Yeah, but 25,000 acres? Like Dolan said, that's a lot of condos."

"Oh, the condos and commercial stuff are only going to be right alongside the highway. Getting the Town Council to approve that isn't any big deal. What Wilson's really worried about is getting approval from the state and the Environmental Protection Agency for this."

He handed Weber a multi-folded sheet of graph paper covered with lines and marks.

"What are these, hieroglyphics?"

"No, they're seismology reports Roger Wilson had done on the sly. According to them, that entire tract sits on top of a huge pocket of natural gas that he plans to lease to an oil company out of Texas that plans to get it out by fracking."

"What the heck is fracking?"

"It's a process of extracting natural gas from deep within the earth.

That's what they're doing that's producing boomtowns in Texas and North Dakota. Until now, it's been pretty much non-existent in Arizona because of the lack of proven shale gas fields. They did some test wells between Springerville and St. Johns a few years ago without much success. If this report is right, that changes things."

"Damn!"

"According to what I've been able to figure out, Wilson's overseas investors don't have a clue about all this, they just think he's building a little old commercial development. He's retaining all mineral rights, and those investors don't know about the rest of the land he's already got. In actuality, he could give a damn about the development, all that is just a smokescreen to get control of the rest of the land he needs."

Parks unrolled a topographic map. "You see, between the Forest Service land and these parcels here, at this point he's still landlocked. All of those parcels border the highway. Because of the terrain, the only possible way to get access to the rest of it is across those properties.

"But why all of it?" Buz asked. "He'd already be richer than King Midas. How much is enough?"

Weber remembered what Roger Wilson had told him on his first visit to the developer's office, "For a true visionary like myself, there is never enough."

"Part of it is because Wilson's greedy and doesn't want to share any of it that he doesn't have to," Weber said. "To him, it's not just about the money, it's about winning. If he leaves any money on the table, even a nickel, it's not a total victory. What else do you have, Parks?"

"Here's a list of the people who are going to cash in if this all goes through. I don't think any of them know anything about the master plan, but at the money Wilson's offering, they all stand to make a lot of money. Do some of these names look familiar to you?"

The list was organized by size starting with the smallest parcel and working its way down the page to the largest. Weber read through the list, seeing several names he recognized, including Juliette Murdoch. But it was the last name on the list that made him do a double take.

"Holy shit! Two million dollars?"

"Right there in black and white, big guy."

"Emma must have got wind of this somehow," Weber said.

"Maybe. Maybe not. Whether she thought she was just stopping another development or a fracking operation, either way the results would have been the same. You can't keep something this big quiet forever. Sooner or later word was going to get out and then some people's big dreams were going to go up in smoke."

Weber sat back in his chair, trying to process everything. It was all falling into place and becoming clear as day. He pulled a telephone book out of one of his desk drawers, looked up a number and called it. A few moments later he hung up and pushed his chair back and said, "Saddle up, boys, it's time to go to work."

Chapter 36

When they drove down the long ranch driveway in a caravan of four vehicles, Jake Gibbons heard them approaching and came out of the barn, where he had been shoeing a dapple mare.

"Howdy Sheriff," Jake said as Weber climbed out of the Explorer. "Looks like you brought a posse with you. If you're looking for Butch and Sundance, I haven't seen them."

"Where's your brother, Jake?"

"Sam? I think he's over there in the equipment shed. What's this all about?"

"Deputy Wright, cuff him," Weber ordered.

"What? What the hell…"

Dan Wright pulled Jake's hands behind him and snapped handcuffs on the bewildered man.

"Wait a minute, Sheriff? What the hell's going on here?"

"You're not under arrest at this point, this is for your safety and ours. Stay here," Weber told him, starting toward the large metal workshop across from the barn.

Weber led Coop and Parks to the big double doors of the building, which were propped open. Dolan and Buz spread out, each checking nearby outbuildings, while Chad went to the back of the equipment shed to secure the rear doors.

Hank Williams, Jr. was singing about all of his rowdy friends settling down over a portable radio that was sitting on a neatly organized workbench, the volume turned up high. Sam Gibbons was deep inside the hood of a white Mack truck with a flat bed that still held traces of hay and wasn't aware he was no longer alone until Weber turned the radio off. Looking up at the sudden silence, Sam saw the three grim faced lawmen and the light seemed to go out of his eyes.

"I hoped it wouldn't come to this, but I kind of figured it would," he said, straightening up and laying the wrench he was holding on the truck's fender.

"Sam Gibbons, you're under arrest for the murder of Emma Moyer," Weber said, then read him his Miranda rights.

When the sheriff finished, Sam said, "Jake didn't know about any of this. I guess him finding out hurts me worse than whatever else is coming."

"You didn't think he'd notice when you were suddenly rich?"

"We been poor so long, fighting the weather and the bank every season just to keep afloat, selling a few cattle every year, guiding hunters, whatever it takes to just hang on. And we still get a little further behind every year. We're gonna be fifty next year and it's been a hard life. I lost my Eva last year when the flu came through here and Jake's got a cough that won't go away. I thought if we could just finally get clear and have enough to live out our lives in comfort…. Oh hell, man, just put them handcuffs on me and lets get on with it."

***

"I still can't believe it," Chad said. "Sam Gibbons of all people."

"You wonder what makes a good man like that turn," Tommy said. "Man lives his whole life doing what's expected of him and then something like this happens."

"I can tell you what causes it," Weber said. "A lifetime of working your fingers to the bone and beating your head against the wall year after year and not getting anywhere. I saw it with my Dad and swore I'd never live that life."

"But your old man never did something like this," Dolan said. "I remember Mr. Joe, he was a damn fine man."

"Who knows? Maybe he wasn't ever pushed far enough? Sam lost his wife last year, now it looks like Jake's got lung cancer and the bank's about to foreclose on the family ranch. Sam's wife had inherited that 1,200 acres Roger Wilson wants back when her Daddy died but it was just raw grazing land, costing him more in taxes every year than it earned. So when Wilson came along waving a big check under his nose, he saw a way out."

"But why kill Emma?"

"Because she was going to ruin the one and only chance he saw to ever get clear. I don't know if he really set out to kill her, but when Jake called him on the radio to tell him about her interrupting the hunt, it must have been the final straw. Sam said Richey Dewitt killed his deer about mid-morning and they spent most of the day getting it out. But they weren't that far off the trail and that side of the mountain is a lot easier terrain than where Jake had his hunters out, so it shouldn't have taken all that long. And it didn't. When I called Conrad Demaris at the meat locker, he said Sam and the Dewitt brothers had dropped off Richey's buck to be butchered a little after noon. He remembered because he was just finishing his lunch when they pulled in. The Game and Fish Department makes him log in every game animal that he gets, and he double checked his paperwork. 12:25 p.m. He said they were there for a half hour, maybe forty-five minutes."

"So Sam had plenty of time to drop the brothers off and get up the mountain," Coop said.

"Yeah. He said he was looking for Emma to tell her off once and for all, and then when he found her car it just pissed him off even more and he slashed her tires. To be honest, I don't think he planned to kill her even then. But she showed up and it happened from there. Then he got the radio call about Lenny Dewitt going missing, and told Jake he'd come help look for him. He didn't mention that he was already further up the mountain."

"Do you think Jake knew anything about it at all?" Robyn asked.

Weber shook his head. "Both brothers insist he didn't, and he seems genuinely shocked. Looking back at what happened with Debbie, I know it can happen."

"Debbie and Sam, like two peas in a pod," Dolan said.

Weber shook his head. "The difference is, my sister did what she did out of pure evil greed. She never showed an ounce of remorse and still hasn't. In Sam's case, he's watching everything him and his brother, and their father and grandfather before them work for slipping away. The only person he's got left in the world is Jake, and they don't have health insurance because they can't afford it. The end result is still the same, but I think the motives were entirely different."

"What do you think?" Bob Bennett asked. "If I go for Second Degree Murder it takes the death penalty off the table."

"Does it matter if he does twenty years or thirty, or fifty, Bob? The chances of him ever seeing daylight again are slim to none. And if he ever did get paroled, what would he come back to?"

There was no good answer to that, so the Town's attorney didn't try to offer one.

Chapter 37

Jake Gibbons was parked off the Forest Service road, in the parking area where Emma Moyer had been killed. The idling engine of his crew cab pickup sent a white vapor trail up into the still mountain air. Stopping his vehicle beside the pickup, Weber opened the passenger door and crawled in beside him, uninvited.

"Evening, Sheriff."

"Jake."

Neither man said anything for several minutes until Jake broke the silence. "I've loved it up here on this mountain since I was a kid. Got a lot of happy memories of this place. Shot my first deer over yonder about a mile or so when I wasn't much more than knee high to a grasshopper. I still remember the look on my old man's face. I think he was more excited than I was. He cut the heart and liver out and started a fire and cooked them up right there. Don't think I've ever ate anything as delicious in my life."

Weber knew that no reply was needed so he kept silent, letting the other man talk.

"That's a way of life that's about over, ain't it, Sheriff? They keep building more and more, it won't be much longer before we won't recognize this place. Won't recognize anything in these parts. I'm not even fifty yet, but I feel like a very old man. Hell, with this thing growing inside of me, who knows if I'll even be here a year from now?"

"You could get help, Jake."

"Never was a man to take charity, Sheriff. Never been a Gibbons who did and I'm not about to be the first one."

"That land of Sam's. You know he wants you to have it."

"Oh, with all of this coming out, that rich man's big scheme is history."

"The land's still got a lot of value, Jake. These developers are buying up land right and left."

"I don't see you rushing to sell yours off, Sheriff. Besides, I'd rather die broke than know I had a hand in helping them destroy this place any more than it is. I kind of get the feeling you feel the same way or you'd have cashed in by now."

"So what happens next, Jake?"

"Do you remember when that young fellow shot his father-in-law?"

"Kind of hard to forget anything that's happened lately, Jake."

"You said something to me about not wearing guilt. Said you knew what that was like. Well, I guess you do. But who'd have thought we'd be sitting up here tonight, both of us sharing a different kind of guilt, you and me? How do you live with that guilt, Sheriff? 'Cause I'm not sure I can."

"What my sister did and what Sam did, that's not us, Jake. At least Sam thought he was…"

Jake held up his hand to stop him. "Don't, Sheriff. I know what you're gonna say, and it sure ain't gonna help. Your sister did what she did for whatever reason she had, and no disrespect to you, she was wrong for doing it. There ain't no other way to say it. But knowing that what pushed Sam over the edge was to help me…. that's an entirely different kind of guilt. One I'm not sure I can wear, but how do I not wear it? How can I open my eyes tomorrow, knowing what happened up here and why it happened?"

Weber nudged the 30-30 Winchester lever-action carbine sitting upright on the floor between them. "That what this is for, Jake?"

"Wont lie to you and tell you it didn't cross my mind." He coughed, then thumped his chest and said, "And won't promise you it won't come to that as this gets worse. I've worked hard all my life, Sheriff. Got nothing to show for it, and not much reason to hold on. But not tonight, and not here. I think there's been enough dying that's gone on up here."

They sat there for a while longer, then Jake said, "I've got horses to feed. Guess I'd better get on home."

He reached his arm across the cab and shook the sheriff's hand.

"You're a good man, Jim Weber. I'm proud to call you my friend."

"You gonna be okay, Jake?"

"No, I'm gonna die. But not tonight. I've got horses to feed."

Weber climbed out of the truck's cab and watched as Jake made a U-turn and waved at him, then drove down the mountain. In a few minutes the sound of his truck was gone and it was quiet. Weber looked up at the inky winter sky and watched a million stars twinkling. Somewhere in the night he heard an owl hoot off in the distance, and closer in, some small animal moved through the brush, making fallen branches rattle. Then it was silent again. Finally, Weber knew that he had made his peace with this place and it was time to go home.

Made in the USA
Middletown, DE
11 May 2021